BAD TO THE CRONE

A SPELL'S ANGELS COZY MYSTERY

AMANDA M. LEE

WINCHESTERSHAW PUBLICATIONS

PROLOGUE

TWENTY-FIVE YEARS AGO

The woman cut through the night, determined, silent.

Her feet made no sound on the pavement even though she wore hard-soled shoes that should've clicked against the cement. She'd cast a spell to muffle the sound because she was on a timetable and it was simply easier to use the magic she had at her command than to risk the wrong person seeing her.

The little girl at her side emitted the occasional sniffle but was otherwise silent. Because of the darkness, it was hard to make out anything about the duo. The only hint came from beneath the child's inky hoodie when a trace of blond hair peeked out.

The woman with the child was careful when they came to a stop in front of a fire station. Light illuminated the windows, but no silhouettes floated past to suggest someone was inside. The woman knew the skeleton night crew was present — she'd checked to make sure before collecting the girl — but she didn't call to them and request help. This wasn't that sort of visit.

"Hey." She forced a tight-lipped smile onto her face as she knelt before the child. "I'm sorry about this ... all of this." She felt strained as she debated what to say. She'd practiced this speech in the mirror several times the last few days. The words never got easier, and they never felt right.

"What am I doing here?" the girl asked, confused. She stared at the building for a long time. "I don't know where I am."

The woman sighed, misery and worry colliding. "I know. I don't want to leave you here, but I don't have a choice."

The child's lower lip trembled. "You're going to leave me here?" Her eyes turned furtive as she darted around, a wave of terror so strong it caused the nearby trees to ripple and bend as they gave way to the power washing over her. "I don't want to stay here!"

"I know you don't." The woman adjusted her position to ease the wear on her knees, hunkering low to stare directly into the girl's eyes. "You don't want to stay and I don't want to leave you. But I honestly don't have a choice.

"You're not safe with me right now," she continued, choosing her words carefully. "I have to run, and where I'm going, well, you can't come with me."

Tears flowed freely now as the girl fought to maintain some semblance of calm ... and failed. "But you can't!" She gripped the front of the woman's dark cloak. "You can't leave me here. I don't want to stay. I ... please!" She was taught never to beg and yet that's what she did now. "Don't leave me. I don't want to be alone!"

Though she had voluntarily taken on the job of leaving the child behind out of a sense of practicality, the woman choked back a sob as emotion got the better of her. This was the hardest thing she'd ever done. That didn't mean it wasn't necessary.

"You'll never truly be alone." She pressed a finger to the girl's forehead and immediately the child stopped whimpering, instead swaying as her eyes went glassy. "We're here," she whispered, pressing a hand to the girl's heart. "We'll also be here." She kissed her forehead. "Hold onto this." She slipped a silver necklace into her pocket and made sure it wasn't poking out in case someone decided to lift the trinket in the melee of the girl's discovery. "You will see at least one of us again.

"Whatever happens, you must know that it wasn't our choice to leave you," she continued. "You're the future, our only hope. We wanted to keep you. You have no idea how much. Your safety is more important than what we want, though."

She cast a terrified look over her shoulder at an unexpected noise and peered into the darkness. She sensed malevolence closing in and knew she must be quick.

"You need to go to the building and knock," she instructed, turning grim. "Tell them that you don't know how you got here, or where you're supposed to be. They'll look for relatives, your next of kin, but we've protected you with an incantation. No one will be able to claim you unless their hearts are pure ... and they can protect you. That second part is the most important, although you might not always see it that way.

"If we can, we'll come for you," she said, sobs clogging her throat as she fought to maintain her demeanor. "I don't think that's going to be possible for a very long time. Even then ... well ... you might never see us again, our magic will sustain you until it's time. You will feel us even if you don't know us."

She ran her finger down the girl's cheek as she fought the over-whelming urge to cry. "You're stronger than you realize. I'm only sorry that we won't have a chance to teach you our ways. You'll have to figure out this world on your own.

"It's not an easy world, or even a good one at times," she said, the hair on the back of her neck standing on end as she registered a dark presence closing in. "It's what you have to overcome. I have faith that you will, that you'll figure everything out in due course. Until then ... you will live in the darkness because that's the greatest gift I can give you."

She pressed her lips to the child's forehead. "Someday you will remember." Another kiss. "May we meet again."

With those words she shoved the girl toward the door. "Knock on the door. Go inside. Leave this behind you." Her tone, suddenly cold and devoid of warmth, didn't allow for argument.

The child was confused but had no choice but to obey. The memory spell had done its job. She didn't remember the past four years of her life. The woman in front of her was a stranger.

"I ... knock on the door," she murmured, staring at the fire station. "Ask for help."

"Yes." The woman was back on her feet and glaring at a shadow detaching from the tree line across the street. "You must go now. We're already out of time."

As the child obeyed, the woman walked away from the past. There was no changing things now. They'd waited too long. All they could hope for was that the child would do what she was born to do.

It would take time, but as long as she was alive there was hope.

How long that hope could sustain them was anybody's guess.

She pushed worry out of her mind and focused on the coming battle. She would have to fight until the child made it out of the danger zone, away from the creatures that stalked the night, to relative safety. Then she would have to fight for an opening to flee. There was no assurance that either would happen. If she didn't fight, though, it was guaranteed she would fail.

So, with only one option in front of her, she did what was necessary. She fought ... and for one day, she won.

The battle was over, but the war had just begun.

ONE

PRESENT DAY

I'm a city person.

I like tall buildings and busy skylines. I like movie theaters that are open at midnight. I like being able to shop in the middle of the night. Heck, I like knowing where the after-hours bars are — and they had better not be too far — so I can party well into the wee hours.

I like action ... and street noise ... and the hint of danger that accompanies both.

So, given all that, how did I end up here?

"Welcome to Hawthorne Hollow."

The words were benign, but they sent chills down my spine as I focused on the man who uttered them.

Rooster Tremaine was in his mid-fifties and burly. He wore a flannel shirt with the sleeves ripped off, which allowed him to display a set of biceps that would've been welcome in a 1980s action movie. He was bald — whether that was a choice or not, I couldn't say — and he wore a red bandanna tied over his bare head.

He was tough and looked mean ... but as a witch, I could read his

5

aura and knew it was all an act. He had a giving heart and soul. He simply didn't want anyone to know it.

"I saw the sign when I was coming in," I said dryly, leaning a hip against the counter at The Rusty Cauldron, northern Lower Michigan's version of a biker bar. It left a lot to be desired ... and yet it was somehow homey, too. "Population four-thousand, huh? That's not exactly what I would call a happening spot."

Instead of being offended, Rooster snorted. "Don't let the town's size fool you. This place finds trouble faster than a Kardashian finds something stupid to say."

The reference threw me for a loop. "You watch the Kardashians?"

"No. I make fun of the Kardashians."

Maybe I was going to like this place after all. "Scout Randall." I introduced myself by jutting out my hand. "I've been transferred here for the time being. I have no idea how long the assignment will last."

Amusement filtered through Rooster's eyes as he rested his weight on his elbow behind the counter. I wasn't sure if the bar served as an office — in Detroit, the local chapter of the Spells Angels rented actual office space — or was simply a hangout, but I was determined to find out without making myself look like too much of a ninny.

Rooster stared at my hand a moment and then took it. "What's your real name?"

I wasn't surprised by the question. "Scout."

He cocked an eyebrow. "Uh-huh. Your parents named you Scout, did they? Somehow I have my doubts."

This was hardly the first time I'd participated in this very discussion. "I have no idea what my parents named me." I wasn't bucking for sympathy but it was best to get this part of the conversation out of the way. "I don't know if I even had a name. I was abandoned when I was four or five — I'm not really sure of my birthday so they made an educated guess — and the firefighter who found me named me Scout after a character in his favorite book."

Rooster's forehead wrinkled. "From *To Kill a Mockingbird*."

I shrugged. "That would be my guess. I don't really remember him either. He died not long after I was found. A heart attack, I believe."

"Wow. That's quite the story." Rooster was somber. "So, your name really is Scout."

"That's what it says on my license." I flashed a smile to put him at ease. My origin tale made most people uncomfortable. I was used to it. I had no idea where I'd come from, but I'd put that behind me.

Er, well, mostly.

"And how did you end up here?" Rooster asked. "I mean ... you don't look the type to willingly choose Hawthorne Hollow."

That was an understatement. As far as I could tell, Hawthorne Hollow was one stoplight and eight churches. It definitely wasn't my chosen place to hang my hat. Still, I was a team player. When my regional boss in Detroit said that Hawthorne Hollow was down a person and needed a body right away, I was eager to help.

Okay, that's a total lie. I wasn't eager and fought the effort. We drew straws between the other available Spells Angels and me, and I lost. Rooster didn't need to know that. There was no need to make him feel bad.

"I'm here to help as long as you need it," I said, forcing a smile. "You're down a witch ... so here I am."

"Uh-huh." Rooster's expression didn't change. "I think you're going to have a rude awakening here, missy. But it's not my place to say. I don't stick my nose in other people's business."

I had my doubts, which were only strengthened when several of the people hanging around the bar cast him derisive looks. I wasn't surprised none of them said anything, though. Rooster obviously wasn't the sort to be trifled with. "I was told to check in with you," I offered. "You're listed as my liaison."

"I don't know that I want to be anybody's liaison, but I'm in charge in these parts," he confirmed. "I guess we should start with introductions."

He made an odd throat-clearing sound as he gestured toward a group of people at the other end of the room. They'd stared as I entered — I was the new element in town so there was a natural curiosity wafting about — but remained silent. They clearly deferred to Rooster, which made me think he was more powerful than he let

7

on. He was magical, there was no doubt about that, but he kept his cards close. I couldn't be sure exactly how much power he wielded.

"I'll make introductions," he offered, moving out from behind the bar and wiping his hands on a raggedy towel. "Come with me."

I fell into step with him because it seemed the thing to do, but I wasn't keen on meeting the rest of the Hawthorne Hollow tribe. They didn't look friendly, to put it mildly. That was fine, of course, because I wasn't exactly known for my manners.

"Gang, this is Scout Randall," Rooster started. "That's her real name so don't give her grief about it. Scout, this is the gang."

I forced a smile that I didn't feel. "It's nice to meet you," I offered awkwardly.

"Yes, we're thrilled to meet you, too," a woman drawled, sipping from what looked to be a glass of bourbon on the rocks. It wasn't even noon, so I had to question her choices ... something I did internally because I wasn't yet sure what I was up against.

"That's Bonnie," Rooster offered. "She's kind of a pain in the keister, but she's good in a fight, which is the most important thing."

The woman's black hair and eyes almost matched, giving her a creepy look that made me indescribably nervous. "Hey." I bobbed my head and refused to give in to the fluttering fear in my belly. She could be a perfectly nice woman, I reminded myself. The black eyes obviously threw me, but I didn't sense so much magic that I was worried that she could overpower me. I was good in a fight, too. I just hoped it wouldn't become necessary.

"This is Marissa Martin." Rooster directed my attention to a second woman, this one with flaming red hair that looked as if it came out of a bottle.

"Foxy," Marissa countered, extending her hand. "My name is Foxy."

A tall man with a cue in his hand snorted as he circled the pool table at the back of the room. He was the only one who didn't rush over to meet me. He had brown hair that brushed the top of his shoulders, green eyes, a noticeable scar through his left eyebrow and an attitude that rankled. He'd barely said a word yet I could already tell I wasn't going to like him.

"No one is buying the Foxy thing," he called out as he lined up another shot. "I mean ... why would you want that as a nickname anyway?"

Marissa shrugged, unbothered by his derisive tone. "Perhaps because I'm foxy." She sent him a flirty wink that turned my stomach, and then focused on me. "Scout is a fun name, I guess. I mean ... were you a Girl Scout? Is that why you have that name?"

"She doesn't know why she has that name," Rooster interjected. "She was abandoned as a kid and doesn't know her real name. The firefighter who found her named her that. Let it go."

I felt put on the spot thanks to Rooster's outburst, but I remained outwardly cool because I didn't want to show my unprotected underbelly to potential enemies. "It's fine," I gritted out, shaking my head and focusing on the older man shooting pool with the younger one. "And you are?"

"Whistler," he replied, his lips curving. His hair was long and gray and he wore it in a loose ponytail. Of everyone here, he seemed the most at home. "I own this place."

"Oh." Well, that explained that. "It's a nice bar."

He snorted. "It is what it is."

"Um ... you own the bar and serve the cause?" I felt stupid asking the question but was obviously curious.

"I'm retired from the cause," he corrected. "I still help when I can. The bar gets most of my attention. That doesn't mean I don't pitch in when it's necessary."

"Oh, well ... ." I honestly didn't know what to say. Thankfully, Whistler wasn't comfortable with awkward silences and decided to fill it himself. He jerked his thumb in the other man's direction. "This is Gunner Stratton. He's our local Mr. Fix-It. If you run into issues with your bike, he's the one to take it to. He's also involved in other club operations, so if you have any questions he's a good guy to ask."

Gunner? Who names their kid Gunner? That had to be a chosen moniker versus a given one. "Is that your real name?"

"It's the only thing I answer to," Gunner replied, leaning on his cue as he regarded me. "It's not as cool as Scout, I'll give you that, but somehow I've managed to survive."

From the moment I saw him I could feel his attitude and judgmental spirit from across the room ... and I didn't like it. There was no doubt that feeling would only continue to grow because up close and personal he was even ruder than he initially appeared. He was also apparently full of braggadocio. The cockiness wafting off him was downright overwhelming, like bad cologne in a stagnant environment.

"Great." I forced a smile that was more of a sneer. "We can get into a fight about our names later. I'm thinking noon, if that works for you."

Instead of bowing to a verbal spat and embracing the savagery I was certain lurked in his heart, he snickered. "I'll see if I can pencil you in."

"Let's not fight," Bonnie suggested, leaning back in her chair as she rested her feet on a nearby table. She looked relaxed ... other than those really odd black eyes of hers, of course. There was something about her that felt "off," though. I simply couldn't explain it. "What kind of witch are you?"

I'd been expecting the question. It was almost always the first thing asked when meeting other members of the Spells Angels. We were a unique group that collected a variety of paranormal soldiers. Witches were the most common members, though, and I'd learned throughout the years that most witches felt the need to typecast new arrivals because it made them feel better about ... well, just about everything. Most witches were neat and liked everything in their place. I didn't happen to fall into that category.

"I'm a hereditary witch," I replied easily. "I also straddle the hedge witch line."

"You're a hedge witch?" Gunner shifted to face me, the pool game forgotten. "Does that mean you can talk to ghosts?"

I shrugged, suddenly uncomfortable with his pointed stare. "I've talked to ghosts here and there," I acknowledged. "I can see through the veil at times when it's necessary."

"Hedge witches are rare," Bonnie noted. "I'm a ceremonial witch myself."

That didn't surprise me. Bonnie looked to be a regimented woman, her hair perfectly in place despite the bourbon and early hour. Ceremony witches love their rituals. I'd met a number of witches who fell into that category over the years and they weren't always fun to hang around. I was more lackadaisical when it came to my magic, something that serious witches don't always appreciate.

"I look forward to discussing philosophy with you," I lied. "What about you?" I focused on Gunner. "Are you a witch ... or something else?" I was uncomfortable asking the question, but I couldn't get a firm read on him. Compared to everyone else, who were apparently open books and didn't care that I could read their secrets from ten feet away, he was an enigma.

"I'm my own man," Gunner replied, his tone easygoing even though something I couldn't quite identify lurked behind his eyes. "We haven't had a hedge witch in these parts for years. It might prove ... interesting. I wonder if that's why they sent you."

The last statement wasn't directed at me — more to himself ... and maybe Rooster, too — but I responded all the same. "I wasn't specifically chosen for this assignment. We were simply told you needed help and an individual was randomly selected to come here."

"Randomly?" He cocked an eyebrow. "What ... did you draw straws or something?"

I saw no reason to lie. "That's exactly what we did."

This time the chuckle he let loose was low and throaty. "Oh, that's just perfect."

I narrowed my eyes. "Do you have a problem?" My tone was accusatory but I didn't care. He bothered me on a level I couldn't quite grasp and his merriment was grating.

"I don't have a problem. In fact ... ." He didn't finish what he was going to say. Instead, his head snapped toward the door as it opened, his lips curving down when a young woman stepped inside.

I followed his gaze, ready for a fight, but the person I saw standing there was hardly a threat. In fact, she was very clearly a child. She might've been careening toward adulthood — at least in years if not maturity — but she obviously hadn't crossed the line.

"Raisin, what are you doing here?" Rooster complained, shaking his head.

"Don't call me Raisin," the girl barked, hands on her hips. "You know I don't like that."

"You wanted a nickname," Rooster reminded her.

"Yeah, but I wanted something like Bone Crusher. Raisin sounds like ... well ... raisins. It's not badass."

"Neither are you," Marissa pointed out. "By the way, shouldn't you be at school?"

"We don't have school today," the girl shot back. "It's a three-day weekend. It's Monday and we still have Monday off."

Rooster looked dubious but didn't push the issue. Instead, he stated the obvious problem with her appearance at the bar. "You can't be here. You're not old enough."

"You weren't at the office," she argued. "I knew you had a new crew member coming in, and when you weren't at the office I decided to track you down here. This isn't my fault. It's your fault. You know how I feel about meeting new people."

Rooster sighed, the sound long and drawn out. "Geez. You're going to get Whistler in trouble if you're not careful."

Whistler merely shrugged. "We have an out if the sheriff shows up." He smirked in Gunner's direction. "Isn't that right?"

"I'm not answering that question," he growled. "Just ... it's your shot. Take it."

Apparently deciding that it was fine if she stayed, the girl they called Raisin hurried in my direction, not stopping until she was directly in front of me. "I'm Ruthie Morton. I'm so happy to meet you." She shoved her hand at me, which meant I had no choice but to shake it or snub her. Since she was obviously a regular fixture around the others, I decided I had no choice but to be nice ... even though children in general make me uncomfortable.

"Scout Randall." I introduced myself with some trepidation. "It's nice to meet you."

"Right back at you." She was so excited she almost tripped over her own feet as she tried to plant herself in such a manner that I had no hope of escape. "I want to hear absolutely everything about you. I mean ... everything. Where did you grow up? Do you have a boyfriend? You look the sort who has a boyfriend. Is he big? Did he come to Hawthorne Hollow with you? Oh, do you have kids? I've never met anyone in the crew who has kids. You would be the first. Not that there's anything wrong with that, I mean. I've just never seen it."

I was flabbergasted by the endless stream of words. "Um ... ."

"Ignore her," Gunner instructed, shaking his head. "If you answer her questions now you'll have to keep answering them for as long as you're here. Raisin can't seem to help herself from sticking her nose in places it doesn't belong."

Indignant, the teenager squared her shoulders. "Curiosity is not a crime."

"Yeah, yeah, yeah." He dismissed her with a wave of his hand. "You should let Scout settle in before you interrogate her. She'll be around for a bit, so you have time."

"Maybe I don't want to wait." Ruthie's eyes filled with fire. "Have you considered that?"

"Not really." Gunner's tone was dismissive. "Seriously, leave her alone. She hasn't even seen her new digs yet. You're being a pest."

"You're a pest."

Rooster smoothly slid between Gunner and Ruthie before the girl could completely lose her cool. "That will be enough of that," he instructed, laying a heavy hand on the girl's shoulder. "Now is not the time. We have a new member of our team. This isn't how I expected to introduce her to everybody."

Yeah, speaking of that ... . "I was under the impression you had a bigger crew," I noted, returning to the business at hand. "I was told you had more riders than this." I tried to refrain from being dismissive as I gestured around the room.

"We do, but this is a larger area than you're used to," Rooster replied. "Some of the team members are out on assignment. We'll introduce you when they come back. As for now, I think you're better off getting a tour of the town."

I was pretty sure I'd seen every highlight — both of them — upon crossing the township line. Still, I forced a smile and nodded. This was standard procedure. I understood the rules and had no choice but to play the game. "Sure." I expected him to give me the tour. He was the boss, after all. Instead, he decided to fob off the responsibility.

"Gunner, you need to show her around," Rooster announced. "I'm going to take Raisin here to school to make sure the story she's telling about a holiday is true. That means you're on tour duty."

The only person more annoyed by the suggestion than me was Gunner. The look he briefly shot me was full of annoyance.

"Is a tour really necessary?" he challenged.

Rooster nodded without hesitation. "It is. You know how it goes. This is a new environment for Scout. We don't want her to be caught unaware."

Gunner sighed, resigned. "Fine. I'm not going to like it, though."

That made two of us.

TWO

I tucked my hands in the pockets of my well-worn Levi's as I
followed Gunner out of the building. When my instructions from the home office told me to meet my new co-workers at a
bar, I'd been suspicious. Now that I'd met the handful of people inside
the structure, I was even more leery.

How did I end up here?

No, seriously. I was starting to wonder if someone had somehow
rigged the straws before we drew.

"Is that your bike?" Gunner slowed his pace as he stared at my
Harley-Davidson Street Glide. It was black — my favorite color —
and polished to a blinding glare because I'd had it detailed the
previous day. If I couldn't take pride in my ride, what could I take
pride in?

I nodded. "Yeah."

"You've modified it so it sits even lower to the ground." The tour
momentarily abandoned, he moved closer to the bike. "You have a few
upgrades, too, including custom foot pegs."

"I like what I like," I replied simply. "That bike is comfortable."

"I don't doubt it." His gaze was thoughtful as he turned back to me.
"Do you do your own work?"

"Some. I can't do everything. I took automotive classes in high school. While all the other girls were in band and acting classes, I was getting dirty and learning about engines. It actually turned out to be a good choice."

"Well, it looks like you keep her up nicely." He gestured toward a black Ducati Monster 797, which to my knowledge wasn't even available in America yet. "That's one of mine."

I arched an eyebrow. "You have more than one bike?"

For the first time since we'd met, he cracked a legitimate smile. "Doesn't everybody?"

"No. What happens if you have to run and can only take one bike? Do you just abandon it?"

The question caught him off guard. "I've never had to run and leave a bike behind for more than a few hours."

"Oh, well ... ."

"Have you?" He seemed legitimately interested in my answer.

I shrugged and turned away from the beautiful motorcycle. It really was spectacular, although not exactly my style. That didn't mean I wouldn't enjoy taking it for a spin if offered the chance. "So ... a tour of Hawthorne Hollow?"

He kept his eyes on me for an extended beat and then nodded. "We might as well walk. I know you're probably like the rest of us and don't want to leave your bike behind, but we're talking about a small area ... and the bikes are safer here because random people won't dare come up to them at the Cauldron."

I nodded. I'd expected as much. "That's fine. I hopped on my bike at four this morning and could use some stretching time after that long ride."

"You came from Detroit, right?"

"Yeah. The chapter is much bigger there."

"I think you'll find the chapter is much stronger here, but that's something you'll have to figure out on your own."

I couldn't tell if he was being truthful or simply bragging because he thought I was talking smack about his club. Either way, I decided to let it go.

"How did Hawthorne Hollow get chosen for a Spells Angels stronghold?" I opted to ask the most pressing question first. "I mean ... this doesn't exactly strike me as a hotbed of paranormal activity."

In truth, the Spells Angels were more than a biker gang. On the surface, people were expected to be wary of us, want to steer clear. Television and movies were supposed to have programmed into their heads the notion that we were dangerous and not to be trifled with. We were made up of paranormal beings and expected to fight the good fight against other supernatural creatures who weren't necessarily worried about making the world a better place, but we were more than the sum of our parts. We kept the truth about our group on the down low. That was by design, so we could operate without law enforcement breathing down our necks.

"You'd be surprised," Gunner countered. "There are creatures drawn to this area because they think they'll be able to get away with murder — and I mean that literally — because it's so isolated up here. The need for a chapter in this area is greater than most areas."

That hadn't occurred to me, but it made sense. "And what do we fight most often here?"

His eyes were heavy as they snagged mine. "Shifters are prevalent."

"Most shifters aren't evil," I pointed out.

His lips curved. "I know that. I was wondering if you did."

"So, that was a test?"

He shrugged. "I was simply feeling you out. This is a weird situation for all of us. Most of the people assigned here are familiar with the area. Some grew up here and others grew up in neighboring towns. You did neither."

"At least not that I know of," I agreed. "It's always possible I spent time here as a kid and simply don't remember."

He narrowed his eyes. "Yeah, about that ... I'm sorry. It sounds like you had it rough."

"There's no need for you to apologize. You obviously didn't abandon me at a fire station."

"Still, that has to be difficult. You don't remember anything from before then?"

"No."

"Doesn't that bother you?"

I immediately started shaking my head. "No."

He looked as if he didn't believe me and was going to continue pressing the subject, but he ultimately changed course. "Hawthorne Hollow is old. It's been here for two hundred years, although the area around it wasn't settled until after that."

"What cities are close?" I asked. "I mean ... I looked on a map. We're close to Lake Michigan, which means Traverse City is about thirty minutes away. I didn't see much else of note."

"That's because there's not much else of note. The only other town that gets any buzz in this area is Hemlock Cove. That's about forty minutes away. If you get time, head over. It's ... interesting."

Something about the way he said the word caused suspicion to rear its ugly head. "What does that mean?"

"It's a town of witches."

"Sounds fun."

"Most of the town consists of people *pretending* to be witches," he clarified. "There are a few real witches there, but most of the town is a facade."

That sounded less fun. "I think I'll pass."

"It's a worth a visit, but it's not necessary now. As for Hawthorne Hollow ... well ... it is what it is." He let loose a sigh as we arrived at the corner of Main Street. "This is it. Almost everything of note is right on this main drive. There's a grocery store that way, but it doesn't offer much. I recommend driving to Gaylord once a week for groceries. They have a better selection."

I pursed my lips as I regarded what could loosely be described as a town. There were fifteen buildings on Main Street and all of them served a specific purpose.

"There's a gas station, the police station, pizza shop, bank, diner, coffee shop, bakery and hardware store," he continued. "There's also a yarn store that's allowed to remain operational because Mrs. Yancy is a hundred years old and no one makes her pay rent on the building. That's it."

"Oh, now, come on," I teased, furrowing my brow when a woman walking on the other side of the street caught sight of us and offered a happy wave. "There's also a bookstore, although I can't figure out how a town this size can maintain a bookstore." Honestly, the bookstore made me happy when I saw it.

"Don't get too excited," Gunner chided. "That's the coffee shop. The selection of books inside consists of about twenty of the current bestsellers. If you're a book fan, I suggest investing in an e-reader, because your selection here isn't great."

That was disappointing. Still ... . "How is the coffee?"

He grinned. "The best in town."

"Is that saying much?"

"You might be surprised." He purposely turned away from the woman, who looked to be crossing the street, and prodded me along the sidewalk. I found his reaction troubling.

"Is that your girlfriend?" I glanced over my shoulder. The woman was still watching us, the expression on her face impossible to read.

"No." Gunner was firm. "I don't have a girlfriend."

"She seems to be trying to get your attention," I pointed out, causing him to sigh.

"It's fine. Come this way." He increased his pace, leaving me no choice but to hurry after him. By the time we got to the end of the block I was out of breath and confused.

"What's your deal?"

He ignored the question. "These are the township offices. There's also a library, but the books in there are as bad as the books in the coffee shop. If you need land deeds, this is the place to go. The woman behind the counter is friendly and helps without getting into your business."

I couldn't hide my amusement. "Do you often need land deeds here?"

"You'd be surprised." He kept walking. "This is one of three cemeteries within the township limits," he volunteered. "There's another out on the highway. It's smaller, but you'll probably find yourself there as well."

I was confused. "Why does a town this size need three cemeteries?"

"You're just asking yourself that?"

"I ... well ... yeah." It hadn't occurred to me even though I'd noted the locations when I was riding through on my way to The Rusty Cauldron. "That seems weird."

"Hawthorne Hollow is a busy place," Gunner explained. "There's a reason you were sent here. It wasn't simply because Rooster whined and they capitulated."

"I didn't assume that, no matter what you think."

"Well, that's good." He sighed and dragged his hand through his hair. "I think we might've gotten off on the wrong foot. You have attitude with me, and it's probably deserved."

"That's because you have attitude with me," I shot back.

"I'm simply not good with new people." He lowered his voice and glanced around, averting his gaze when an elderly woman kneeling next to a tombstone in the cemetery excitedly waved at him. "People have attitude when it comes to Hawthorne Hollow. Some, like yourself, can't seem to help themselves. I'm defensive, which isn't a good thing."

I scratched the side of my nose. "Is there a reason everyone seems to know you?"

"Give it a few days. Everyone will know you, too."

"Maybe. But you seem to be popular." The woman kept waving, almost frantically so. "Why is that? I mean ... are you a local celebrity on your downtime? Also, if you don't wave back at that woman she's going to break a hip or something."

He groaned but slowly turned in the woman's direction. The half-wave he offered made me smile. "Hello, Mrs. Kapinski," he called out. "How are you today?"

"I'm just fine, dear," she replied, exhaling heavily and finally dropping her arm. "How are you? I saw your father a bit ago. You're starting to look more and more like him."

I had no idea who Gunner's father was, but he obviously didn't like the comparison. Still, he kept his manners in check and nodded. "Thank you, Mrs. Kapinski."

It took everything I had not to burst out laughing at his hangdog expression. Instead I merely pressed my lips together and waited.

"I know what you're thinking," he started.

I seriously doubted that. "I'm not thinking anything."

"You are." He made a face. "You're thinking that I'm popular with certain members of the population. I can't help that. I grew up here. Everyone knows me."

Things slipped into place. "You grew up right here in Hawthorne Hollow?"

He nodded, morose. "I did. The town is small. You'll be a familiar face in days. I'll always be one of the prodigal sons. I left for a bit and came back. I thought I wanted to get away, but ultimately that turned out not to be true. I'm a Hawthorne Hollow boy at heart ... and I'm loved here."

"That's not a bad thing," I pointed out, falling into step with him as he turned the corner. We were heading along a residential street, although I had no idea why. "There's no reason to be embarrassed."

"I'm not embarrassed." As if to prove himself, he changed the subject. "Most people here take pride in the town. They keep up their lawns and don't leave trash lying around. That's probably different from the city."

"Only *some* parts of the city," I clarified. "People have pride in their homes wherever they live. There's always going to be a good or bad element. That doesn't come from where you live but rather who you are."

"That's a fair point."

We lapsed into easy conversation, mostly about the town. I was curious about how Gunner fit into this specific town, but I figured that would become obvious after a short amount of time. He led me in a big square, and before I realized it we were on a path cutting through some rather thick woods and looked to be heading to nowhere.

"What are we doing out here?" I wasn't exactly nervous — I'd been in enough fights for my life that I barely batted an eyelash these days when things popped up — but the change in the scenery was cause for alarm. I wasn't exactly a woodsy girl. I preferred urban streets, as I said.

"This is a shortcut you should know about," Gunner replied. "You can bring your bike down this trail. We've smoothed most of the ruts. On the other side of the trees you run smack into the parking lot at the back of the Cauldron."

"Oh." I was momentarily chagrined. "That's a good tip."

He smirked. "I didn't bring you here to do anything untoward. In fact ... ." He slowed his pace and reached over to snag my arm when I didn't follow suit. "Wait."

I was already moving ahead of him when I sensed a hint of movement to my right. My instincts took over and I dodged to my left, narrowly escaping when a thin creature — one that looked like a moving twig with leaves for hair — threw itself at me.

"What the ... ?" I cursed under my breath as I overbalanced and tipped to the side. I hit the well-worn pathway hard enough that my breath was momentarily knocked from my lungs.

"It's a spriggan," Gunner announced, drawing a knife from a sheath on his belt. I hadn't noticed the weapon earlier, which made me feel stupid. He was obviously ready for something to happen. This was another test, one that I'd failed miserably.

"I have no idea what a spriggan is," I gritted out as I glared at the creature. It had gnarly long teeth and its hands boasted three fingers. "I'm assuming it needs to die, though, right?"

"Don't worry about that," Gunner growled, dodging when the creature lashed out at him. "I've got it."

He was doing that manly "It's my job to save a woman" thing. It grated even though I was out of my element.

"No, I've got it," I countered, unleashing a smattering of magic from my fingertips and shoving it as hard as I could in the direction of the spriggan. "You just sit there and look pretty."

The magic flowed freely and smacked into the creature with such force that the spriggan was knocked back on its heels. The creature's eyes went wide as — at the exact moment of impact — fire exploded from the magical tendrils I slammed toward it. The creature screeched as it instantaneously went up in flames.

Gunner was moving to stab it with his blade, but he had to rear back to keep out of the way of the fire. "Hey!"

I merely shrugged, calling back the magic so the flames died. The spriggan collapsed on the ground, a charred mess.

"What did you just do?" Gunner asked, his face pale. "I ... what was that?"

I wasn't expecting the question. "Magic," I replied simply. "Isn't that what we're supposed to do?"

"I thought you were a hedge witch," he countered. "That's what you said."

"I also said I was a hereditary witch," I reminded him, accepting his hand when he reached out to pull me to my feet. "I'm more than one thing."

He worked his jaw but didn't back down when I regained my footing. My chest was parallel to his and he searched my face for answers he apparently didn't feel he was getting. "What kind of witch was your mother?"

"I don't know." That was the truth. "I already told you I don't remember anything from before I was five or so. It's simply not there."

"Or maybe you're too traumatized to remember," he offered.

"Maybe, but ... it doesn't matter. I've known about my magic since I was a kid. I don't know where it came from, but I can do more than most other witches I've come into contact with."

"I can see that." Gunner let loose a sigh as he glanced at the dead spriggan. "You handled that well."

"It was just a tree with a mouth."

He smirked. "It was more than that, but ... I guess we don't have to worry about you taking on your new environment. You handled that well."

"Yes, I'm a masterful witch," I drawled, moving back to the path. "Were you really going to stab that tree?"

"I don't have fire magic. That was my only option."

"I guess. Still, it doesn't seem very prudent. I ... ." I was feeling full of myself, enjoying the fact that he was impressed. I was so caught up in what I was saying that I didn't pay attention to where I was walking and tripped over what I initially thought was a branch jutting out at the edge of the trees.

"Oomph."

Gunner attempted to grab my arm to save me, but it was already too late. I pitched face forward and hit the ground for the second time in less than ten minutes. My ego didn't like the bashing it was taking.

"Well, that sucked," I complained, rubbing my shoulder to attack the small jolts throbbing through it. "I thought you said this path was clear."

When Gunner didn't immediately respond, I forced myself to shift so I could look at him. He wasn't focused on me. Instead, his eyes were pointed at an object on the ground.

What I initially thought was a tree branch turned out to be something else entirely ... and it made my blood run cold.

"Is that a ... leg?" I swallowed hard.

He nodded as he dug in his pocket for his phone. "Yeah, and it's attached to a body."

I wasn't sure I wanted to see anything else. "Is it a human?"

"Yeah."

"How did he die?"

"Badly." He hit a button on his phone and pressed it to his ear. "I need to report a dead body," he announced when someone picked up on the other end. "I definitely don't think it was natural causes."

THREE

*I*t was hardly the first body I'd come into contact with. You couldn't be in my line of work — monster hunter extraordinaire, for those still asking questions — and not see bodies.

Still, mere hours after landing in my new home, seeing the body was something of a jolt.

"The police are on their way," Gunner announced as he knelt next to me. His expression was hard to read, but I thought I recognized sympathy and worry rolling around in the depths of his eyes.

"That's good." I worked overtime to calm myself. I wasn't the sort of witch who panicked in the face of danger. "It's a man."

"What?" Confused, Gunner shifted. "What do you mean?"

I gestured toward the body. I was still on the ground, no longer sprawled but not on my feet either. I couldn't make myself look away from the body no matter how hard I tried. "It's a man."

Gunner slowly shifted his gaze to the body. "Yeah. The facial features are obliterated, but it's very clearly a man."

That was a harsh way to put it. *Obliterated.* I wasn't sure how to respond. "Do you recognize him?"

Gunner arched an eyebrow. "Should I recognize him?"

"You're Hawthorne Hollow's favored son."

He scowled. "That doesn't mean I recognize every resident," he pointed out. "I mean ... his face is kind of gone."

He wasn't wrong. Whoever the man had been in life was a mystery. The features that had defined him — eyes, nose, lips, cheeks ... even his brow ridge — were gone. It was almost as if someone had purposely tried to remove his identity, which I found interesting.

"I don't see any tattoos or anything on the skin that's visible," I noted, rolling to my knees as I studied the body more closely. "Fingers are dirty, as if he's been working outside, perhaps in a garden or something. The clothes are relatively new, though, and not something you would wear when doing yard work."

Gunner stared hard. "What are you getting at? Are you suddenly a detective?"

I shrugged, noncommittal. "I've simply seen my share of bodies. They're prevalent in Detroit ... and it's not always because of the job."

Gunner's expression softened. "Oh. I ... yeah, I can see that." His eyes lingered on me for a beat before moving to the body. "We don't have a large indigent population. There are one or two people who have taken over abandoned homes. It's not easy to live up here if you don't have gas and power in the winter. It's too cold."

That hadn't occurred to me. Michigan was known for brutal winters, but they mostly occurred in the Upper Peninsula and north of Bay City. The southern part of the state saw snow, but it was nowhere near the levels Hawthorne Hollow was probably used to. "So, you're saying this is a local," I supplied as I hunkered lower to stare at what should've been the man's profile. "Huh."

Gunner slid me a sidelong look. "Huh, what?"

"Nothing. It's just ... weird."

"You think it's weird that the body has no face?" He was incredulous. "Well, isn't that convenient? We finally have something we agree on. I think that's weird, too."

His tone set my teeth on edge. "Is there something you want to say to me?" I felt I'd been more than patient. He was trying to agitate me, but I had no idea why. "You've been up my butt since I got here."

He made a face. "I most certainly haven't been up your butt. That is just ... stupid."

"What would you call it? You haven't been friendly."

"I didn't know that was a requirement of the job." He planted his hands on his narrow hips. "You're the one who flew into town with an attitude. Don't think I didn't notice. You can't turn things around on me now and expect me to simply absorb the responsibility for your attitude."

He was daft. There was no other way to explain his reaction. "Attitude? What attitude? I've been nothing but pleasant despite the fact that I've been forced to move to a town the size of a postage stamp."

"There!" He jabbed out a finger. "That right there. You've had attitude about the town since you landed and I don't appreciate it."

"I have not!" I was offended on behalf of ... well, people who were often offended for reasons they couldn't identify. I honestly had no idea why I was so worked up. His need to jump on me for no apparent reason rankled. "I haven't said a thing about this town."

"You might not have said anything, but you've wrinkled your nose left and right during the entire tour," he shot back. "It's unpleasant ... and disrespectful."

I narrowed my eyes. "I don't wrinkle my nose."

"Oh, please. You're the poster girl for mothers everywhere who say, 'Your face is going to freeze like that.' I bet your mother said that to you a million times when you were a kid because of that face you make."

"I wouldn't know. I don't remember her."

He stilled, the simple statement taking the wind out of his sails. "I ... that's neither here nor there." He recovered quickly and shook his head. "I'm being serious here. You've had attitude since you landed and I don't appreciate it."

"I have not!" Even as I barked the words I couldn't stop myself from mentally going over my demeanor since I'd hit town. I was almost positive I hadn't said one negative thing. Sure, I'd thought them — this wasn't exactly my dream assignment, after all — but I hadn't said a single word. "I think you're worked up because you have a complex about the size of the town. That probably ties into your complex about the size of other things."

His mouth dropped open. "Listen here, I ... ." Whatever he was going to say died on his lips when a large figure appeared on the path behind him.

Instinctively, I leaned forward to shove him out of the way so the shadow that was closing in on us wouldn't be able to attack him from behind. Confused because I was attempting to touch him, Gunner caught my wrists and glared.

"What do you think you're doing?" he complained. "This is a no-touching zone."

"She was trying to save you from me," the interloper announced, causing Gunner to jerk in surprise as he turned and frowned.

The newcomer was probably in his mid-fifties, perhaps early-sixties, if I had to guess. He had salt-and-pepper hair and wore a uniform that declared him Chief Stratton. The name accompanied by a badge and a weapon secured to his utility belt told me all I needed to know. The police had finally arrived.

"I'm sorry." I breathed heavily as I recovered. "You simply took me by surprise. I didn't hear you coming."

And that was a problem all on its own. Why hadn't I heard him coming? My senses were generally over-tuned and I heard things that weren't necessary ... or important. I couldn't remember the last time I didn't sense when someone who posed a potential danger was approaching.

"You could've made a noise," Gunner complained, releasing my wrists as he focused on the man. "That's the polite thing to do."

"I don't remember agreeing to be polite during our interactions," the chief shot back. "I mean ... was that in an agreement I signed and forgot about?"

Gunner let loose a weary sigh as he dragged a hand through his hair, leaving it more of a mess than when he started. "No. I simply didn't hear you. I ... you surprised me."

"I don't think it was me being sneaky that caused you to forget where you were." The man's eyes were heavy as they landed on me. "Who's your new friend?"

"No one," Gunner answered automatically. "She's not important."

And he thought I was insulting. I straightened, murdering him with a dark look before focusing on the chief. "My name is Scout Randall. I'm new in town."

"Oh?" Stratton didn't look impressed as he arched an eyebrow. "I didn't realize Hawthorne Hollow was getting a new resident." The look he shot Gunner was accusatory. "I wasn't informed that I should be expecting anyone."

Now it was my turn to be confused. "Is there a reason you should be informed?"

He shrugged. "Well, some think it's polite to tell me when things happen in my town. Not everyone, mind you, but some people."

"Oh, don't give her grief," Gunner snapped. "It's not her fault that you constantly walk around with a stick up your ... ."

Stratton cleared his throat and cut Gunner off. "You probably don't want to finish that statement, son. It won't go well for either of us if you do."

Reality smacked me across the face — hard — and things slipped into place. "Holy ... you're his father!"

Stratton slowly turned his gaze back to me, amusement curving his lips. "You're just figuring that out?"

His tone bothered me as much as that of his son's. "I guess the last name should've been a hint. Gunner Stratton. Chief Stratton. In a town this size you would have to be related."

"And here we go complaining about the town again," Gunner muttered.

"I'm not complaining." For some reason, I wanted to poke him ... with a big stick, or an ax. "I was simply stating a fact. You can't get uptight every time I mention the size of the town. If you do, we'll be fighting nonstop. Is that what you want?"

Instead of responding with a "no" as I expected, he merely shrugged. "I'm fine with fighting. You look as if you can hold your own."

"Ugh." I slapped my hand to my forehead as I groaned. "You're going to drive me insane. I can already tell."

Chief Stratton took me by surprise when he chuckled. "Oh, geez. Is this you guys' version of foreplay or something? If so, you've got a lot to learn."

Gunner scowled. "Don't add to this madness."

"I'll add to whatever madness I want, *Graham*," he snapped, drawing out the name and causing me to tilt my head to the side.

"Graham?"

"Don't!" Gunner extended a warning finger in my direction. It was too late.

"Is that your real name?" It made sense now. He didn't like his name, and they both started with G. Although ... Graham sounded less ridiculous to me than Gunner. "Why don't you like the name Graham?"

"I didn't say I didn't like it," he replied, his eyes flashing. "I simply don't respond to it."

"He doesn't like it because his name is Graham Stratton Jr.," the chief volunteered, dragging my gaze back to him. "He's got a complex about sharing his name with me."

Ah, and there was the rest of it. That made so much sense. "I knew he had a complex," I admitted. "I didn't know it was about his name."

Stratton snickered. "Yes, well, my son is nothing if not ... stupid."

I straightened, surprised by his tone. "It's just a name."

"It's more than that." Stratton's gaze landed on his son before he turned to the body. "What do we have here?"

"It's a body," I answered automatically.

"Really?"

My eyebrows drew together as annoyance flowed through me. "Then why did you ask?"

"It's not so funny now that you're getting to know him better, huh?" Gunner challenged. He'd moved to lean against a nearby tree, arms folded over his chest.

"I'm not sure what to make of any of it," I admitted. "I'll get back to you once I've settled."

"I'm waiting on pins and needles."

Stratton's gaze bounced between us before he shook his head and turned back to the body. "This isn't normal." He sounded as if he was talking to himself rather than us. "I mean ... it can't be."

"Oh, really?" Gunner's tone dripped with sarcasm. "What was your first clue? I'm guessing it was the lack of a face."

I never had a father — at least that I remembered — but the look on Stratton's face now was straight out of a how-to book for fathers. It was hilarious enough that I had to bite the inside of my cheek to keep from laughing.

"The missing face is definitely a hint," Stratton shot back. "I mean ... especially since it was removed by magical means."

Even though I was enjoying myself despite the surreal situation, the words knocked me for a loop. I looked to Gunner for leadership on how to handle the situation — in Detroit, you never used the M-word with people not in the club — but he was so focused on his father he barely looked at me.

"How do you know it was done magically?" he asked after a beat.

Stratton pointed toward the man's profile. "There are no jagged cuts. If this was done with a knife, then the tissue would be an absolute mess ... like wet dog food or something."

My stomach turned at the comparison as Gunner tilted his head and stared at the smooth area that rested beneath the blood.

"I can see that." Gunner dropped to a crouch to stare at the body. "What about a laser? There are things like laser scalpels, right?"

"There are, but I don't see how anyone could get one out of a hospital," Stratton replied. "Of course, even if we overlook that, this isn't one big wound as much as an absence of flesh."

"Really?" I wasn't squeamish but the turn of that particular phrase was enough to make me swear off meat for the foreseeable future. "Do you have to put it that way?"

Stratton chuckled. "You're going to be fun. I can already tell."

"No, she's not," Gunner shot back. "She's going to be a pain in the you-know-what."

"Maybe." Stratton was momentarily thoughtful as he regarded me before turning back to the body. "This was definitely ritual. I mean ... look at his wrists. There are symbols carved into them. The face has been ripped off, but it wasn't done physically. This is definitely magic."

All the signs were there. I simply hadn't put them together. I felt like a dolt for missing what should've been obvious.

"So, the question is, what manner of creature can make something like this happen?" Gunner mused, rubbing his hand over his chin as he regarded the body. "You don't have any ideas, do you?"

It took me a moment to realize he was talking to me. "Definitely not." I vehemently shook my head. "I've never seen anything like this before in my life. Heck, I hadn't seen anything like that spriggan either. It's starting to become obvious that I'm out of my depth."

"Spriggan?" Stratton lifted his chin. "Is that the thing I saw dead in the woods? I couldn't be sure if it used to be something or if kids were just out here setting fires again. I was going to ask you about it."

"It's a spriggan," Gunner replied. "I was going to take it out the normal way, but Scout here had other ideas."

"I see." Stratton's gaze was heavy when it landed on me. "What kind of name is Scout?"

I shrugged. "What kind of name is Graham?"

"A family name."

"Well, Scout isn't. I was named by the firefighter who found me when I was a kid."

Stratton looked to his son for further information but Gunner merely shook his head. "It's a long story," he said. "You can ask her about it later. We have a bigger problem."

"You mean the guy without a face?" Stratton gestured toward the body again and shook his head. "Yeah. He's definitely a problem. First, we have to find out who he is. After that, we have to figure out who did this. Then, after that, we'll have to put the public at ease without telling them the truth. It's going to be a lovely couple of days. I can already tell."

"Not just that," Gunner countered. "If some manner of creature is strong enough to let loose a spell that can do this, that means we're dealing with a dangerous individual. I'm guessing jail won't be an option at the end of this tale. That means we'll have to eradicate what-ever it is."

"I don't want to hear about that." Stratton held up his hand to silence his son when Gunner started to argue. "I'm serious. I can't sit here and listen when you're talking about murder."

"I'm not talking about murder. I'm talking about protection for the town. We can't have this happening over and over again. It's ... an abomination."

"It is that," Stratton agreed. "I'm not the type who thinks an eye for an eye is always the correct response, though."

"Is that what you think I'm suggesting?" Gunner's temper was back on full display.

"I think that you're feeling the need to wreak havoc," Stratton replied without hesitation. "I'm here to tell you that I don't agree."

"And what are you going to do about it?"

Stratton shrugged. "I don't know. I guess we'll have to see how things play out."

The way the two men eyed each other told me things were hardly settled. If this was a truce, it was an uneasy one.

Well, great. If we didn't have enough on our plates, what was one more little problem?

FOUR

*T*he rest of the day passed in a blur.

By the time we got back to the Cauldron, news had spread around town that a body had been found in the woods. Rooster was happy that Gunner and I were on the scene so we could explain the disposition of the body, but he looked as flummoxed as we felt after we described what we'd discovered.

"There's no way a spriggan did that," he mused, a glass of bourbon clutched tightly in his hand. The bar was dead, although that wasn't a surprise given the time of day. I had a feeling things would pick up later in the evening.

"I'm not familiar with spriggans," I admitted, taking a seat on the stool next to him. "What are they?"

"They're old and of another world. They originated in Ireland — and weren't always dangerous — but they moved to the New World during times of mass immigration. Once here, once in the wilds of a new world, they took on a life of their own."

That wasn't really an answer. Or at least not as much of an answer as I wanted. "How many of them live around here?"

"Enough that we have to watch things closely during hunting

season ... and morel season ... and camping season ... and snowmobile season."

"So ... year-round?"

He snickered. "Pretty much. They're not very bright, so it's not hard to catch them. Still, setting it on fire was a dangerous proposition. It's the dry season. What would've happened if it ran into the trees after the initial attack?"

"I don't know. I wasn't expecting the attack. I guess next time I'll know to try something else."

"Just keep it in mind." Rooster downed the rest of his drink and glanced at the clock on the wall. "It's getting late. I should probably show you to your new digs and let you get settled. I didn't mean for you to be plunged into a big job so quickly." He flicked his eyes to Gunner. "I expect you to touch base with your father later, get whatever information we might need to start looking for our culprit."

Gunner didn't appear happy with the suggestion. "He doesn't enjoy sharing information."

"Yeah, well, in this case I don't see where he has many options. He can't handle it himself."

Gunner obviously agreed, because he didn't offer further argument.

I FOLLOWED ROOSTER OUT of town. The road to my new lodging was dirt, which meant ruts. I paid close attention as I traversed it, although Rooster appeared more comfortable with the route, barely glancing down as we chewed up miles. I figured I would eventually get comfortable with the road, that is if I stayed long enough.

Once we stopped, I immediately wanted to turn around and flee back to Detroit. The mystery and intrigue of faceless bodies and spriggans aside, the cabin he led me to was not what I would call comfortable. In fact, it looked straight out of a horror movie.

"Oh, well ... ." I didn't know what to say so I merely stared.

More amused than contrite, Rooster shrugged. "It belongs to the company. If you decide to stay after your initial placement, I'm sure you can find something that's up to your standards."

He made me sound like a snob. As someone who grew up in a bevy of foster and group homes, that wasn't the case. Still, this wasn't what I was used to.

"Are you sure the roof is going to hold?" I asked, dubious.

"I have no idea. If you want to fix it up, I'll pay for supplies. You're in charge of the labor, though."

It was better than nothing ... which wasn't saying much. "I'll take you up on that." I was fairly handy when I put my mind to it. "Where can I get supplies?"

"There's a lumberyard on the north side of town. Just tell them you're with me. If they have a question, they'll call to confirm. Get whatever you need."

I nodded. "Okay, well ... are there keys?"

"You're a witch," he reminded me. "You don't need keys."

That might've been true, but I was used to being able to lock my doors to keep humans out once I was safely inside. It was simply one less worry. "So ... I should get new door handles, too. That's what you're saying, right?"

He choked on a laugh. "If you feel the need. You're perfectly safe out here. The perimeter has been salted — at least for the most part — which means that most creatures wouldn't dare cross the boundaries. If they do, you're more than capable of taking care of yourself."

He sounded far more convinced of my abilities than I felt. "What time should I report for work tomorrow?"

"Take the day to look around, do whatever you want around the cabin," he instructed. "If you have questions, you have my number. If you need help, don't hesitate to call."

He said the words, but I couldn't help but wonder if he meant them. Obviously I was the outsider here, not part of the crew. I would either have to fix that or suck it up. I wasn't sure which option was more appealing.

"Well, I'd better get to work."

"I was serious about helping. All you have to do is ask."

That was harder than he realized. "I need to look around first. I'll let you know when I have a better handle on things."

"Good enough."

I SLEPT BECAUSE I WAS exhausted. Otherwise I'm not sure I would've been able to close my eyes for more than twenty minutes at a time. The cabin had good bones, but that was all that could be said about it. Whoever lived in the space before was a pig ... and that was putting it nicely.

I spent hours cleaning the living room and kitchen before ceding to the wishes of my body and passing out. By the time I woke the next morning, all I wanted was a shower. That meant cleaning the bathroom, because I was too skittish to shower in a space that reminded me of a bad *Friday the 13th* movie.

The bathroom project took the better part of the morning. By the time I was finished (and showered), I was already feeling aches and pains that caused me to make a mental note to track down a pharmacy later to get some Advil.

I had my breakfast on the front porch, which also needed to be cleaned, and munched on a granola bar as I surveyed the cabin. In truth, it could be cute with some work. The amount of work for that to happen, though, was mind-boggling. Most everything I could do myself — including roof repair and plumbing tweaks — but I couldn't decide if I wanted to put in the effort.

When the assignment came up, no one wanted to leave the comfortable confines of Detroit to volunteer his or her time in the sticks. That's why the boss insisted we draw straws. I put on a brave face when I lost, but moving wasn't high on my to-do list. Still, here I was. If I didn't put forth the effort I would essentially be proving to Rooster that my heart wasn't in the gig. In truth, the Hawthorne Hollow assignment offered me a chance to learn about creatures I'd never come in contact with ... and I was always up for learning.

"Good morning."

I jerked my head up at the greeting, frowning when I recognized

Raisin's red head. She'd managed to sneak up on me thanks to a generous tree line, and I couldn't help but wonder if she'd taken the time to watch me before making her presence known. I didn't like the thought.

"Hey." I wiped my mouth with the back of my hand — there were no napkins inside, so I had another thing to add to my shopping list — and watched the girl approach. "Where did you come from?"

"I live over that way." Raisin's wave was vague. She could've been pointing in almost any direction. "Rooster told me you would be living here, so I decided to play a hunch and see if you needed any help."

The girl almost looked hopeful, which instantly made me suspicious.

"Help with what?"

Raisin shrugged. "Whatever needs to be done around here. The last person who stayed here really let the cabin go."

That was an understatement. "And who was that?"

"Her name was Rain and she had a personality like burnt toast."

"Crunchy?"

"Stinky."

I bobbed my head, amused. "Well ... I'm sorry she wasn't friendly."

"She wasn't unfriendly," Raisin said hurriedly. "She simply didn't get how hard it is to live out here, what with all the monsters and everything."

I was instantly suspicious. I didn't sense a whiff of witch on the girl, yet she obviously knew the Spells Angels were more than they appeared. "What kind of monsters?" I asked, testing a theory.

"All kinds." Raisin warmed to her subject as she sat next to me on the porch without invitation. "There are spriggans ... and werewolves ... and ghosts. I mean ... a lot of ghosts. Have you seen how many cemeteries we have?"

"Yeah. A lot."

"There are also wendigos, Bigfoot, the Mothman and Hellhounds."

I pressed my lips together, unsure how to proceed. "Bigfoot, huh?"

"Oh, I know that some people don't believe he exists, but I know he does," Raisin replied. "I've felt his presence outside my house. He likes to lurk, be on his own, but he's out there."

In other words she'd heard a lot of talk but had no idea what to make of it. That made sense. She was a young girl trying to get a foothold in a world she didn't understand. Of course she talked big. She might even have the guts to back up her words. That didn't mean she understood what was happening around her.

"Have you actually seen him?"

Raisin shook her head. "I tried to get Gunner to come out and search the woods behind my house once, but he says I'm crazy. But I know what I saw."

"Gunner, huh?" I pursed my lips, sensing a bit of emotion roiling underneath the girl's relaxed demeanor. "He's attractive, isn't he? Is that why you called him out to your property?"

Raisin's gaze was withering. "I know what you're suggesting. You think I have a crush on him."

"Don't you?"

"I ... no ... why would you even ask that?"

Her reaction convinced me even more that I was on the right track. "It's okay to have a crush on him. I don't think he minds. In fact, after spending a few hours with him yesterday I'm convinced that he has a whopping crush on himself."

She snorted. "He likes to look at himself in mirrors."

"Oh, yeah? How do you know that?"

"Because he's always staring at himself in the mirror behind Whistler's bar," Raisin replied, matter-of-fact. "He does it when he thinks no one is looking. He also mows his yard shirtless and he always spends extra time walking in front of the windows so he can catch his reflection."

I was amused. "Well ... I guess that's okay. It's not as if he's hurting anyone."

"No." Lips pursed, Raisin studied the cabin. "It's going to take a lot of work to get this place looking how it should."

"It will," I agreed.

"Are you going to do the work?"

I knew what she was really asking. I wasn't sure how to answer. "I'm going to at least start fixing it up," I replied finally, earning a wide smile from Raisin. "I have to find the lumberyard on the north side of town. I need some supplies ... and to figure out a way to have those supplies delivered."

"I can show you where the lumberyard is," she offered, earnest. "I mean ... I've been there before and everything. They have guys with trucks who will deliver the supplies for free."

That was exactly what I wanted to hear. "Okay. That sounds like a plan." I stood and balled up the granola bar wrapper. "I need to throw this away and grab my coat." I shifted my eyes to my bike. "Are you allowed to ride on a motorcycle?"

"Oh, yeah." Raisin bobbed her head so fast I was instantly suspicious. "Motorcycles are my thing. I'm totally getting one as soon as I'm old enough ... and have enough money to buy one."

I took a moment to eye her clothing. It wasn't ragged or dirty. It also wasn't designer. I was fine with that. I never understood the need to spend six-hundred bucks on the same sweater you could buy for thirty. Still, my guess was the girl lived on a tight budget. If she wasn't below the poverty line she was probably close to it. Money wasn't important to me, so I didn't care. That didn't mean I wasn't leery of crossing another line.

"Does your mother allow you to ride motorcycles?" I asked, stressing the question this time.

Raisin swallowed hard. "My mother is dead. I live with my father – and he doesn't care."

There was a defiance to her stance that I couldn't quite identify. I wasn't familiar with fathers or mothers, so I wasn't sure what to make of the girl's change in demeanor. Still, she hung around with people who spent all their time on bikes. She'd obviously been on one before.

"I have an extra helmet," I said finally, resigned. "I'll grab my coat from inside and get it for you while I'm in there. We're not going far."

"Definitely not." Raisin's eyes sparkled. "That's a nice bike, by the way. Did you have to save up long for it?"

Only my whole life, I answered silently. It was the one thing I owned outright. "A good bit of time," I replied after a beat. "I wanted to wait until I could pay cash."

Raisin's mouth dropped open. "Cash?" I didn't even realize she was calculating until it was already too late. "That's like, twenty-two thousand dollars without taking in the enhancements."

Raisin was officially impressed as she moved toward the bike. "You have updated foot pegs, a non-standard windshield, tweaks to the engine. That's really amazing."

Because I couldn't remember ever being quite as young as her — and definitely knew I was never as enthusiastic — I merely smiled. "That's why I saved up for a really long time."

"This is the kind of bike I want when it's my turn to join the team," she volunteered. "It's lower so it's not difficult for shorter individuals to climb on, and you can actually modify it shorter if you want."

"You know a lot about bikes," I noted. "Who taught you, your father?"

Raisin immediately started shaking her head. "No. My father doesn't have time for things like that. He works hard ... has to stay late at the office a lot of the time. He doesn't have time for motorcycles."

It sounded like a rehearsed response. "Well ... ."

"Gunner taught me," Raisin added hurriedly. "He lets me watch him when he's in the garage. You haven't seen the garage yet. It's awesome. Rooster has all the tools and he's real good at fixing things."

"Then I can't wait to see the garage," I said. The girl was an enigma, excitable and happy one moment, worried and skittish the next. I couldn't get a firm read on her, which vexed me. I was used to knowing more about people than they were willing to reveal. Raisin was something else entirely. "Let me drop this wrapper in the garbage and grab my coat. We'll head to the lumberyard and you can tell me all about Rooster's garage."

Raisin's smile was so wide it threatened to split her entire face. "Okay. That sounds fun. Did I mention I'm good at fixing houses, too? I can totally help you get this place up to snuff. I'm great at following directions and I can do almost anything."

Now she was getting ahead of herself. "Let me look around the lumberyard. I don't even know what I need yet."

"Sure, sure, sure. Did I mention I can help with shingles? I'm good with shingles. Whistler taught me last summer when he needed to patch his roof."

It sounded as though Raisin spent a lot of time with the group, so much so I couldn't help wondering if someone wasn't missing her at home. Of course, that wasn't my business ... and yet I was worried all the same.

"Five minutes and I'll be ready to go," I promised. "Don't touch anything while you're waiting."

"Hey, I'm not new." She rolled her eyes. "I know exactly how to respect a bike. Gunner taught me that first thing."

"Well ... good for him."

"He's a great guy."

"He's ... something."

FIVE

*T*he Hawthorne Hollow Lumberyard wasn't what I expected. Since everything else in the town was old and rundown, I thought the lumberyard would be more of the same.

I was wrong.

"Wow!" I hung my helmet from the handlebars of my bike and unzipped my leather coat. "This is ... wow!"

Raisin, who was all wide eyes and giggles, took off her helmet and did a hip-wiggling dance. "That was awesome!"

Confused, I glanced over my shoulder to see if I'd somehow missed something. The parking lot was busy with people loading their vehicles, but nobody stood out. "What was awesome?"

"That ride," Raisin replied, not missing a beat. "I knew it would be cool, but ... that was, like, the best thing ever."

"What ride? The ride you were just on with me. I ... ." Lost, I turned forward again and internally cringed when I noticed a familiar figure detaching from the group of workers standing by the front door of the office and heading in our direction. "Oh, geez. What is he doing here?"

Gunner was too far away to hear the question, but the look on his face told me I was about to hear an earful. I decided to head him off before he could start bellowing, although I wasn't sure what he had to gripe about.

"Are you following me?"

He ignored the question and focused on Raisin. "What do you think you're doing? Why aren't you in school?"

Caught off guard, I slid a suspicious look to the girl. I'd forgotten about school. When I was her age I rarely went, so I should've realized she was up to something. "You didn't skip school, did you?"

"Of course not," Gunner answered dryly. "There's no way a teenager would figure out a way to skip school two days in a row. I'm shocked you would even ask anything of the sort. In fact, I'm more shocked that you didn't ask."

I felt like an idiot. To buy time before responding — and saying something I might regret because I rarely think before I speak — I pressed the tip of my tongue to the back of my teeth.

"I'm not missing anything important," Raisin said earnestly, batting her eyelashes at Gunner in a manner that made me think she'd done it before. "I swear. I'm all caught up on everything ... including the algebra you've been working on with me."

The fact that Gunner helped an annoying teenager with her home-work was enough to dull the cutting edge of my agitation. What kind of guy helps with algebra? A nice one, that's what kind. Sure, he hadn't been overly nice to me. He clearly had a soft spot for Raisin, though.

"I didn't think about school," I admitted after a beat, feeling foolish. "I should have, but ... she came out of nowhere. I was sitting on the front porch. I'd been cleaning for hours. I ... didn't think about it."

He slowly slid his eyes to me. "You didn't think about a teenager not being in school during the middle of the week?"

The truth was, I rarely thought about school. I hadn't finished high school. When I interviewed for the job with Spells Angels, they granted my application with the stipulation that I pass my GED. After three weeks of hardcore studying — and rampant terror — I managed to pass. I still wasn't sure how it happened.

"It was a mistake." I'm not often wrong, but when I am I admit it. "I didn't think. I just ... wasn't expecting her to show up the way she did. Besides, it's spring. I thought maybe school was already out."

"Not for another month," Gunner replied, irritation causing his nostrils to flare. "If you had questions, you should've asked."

"Who?" My temper flared. "I was out there alone when she showed up. I was up late last night cleaning and again this morning because the place needed even more cleaning. I'm sorry I didn't put it together right away."

Gunner's expression was hard to read. If I had to guess, something nasty was sliding over his tongue and he couldn't wait to spew it in my direction. I didn't find out, though, because another man had detached from the group of workers and closed the distance between us.

"You must be the new woman in town," he said, his brown eyes lighting with good humor. "I'm Brandon Masters." He extended his hand. "Gunner and I went to high school together. She's even prettier than you said, Gunner. I can't help but wonder if you played down her looks so you could keep her to yourself."

I was flabbergasted by the greeting. "I ... what?"

"Brandon Masters," he repeated, waving his hand to get my attention. "I've heard a lot about you."

That sounded frightening. "Whatever he said isn't true," I blurted.

"Really?" Brandon's eyebrows hopped. "How do you know he didn't say something flattering?"

"Because I don't think he's capable of that," I replied without hesitation.

"Uh-huh." Brandon's gaze was heavy as it bounced between us. "Well, he is capable and he said you were helpful to him yesterday when it came to finding Hal's body. He might not have said that to you, but he said it to me ... and he seemed to mean it."

"Well ... ." I glanced at Gunner, who steadfastly refused to meet my gaze. "Who is Hal?" I asked, opting to change the subject. It seemed like the safest course of action.

"Hal Crosby," Gunner replied, collecting himself. "He's the man we found in the woods."

"Hal Crosby is dead?" Raisin's eyes widened until they reminded me of saucers. "Are you serious? How did he die? Why am I just hearing about this? How could you keep this from me?" The look she shot me was accusatory.

"First of all, it's not her job to keep you updated on Spells Angels business," Gunner answered for me. "Secondly, she didn't have any idea who we found."

"How could she not know?"

"Because ... ." Gunner didn't immediately answer. I knew why. He didn't want to frighten a teenage girl.

"Because it was hard to see in the light we had," I lied smoothly, earning a cocked eyebrow from Gunner. "I also didn't stick around long enough to hear the information from Chief Stratton. I had to get to the cabin ... and de-louse it."

For the first time since I'd arrived, Gunner cracked a smile. "I heard you got the place Rain was living in. I'm ... sorry."

"Was there an option for a different place?" I was suddenly suspicious. This felt like a test they expected me to fail, which only propelled me to want to dig my heels in deeper.

"Rooster owns several cabins," Gunner shrugged. "I think the other two are inhabited right now. I suggested you hit the hotel until you found something else, but Rooster said you had a certain reputation and you would be fine."

Yup. Definitely a test. "I *will* be fine," I agreed, straightening my shoulders and glancing around the lumberyard. "I just need to find a way to get what I need back to the cabin. I can't ride with them on the bike."

"Sure you can," Raisin countered. She was a bundle of fluttery energy and most of her attention was directed at Gunner. Obviously she had a crush on him — something he didn't discourage — but she was also interested in me. I was having trouble with the influx of young energy because I never remembered being that bouncy when I was her age. "I'll hold the lumber while you navigate."

"You will not," Gunner shot back before I could find a gentle way to explain that wasn't going to happen. "You're not even supposed to be on motorcycles. Your father warned us what would happen if we allowed it."

My stomach twisted. "Aw, man!" I slapped my hand to my forehead. "I knew that was going to come back to bite me. I just knew it."

Instead of railing again, Gunner decided to take pity on me. "I'm guessing she didn't tell you."

"Nope."

Suddenly sheepish, Raisin found something on the horizon to stare at. "I'm going to look around and see what you need, Scout," she said hurriedly. "We should put together a list or something."

I pressed the heel of my hand to my forehead as she scampered off, a mixture of annoyance and amusement washing over me. "I shouldn't have let her talk me into giving her a ride." I had no idea why I was apologizing to Gunner when I should've been tracking down Raisin's father and explaining my actions to him. "She caught me off guard."

"She's good at that," Brandon offered, grinning. "Don't let Gunner's big brother act get you down. He's fallen for more than one of Ruthie's manipulations. She's very good at getting what she wants."

"And still needs to be watched," Gunner stressed. "She can't help herself from being drawn to us ... especially you. You have everything she wants, even though she doesn't know what that is. She was drawn to Rain, too. It was hard on her when ... ," he trailed off.

"When what?" I racked my memory for information regarding the woman who held the position before me. "What happened to Rain?"

"She went away," Gunner replied simply. "She's gone, and it was a hard blow for Raisin. I don't want to see her go through the same thing if you decide to leave."

I found the comment insulting. "I haven't decided to fix anything but my roof."

"Then find what you need," Gunner suggested. "I have one of the yard trucks at my disposal. I can deliver the material to you at the cabin and take Raisin home at the same time. She'll put up a fight, but she's not getting back on the bike."

All I could do was nod. "Okay. That sounds like a plan."

. . .

THE LUMBERYARD WAS EVEN BIGGER than I estimated upon first glance. There were at least four structures holding already-cut beams, and I lost myself in the vastness of the property before I realized what was happening. In fact, I was so lost that I didn't even realize I wasn't alone in one of the sheds until I heard a plaintive cry behind me.

When I turned, I found what had to be the world's smallest kitten — mostly black with a few white accents — staring at me from the middle of the floor. It was so tiny I briefly wondered how it had managed to get away from its mother.

"What are you doing here?" I crouched down and stared into the doleful eyes of the kitten. "Shouldn't you be nursing in a lair somewhere?"

The kitten responded by moving closer to me. It seemed to trust me despite the fact that I'd never considered myself an animal person.

"What are you doing?" Gunner asked, walking into the shed behind me. He tilted his head when he saw I was staring at something on the ground and then smiled when he caught sight of the ball of fluff. "Ah, there it is. We knew one got away but couldn't figure out where it went. We assumed it climbed under the piles and died."

I wrinkled my forehead, confused. "Where is its mother?"

"Relocated to another barn. The lumberyard isn't safe for cats because of all the activity. Brandon has dogs that roam the property at night. They're not bad dogs, but they've been known to shred a cat or two ... or eight. When the mother showed up with a litter two weeks ago, we let her stay until we could get close enough to capture them all. I sent her to my Uncle Bill's farm ... right after I paid to have her fixed."

"You paid to have a stray fixed?" Every time I wanted to write him off as a jerk I found out something about him that I liked. It was beyond annoying. "Well, I guess you should take this one and move him out with the others." I grabbed the kitten before it could scamper away and held it up. "He should be with his family."

Gunner smiled as the kitten swiped at me and crawled up my arm and perched on my shoulder. It hid behind my hair and I felt it purring against my neck. "I think he's picked his family."

It took me a moment to register what he was saying. "I can't take him with me."

"Why not? I happen to know Rooster loves cats. He won't give you grief over a kitten."

"That's all well and good to say, but ... he's probably missing his family."

Gunner lifted his nose, almost as if he was scenting something, and then shook his head. "He's decided that you're his human. That's why he came out."

That was the most ridiculous thing I'd ever heard. "Oh, really? Did he tell you that?"

"No. He's telling *you* that." He pointed to my shoulder.

Even when I turned I couldn't see everything. I knew enough to realize the kitten had settled down and was preparing to sleep, as if this was his favorite spot in the world and always had been. That didn't mean I was in the market for a pet.

"I don't have anything to take care of a kitten," I said, trying one last time. "I don't think they eat granola."

"I'm sure you'll figure it out." He amiably patted my shoulder before moving to look at the items I'd been hauling around on the dolly provided by Brandon. "Is most of this for the roof?"

I nodded. "It has a few issues. I think I can fix it."

He slid me a sidelong look. "Who taught you how to fix a roof?"

"My third foster father. He was the one after the guy who blew all the money the state gave him for my care at the casino. The second guy was a dink. The third guy was cool."

"But you didn't stay with him?"

The question made me uncomfortable. "He was shot on his way home from work. His wife couldn't hold it together and ... it doesn't matter. I was there only a few weeks. No one ever wanted to keep me. They all sent me back with a stamp on my forehead that said 'return to sender.' I don't blame them. I think they sensed I was different."

"Well, I blame them." He was calm as he shook his head. "Still, it's a good talent to have. I can help if you need me."

The offer made me uncomfortable. "You don't have to. Delivering the supplies is enough."

"Still ... I want to help if I can. After all, I came down pretty hard when you showed up today. Upon further reflection, that wasn't fair. I know how Raisin can be. She manipulated you because she figured you hadn't been here long enough to know the rules. That's not your fault."

It wasn't, but I still felt guilty. "Let's talk about something else," I suggested, sliding a bundle of shingles off the rack and onto the dolly. "Tell me about Hal Crosby."

"There's not much to tell," Gunner replied, snagging a box of nails from a nearby shelf and adding them to my collection without asking. Since I needed them, I refrained from sniping at him. "He was a quiet guy. I didn't know him very well."

"I would have thought the son of the chief would know everybody in town," I teased.

"I knew him," he clarified. "I just didn't know him well. He spent all of his time at All Souls Church."

I waited for him to continue. When he didn't, I pressed harder. "Is there something wrong with the church?"

"Not as far as I can tell. I've never been inside. We have a lot of churches for a small town."

"Kind of like cemeteries?"

"Exactly." He bobbed his head and grinned, showing off the hint of a dimple that I hadn't previously noticed. "That particular congregation keeps to itself. They don't cause problems. They don't create issues when it comes time for us to go to war — which the other churches have been known to do — so I haven't paid them much attention."

"Don't you think we should go to that church and question them about Hal?" I asked. "I mean ... he did end up dead in the woods without a face."

"He did," Gunner agreed. "We're not cops, though. If we identify a specific threat and it's something we can go after, that's what we do. We're not there yet. Until then, it's my father's case."

"And you're okay with just letting him take over like that?"

"I'm as okay with that as you are with the kitten on your shoulder," he replied. "There's nothing else I can do. Until we know more, we're stuck."

"So ... let's find out more."

"You seem eager to poke your nose into business that might not involve us," he pointed out.

"The dude was missing a face. You know as well as I do that we're going to get involved eventually."

"I don't *know* that."

"You do."

"I don't."

"Oh, now you're just trying to be difficult."

His smile was back, wider this time. "You believe that because you like being difficult. Not everyone gets off on climbing beneath the skin of others and scratching and screaming."

"How do you know that's what I do?"

"Call it a feeling. I'm right, aren't I?"

"No. Definitely not."

"You're full of it."

"And I'm done talking to you. Come on. I have everything I need. If you're going to deliver it to the cabin for me, I want to get going. There's something I need to do before I leave town."

"Pick up supplies for your new cat?"

"Two things I need to do."

SIX

*R*aisin wasn't happy. She tried everything in her repertoire to convince Gunner that it was best if she traveled with me. He was having none of it.

"We promised your father that you wouldn't get on a motorcycle," he reminded her, calm as he folded his arms over his chest. "He pitched a fit about you hanging with us, we compromised with him, and you purposely helped us break that promise. What do you think he's going to do if he finds out?"

Raisin didn't scowl as much as grimace, and for a brief moment I saw a flash of something in her head that caused my heart to skip a beat. I couldn't be sure what I saw — I didn't know her well, after all — but I heard screaming. The noise was gone as quickly as it appeared and I took a moment to clear my throat before focusing on Gunner. He looked normal, at least for him.

"It should take me about an hour to finish up here and then I'll drop the load by your cabin," he offered, seemingly distracted by movement close to the lumberyard's busy main office. "I'll take Raisin home first, but it shouldn't take long."

"I'll come with you," Raisin suggested. "You'll need extra hands to help if you expect to get that cabin looking like something that's not straight out of a Stephen King book. I have hands." She wiggled her fingers in my face for emphasis.

"You do," I agreed, shifting when I felt the kitten knead its claws against my neck. He'd been hiding under my hair, almost as if he sensed I was going to try to find a way to ditch him. He was so well hidden, in fact, Raisin hadn't noticed him. "You're supposed to be in school. From now on, you're not allowed to visit the cabin during school hours." I was firm despite the dejected look on the girl's face. "I'm sorry, but ... you have rules you're supposed to follow. I broke those rules today without even realizing it."

"What she's saying is that you screwed yourself this go-around," Gunner interjected, ignoring the way Raisin huffed and puffed. "Don't look at me that way. Your father doesn't like it when you hang around us. We agreed to certain rules. You broke those rules today and took advantage of Scout. You knew she wouldn't argue because she had other things on her mind. Don't bother denying it."

Raisin made a face that was straight out of a teenybopper television show. "I think you're making way too big of a deal about this," she complained.

"Yes, well, that's not really your call." Gunner rested a hand on her shoulder and focused on me. "Give me about an hour and a half to get to your place, Scout."

"Thanks." I meant it. "That works out well. I have a stop I want to make on the way home."

He pursed his lips. "All Souls Church?"

I nodded without hesitation. "We have to start somewhere, right?"

"I told you to let my father handle the investigation. He'll tell us if there's something he feels we should know."

"Yes, well, perhaps I simply think waiting is a bad idea."

"I agree with her," Raisin announced. "Waiting is a terrible idea. I'll go with her."

Gunner and I turned twin looks of disgust in the girl's direction.

"Don't push me," Gunner warned. "You're sticking with me. No motorcycles. You know how your father feels about them."

"That's because he doesn't understand them," she protested.

"Maybe not, but we made a deal with him." He refused to back down. "You're coming with me, and Scout is going to find her own brand of mischief." His gaze was heavy as it locked with mine. "Try not to tick off the religious folk. Most of them are fine, but a few of them are nuts."

"Isn't that the way it is with almost everything?"

"Just remember that I warned you."

"Yeah, yeah, yeah." I waved off the comment. I was more than capable of taking care of myself. "I've got this under control."

ALL SOULS CHURCH WASN'T what I was expecting. I thought I would be dealing with happy-go-lucky churchgoers and a friendly pastor who would invite me over the threshold in the hopes of turning me to his religion.

Instead I got a handful of dust in the face.

No joke. A woman stood by the door and blew dust in my face the moment I tried to cross into the sanctuary.

"Welcome to those with pure hearts and minds," she announced, her expression benign.

I swiped my hand over my face and glared at her. "What's with the dust?"

"You've been anointed in the body of our savior."

Hmm. That was a slight variation of the tale as far as I knew it. "The body of your savior, huh? Are you talking about Jesus?"

The woman straightened. "I'm talking about he who is the resurrection and the light."

Good grief. She acted like a puppet with a hand stuck up her bottom, parroting information someone had clearly fed her but she didn't understand. This is why I was always leery about organized religion. There were those who understood what they were preaching and believed wholeheartedly. That wasn't my thing, but I understood it. On the flip side, there were those who mimicked faith, basically spouting off what they believed they overheard others saying. To me, those were the people to be wary of. And that's exactly how I felt now.

"And what does the dust do for you?" I asked. "Where do you get the dust? Is it magic dust?"

I felt a presence move in behind me at the moment the final question escaped. I managed to keep my cool as I swiveled — I have issues with people sneaking up behind me, although I try not to show it — and came face to face with an odd-looking man in a brown robe.

"Hello," I mumbled, surprised.

The man, who looked to be in his forties, arched an amused eyebrow. "Welcome to our sanctuary."

I stared at him a moment, uncertainty flowing over me. He was dressed differently than the others. Even the goofball who blew dust on me wore standard jeans and a sweater. He was something else. The bemused way he watched me — as if he was above everything and deigned to check in on the interloper — told me he was in charge.

"My name is Scout Randall." I jutted my hand out to see if he would take it. "I'm new to Hawthorne Hollow."

"It's nice to meet you, Scout Randall." His tone was condescending and he made no move to shake my hand. After waiting another few seconds, I dropped it. "What brings you to Hawthorne Hollow?"

"She's hanging with the devils," the woman hissed, her eyes going narrow. "You know the ones I'm talking about. They spend their time at that pit of passion they call a bar."

Pit of passion? "You mean The Rusty Cauldron?" I asked. "Is that what you're talking about?"

"Cecily, my dear, I don't think now is the time for this conversation," the man soothed, offering the woman a look that set my teeth on edge. For some reason, I disliked him on sight. That was usually a sign that there was something off about the individual in question. In this particular instance, I seemed to have a lot to choose from.

For her part, Cecily made a face as she glanced between us. "I'm the head of the welcome committee," she reminded him.

"Well, Ms. Randall has already been welcomed." He kept his smile in place, but it was obviously a facade. "I'll take over from here."

Cecily looked as if she wanted to argue but instead snapped her feet together, as if getting ready to salute, and nodded. "As you wish." Slowly, she turned to me. I thought she was going to say something. Instead, she opened her hand and blew a fresh coating of dust in my face. "Remember that he is the resurrection and the light."

It took everything I had not to punch her in the face. "I'll try to remember that." I waited until she moved into the inner bowels of the church to wipe my face. I didn't want to give her the satisfaction of seeing me do it. "She's lovely," I drawled.

The man, who remained next to me and seemingly at ease, chuckled. "She has a few quirks. We don't dissuade people from having quirks here, though. We want everyone to be who they are."

"Oh, yeah?" I wiped my hands on my jeans to get rid of the dust. "And who are you?"

"Oh, where are my manners?" He made a tsking sound with his tongue. "I'm Father Bram."

"This is a Catholic church?" I was understandably confused. "It doesn't look like a Catholic church." I peered inside the nave to be certain. "What kind of church is this?"

"We're not Catholic," Bram replied, grinning. "We're non-denominational."

"Then how are you a father?" It was an honest question. "I thought that term was a Catholic thing."

"No one has jurisdiction over a title."

"I think the folks at Marvel would argue that point when it comes to the Hulk ... and Thor ... and Captain America. Well, quite frankly, all of them. You know what I mean."

"I do and I'm not talking trademark issues." Bram kept his smile in place, but there was something about the way he looked at me that made me uncomfortable. "We don't cling to old ways. We've created our own rituals ... and belief systems."

I was intrigued. "So ... you're like a cult, huh?"

"I don't believe I said that."

"I'm not trying to upset you," I said hurriedly. "I wasn't raised in a religious household. Most of this is new to me."

"And where were you raised?" He gestured toward a small table and chairs placed close to a wall. I was trying to ingratiate myself, so I figured it was best to do as he asked.

"Not here," I replied, taking the seat that faced the door so I could monitor those coming and going from the church. "I grew up close to Detroit. I was in various foster homes at times, but for the most part I spent my time in a group home close to the Ambassador Bridge."

"I'm sorry to hear that." Bram looked legitimately contrite. "I believe children are our greatest assets. They should be revered, not thrown away with the trash."

His words grated. "I don't really know how I ended up where I ended up. Ultimately, it doesn't matter."

"Doesn't it?" He was clearly not convinced. "You seem the sort of person who is straightforward and says whatever comes to her mind. Is that not true?"

"It's true."

"So, why lie about your feelings toward your childhood? They're written all over your face. I can feel the pain that emanates from you when you think about the life you could've led compared to the one you were afforded. There's no shame in wishing things had been different.

"Honestly, you would be surprised at the individuals who come through our doors," he continued. "Many are like you, searching for something. They don't believe we can help but are just desperate enough to try."

He was definitely full of himself.

"Well, I am looking for something," I conceded, leaning back in my chair and stretching my legs out in front of me so I could admire my boots. They were new and still being broken in, but they were handsome. "I'm looking for information on Hal Crosby."

Whatever he was expecting, that wasn't it. Bram leaned forward, the arm of his robe brushing against the table as he rested his palms on the metal surface. "Why would you be searching for information about Hal?"

His reaction was more intense than I thought it would be. "My understanding is that he was part of this church."

"He is."

"*Was*," I corrected, playing a hunch. "He's dead."

Bram sucked in a breath and rubbed his hands over his knees. He looked genuinely shocked. Of course, it was possible he was simply a good actor. His demeanor gave me pause, and I wasn't the sort to openly trust someone if they hadn't yet earned it.

"You didn't know," I prodded finally.

"No, I didn't." Bram shook his head. "It's a shock. I saw him just the other day."

"What day would that be?"

"Um ... Saturday. No, Sunday. It was Sunday I'm sure. He was here for my sermon."

"And you haven't seen him since then?"

"No. Hal was a dedicated soul who believed there was only one true path to his salvation."

Bram uttered the words as if they were normal, but I couldn't help being agitated. The statement was an example of why I had shunned religion since childhood. That and the fact that I hated the idea of anything being foisted upon me when I didn't get a choice to exert control.

"I would think, as a progressive church, you would be more open to multiple paths," I countered.

"We're open to different life paths," Bram conceded. "Faith paths are another story. Still, you haven't told me how Hal died. I'm confused ... and wondering why you're here."

"I was with a gentleman from town when the body was discovered," I offered, debating how much information I should share with him. "It was a shocking discovery, especially since I just arrived in Hawthorne Hollow yesterday. I was upset by what happened and simply wanted to make sure I was doing all that could be done."

"And what is it you think could be done that is not being done?"

He sounded rational, as if he was making a point I should've realized on my own. I still didn't trust him.

"I'm wondering about his family," I answered truthfully. "As I said,

I'm new to the area. I would like to meet with them and express my sympathies on their loss."

"Hal had no family," Bram responded. "He had the church and nothing else. I mean ... he had family at one time. They were no longer a part of his life, though. We were his family."

Bram seemed so sure of himself, that I very much doubted the general public found reason to question him. He seemed a benevolent soul, a man who was comfortable in his skin and eager to help those around him. But that was a veneer. Something else lurked beneath the surface, and I was dying to find out what.

"He had zero family? No children? No wife? No brothers or sisters?"

"Not to my knowledge," Bram replied. "He never mentioned them. He was completely about the cause."

"And what is the cause?"

"It doesn't really matter, at least to you," he answered. "You're not interested in learning. You might be one day, but for now your heart is closed to the process. I'm not interested in wasting my time."

It was a convenient out. "Well, that's disappointing." I forced a smile for his benefit. "I really wanted to make sure that Hal's memory would be preserved. I feel bad for him, dying in the woods the way he did."

"Death is always tragic, but that doesn't mean he's not in a better place."

"You think he's better off dead?"

"I don't believe I said that. I simply said he's in a better place."

"Heaven?"

"If that's what he believes in and wishes for."

"What do you believe?"

"That you're digging for answers you're not going to get here," Bram said, slowly getting to his feet. "I don't expect you to understand our way of life. You're not open enough to the process. I have a feeling you will open yourself to it eventually. I will continue to pray for you until then."

I held his gaze, frustrated. We were at an impasse and there was absolutely nothing I could do about it. "Well, thank you for your hospitality." I slowly got to my feet. "It's been a real ... pleasure."

"I'm sorry you didn't find what you were looking for."

His smug tone made me want to slam my fists into his face. "Yet," I corrected. "I haven't gotten what I'm looking for yet. I have plenty of time."

"Yes, well, eternity is an endless loop."

I pressed my lips together as I moved toward the door, slowing my pace when I decided to ask one more question. "What's with the dust?"

"It's the remnants of our savior," he replied simply. "It's supposed to keep the false of heart from darkening our doorstep."

"Does it work?"

"You made it inside."

"That wasn't really an answer."

"No? And here I thought it was." He smirked. "Be careful on your way out. It's a dangerous time ... especially given what happened to Hal. We wouldn't want anything to happen to you before your time."

It sounded like a threat. It was uttered in such an amiable way, though, I knew it would be impossible to convince anyone else that it was anything other than a simple statement.

"You don't have to worry about me," I called out. "I'm like a cat. I have nine lives." Speaking of cats, the kitten I'd left wrapped warming in a blanket was sticking its head out of my helmet, causing me to sigh. It really was a cute little thing, and apparently it wasn't going anywhere. "I'm sure I'll see you around, Father Bram."

His smile was indulgent. "I'm sure you will. I look forward to it."

SEVEN

*G*unner was unloading supplies at the cabin when I arrived. He wore a form-fitting black shirt that showed off his impressive arms and his hair pulled back in a loose ponytail that somehow made the bones of his face look as if they'd been carved from marble.

Not that I notice those things, mind you.

"I wondered if you forgot the way home," he called out, grinning and causing me to jerk my eyes away from his biceps. "I was about to send a search party out for you."

"Yeah, well, it's always nice to know that you're missed." I moved closer so I could help him lift some two-by-fours from the back of the truck. "Did you get Raisin home okay?"

He met my gaze and nodded. "Yeah. She's not happy. In fact, she's threatening to break into my place and cut my hair in the middle of the night because I stole you away from her. No matter what I said, she refused to listen."

"You stole me away from her?" That didn't make much sense. "She's not a creepy stalker, is she?"

He shook his head. "No, but she desperately wants to fit in. It's not happening at school, so she kind of latched on to us to make up for the emptiness she was feeling. We do our best to accommodate her because she's not a bad kid, but ... it's not always easy."

I dropped my end of the lumber and wiped my forehead with the back of my hand. "You kind of sound like a therapist. Has anyone ever told you that?"

He barked out a laugh. "Actually, you're not the first person to say that to me. My father used to say it all the time when my mother went off the rails. I was the only one who could talk her down."

"What do you mean? Off the rails how?"

"She was a drunk." Gunner was matter-of-fact as he uttered the words. "She used to start drinking in the morning, adding Kahlua and Bailey's to her coffee. By lunch she was adding Jack Daniels to her coke.

"At night she would only drink wine or beer," he continued. "She explained to anyone who would listen that she couldn't possibly be an alcoholic because she slowed her pace as the night wore on. Alcoholics drank more as it got later in the night."

"That sounds rough."

"You grew up in foster homes," he pointed out. "I'm betting you had it worse."

"Not really." I felt exposed, vulnerable, as I followed him to the truck for shingles. I couldn't remember the last time I'd talked this much about my past, especially with a near stranger. He made it easy to open up, which was something I couldn't quite wrap my head around. "Most of the foster homes they show you on television are either filled with angelic do-gooders who want to help or evil sociopaths who want to maim. Neither of those is the norm."

"No?" He cocked an eyebrow as he grabbed the shingles from my arms. "I've got these. They're heavy. You grab the ladder and I'll carry them to the roof."

I narrowed my eyes to dangerous slits. "I can carry them. I'm not helpless."

"I don't believe I said you were helpless."

"No, but you insinuated."

"I'm pretty sure you're imagining that."

"And I'm pretty sure I'm a keen judge of character." I poked his chest. "I don't need a knight in shining armor."

He held my gaze for what felt like forever and then dropped the shingles so they landed at my feet. Luckily they scattered in a variety of directions before impact, because otherwise he might've broken a bone or two. "Fine." His eyes flashed with annoyance. "Are you happy?"

My mouth dropped open. "I can't believe you just did that." I hunkered to the ground to gather the shingles. "I mean ... you could've broken them."

"What do you care? Rooster paid for them."

"Yeah, well ... I still would've had to run back and pick up more."

"Oh, the horror." He mocked me and hopped on the tailgate to get comfortable as I scrambled to pick up the mess he'd made. "Where is the kitten?"

"What?" I was flustered. "I didn't hear you."

"The kitten," he repeated. "Where is it? If you abandoned it, I'm going to be really angry."

"Do I look like the sort of person who would abandon a helpless kitten in the middle of town? I mean ... good grief. The kitten is perfectly safe."

"Where is it?"

"You act as if you don't trust me."

"Where is it?" he repeated, annoyance curling his lips into an unattractive sneer. "You don't have it, do you? Where did you leave it?"

If I was frustrated with him before, I was beyond the point of no return now. "I didn't 'leave it'!" Abandoning the shingles, I stomped around him and toward the bike. The saddlebags I used to transport my belongings from Detroit to Hawthorne Hollow were still affixed to the seat, and after rummaging inside, I came out with a worn blanket and the kitten.

The small ball of fluff looked annoyed at being awakened. He blinked several times in rapid succession and glared at me when I held him up to the light.

"Not only do I still have the kitten, I picked up food, too." I carefully placed the animal on the ground so he could look around. "I have soft food ... and dry food ... and chicken broth to soften the dry food ... and some bottles of something that's supposed to be better for his digestive tract than milk because — believe it or not — milk is bad for cats." I pulled all the items out of the saddlebag for emphasis as I mentioned them. "So, no, I'm not mistreating the cat!"

Gunner ran his tongue over his teeth before holding his hands up in mock capitulation. "I think we got off on the wrong foot."

"And I think that you've said that very thing to me more than once," I complained.

"Yeah, well, I like to repeat myself when I'm being a jerk." He winked to let me know he was trying, and hopped out of the truck to gather the shingles. "I really do want to help. I know it doesn't seem like that because ... well, because I've been rude on more than one occasion, but I don't mean it."

"No?"

"No. I think you're actually a good fit for our outfit ... although the growing pains probably won't be easy."

He was making an effort, so it felt the only fair thing to do was meet him halfway. "I'll let you help with the roof."

He chuckled. "Oh, well, thank you for that."

"No, seriously." I clutched the cat items to my chest. "I'll let you help and we'll talk about Hawthorne Hollow and the people in it. I'll try to understand where you're coming from, and you can attempt to do the same with me."

He stared at me for a long beat. "Okay. I agree to your terms."

"Great. First I have to get the kitten set up. I noticed a washing bin out back that looks to be in one piece. I plan to use that for a litter box."

"Smart and practical." His dimple was back when he smiled. "A lovely combination."

I rolled my eyes. "This isn't going to work if you're constantly snarky."

"If you're going to be snarky, then I have no choice but to match your tone."

"Says who?"

He pointed to the sky.

"Crows?" I challenged.

He snickered. "I don't make the rules, but I do have to follow them. You're setting the snark tone."

Sadly, I had a feeling he was telling the truth. "Fine. I'll make an effort."

"That's all I ask."

"Great." I strode toward the cabin. "I'll order pizza in a few hours if we actually manage to get some work done. Dinner will be on me."

"I can't wait."

THREE HOURS LATER, WE SAT ON his tailgate and inhaled pizza and soda as we surveyed our hard work.

The roof was patched. We'd spent twenty minutes at the start arguing about who would go where, but once we agreed that two chiefs made for a bad tribe we finally managed to get in the flow of things. The finished product was actually fairly impressive.

"You know your way around a hammer," Gunner noted, his mouth full of pizza. If he hadn't just spent hours sweating and toiling on my roof for no profit other than pepperoni and cheese I would've found his penchant for talking with his mouth full fairly disgusting.

Well, most likely. Even talking with his mouth full of food he was ridiculously attractive. I hated that about him.

"I told you, one of my foster fathers was handy. He taught me a lot of things, including how to affix shingles and fix drywall."

"The only thing my father can do with a hammer is beat things."

I stilled, uncomfortable. "You mean like ... ."

It took him a moment to grasp what I was insinuating. "God, no!" His eyes flashed. "My father doesn't mistreat me ... at least not *that* way."

That was a relief, but only marginally. After getting a gander at Gunner's interaction with his father, I had certain suspicions. I was glad to see that the worst of them were off. "He doesn't speak very nicely to you," I noted.

"He's ... troubled ... by my life choices."

I picked a mushroom from my pizza slice and popped it in my mouth. "Are you gay?"

"What? No!" His face flushed with color.

"If you are, there's nothing wrong with it. I get it."

"Oh, geez!" He shook his head. "I'm not gay. Those aren't the life choices I'm talking about."

"Oh." Realization dawned. "You mean Spells Angels."

He nodded. "That's exactly what I mean. My father doesn't understand why I would choose to live the life we've dedicated ourselves to. I'm guessing at least that part of things is easier for you because you don't have parents to disappoint."

Instead of making me feel better, the statement was like a sharp jab to the heart. "I think some things are worth the tradeoff."

He blew out an extended breath. "That came out wrong."

"So you keep saying."

He chuckled, the sound low and throaty. "I think it's you. For some reason, you bring it out in me. This rudeness I'm not used to, I mean."

"Believe it or not, that's not the first time I've heard that," I noted, accessing one of the few "bad" memories that could still make me laugh. "One of the foster homes I visited as a teenager — it was a very brief stay — anyway, the woman in the home was very religious and she swore I was the devil sent to lead her astray. She took to locking me in the bedroom at night and surrounding the door with crucifixes."

His pizza forgotten, Gunner briefly ran his hand down my arm. "I'm sorry."

"I was there less than a week." He couldn't understand how the timeframe played into things but I did. Truly, the memory was barely a blip. I told the story now because I found it funny. "I think she picked up on the witch in me, although I can't be sure. I was fourteen at the time, confused. I could feel the power building. It was ... weird. I definitely think she felt it, too. She couldn't get me out of her house fast enough."

Gunner swore under his breath. "How many foster homes were you in?"

"Twenty or so. They kept trying to find me a permanent home even though I was convinced it would never happen. I was fine in the group home. Still, every few months they would trot me out to another set of prospective parents. Every few weeks after that they would send me back."

"That is horrible." He looked legitimately distressed. "I'm sorry."

"Why? You didn't send me back to the group home."

"No, but ... I used to think what happened with my mother was the worst thing ever. I was wrong. At least I had a home and wasn't being dragged all over the countryside."

"You also had a father," I reminded him. "He doesn't seem like the easiest guy to get along with, but I'm guessing he cares."

"He cares," Gunner agreed. "Sometimes I think he cares too much. It might've been better for me if I had a brother, but as the only son, I was his focus. For years he tried to pretend that things were fine with my mother. Then there was an incident and he couldn't pretend any longer. That made things worse."

I wasn't sure I should infringe on his privacy — I hated when people asked invasive questions of me — but I couldn't stop myself. "What happened to your mother? Did she ... die?"

He shook his head, taking me by surprise. "She's in a sanitarium," he replied, his voice cracking. "It's about an hour from here. She was placed there on an involuntary hold after she tried to burn the house down with me locked inside when I was eleven. My father managed to get me out ... and go back for her.

"He has scars on his back from what happened. Part of the roof collapsed," he continued, adopting a far-off expression. "He saved her, though. He never left me alone with her again, and she was locked away pretty quickly. He made sure she could never get out."

I was horrified. "I'm sorry. That's terrible. Do you ever see her?"

"No. I haven't seen her since I was a teenager. My father tried to make me visit her right up until I was eighteen, even though I fought every effort. I simply refused after that. That's part of the reason we fight."

"Surely he can't blame you for not wanting to be around her," I countered. "I mean ... that's not fair to you. She tried to kill you."

"He says she was out of her mind and I shouldn't hold a grudge. I think I'm well within my rights to hold a grudge."

I had to agree with him. "Well, that sucks." I offered up a rueful smile. "I think it's interesting that you won't see your mother and yet you've dedicated your life to helping people with the Spells Angels. It's awesome that you recognize the need and want to give of yourself."

"I think you're giving me too much credit," he countered. "I joined because I wanted to fight. It's in my blood. I like a good battle."

"I think you're exaggerating."

"What makes you say that?"

"Because you're the sort of man who worries about a kitten and puts up with a teenager who creates drama wherever she goes. If you were all about the fight, you would be over both of those."

He sighed. "You're going to ruin my street cred if you spread it around that I asked about the kitten," he said finally. "My street cred is all I have."

"I think you're full of it. Although ... what were you doing at the lumberyard earlier? I forgot to ask. Did you somehow know I would be going there?"

"Actually, I did. Rooster mentioned the cabin needed work and you were going to do it yourself. I would've been there regardless. I work for Brandon one day a week for extra money. As you know, working for the company doesn't exactly allow you to put a lot of money away."

"Definitely not," I agreed. Everything I owned I could carry on my back. Still, I'd managed to tuck away a nest egg. "You're basically saying, on top of everything else, you're a hard worker."

"I like to keep busy."

I cast him a sidelong glance. "Are you sure you're not gay?"

"No ... and stop asking that."

"If you're not gay, there has to be something else wrong with you." I was adamant as I wiped my hands and got to my feet. "No guy who cares about kittens and teenagers is going to stay single otherwise."

"Have you ever considered that I'm merely picky?"

"No."

He snorted and grabbed a napkin from the stack. "My life isn't conducive to romance. I live a hard life ... and could die at any moment. Most women don't understand that."

I felt the same way, so I understood where he was coming from. "That's a bummer. You have a lot of potential being wasted."

"People might say the same about you."

The sound I let loose from deep in my throat was derisive. "What potential do I have?"

"Well, you conjured fire and took out a spriggan without thinking twice about it," he replied without hesitation. "You allowed Raisin to hang around even though you were obviously uncomfortable with her presence. You took in the cat even though you keep telling yourself that having an animal is a mistake given how often you move. Oh, and you can repair your own roof and plumbing. How is that not great potential?"

I had no idea how to answer. Instead, I decided to change the subject. "We should probably give the roof one more once-over and then call it a day. I also need to change the door handles so I have actual locks. Rooster doesn't seem to think I need them, but I disagree."

Instead of being offended, Gunner laughed. "You're also a slave driver. Seriously, the potential is off the charts."

I decided to let the comment go because it felt too much like flirting, and that was the last thing I needed. "Let's get to work."

"Yes, ma'am. You're the boss."

"And don't you forget it."

EIGHT

*G*unner stayed until the sun set, talking up a storm as he helped me switch out door handles and check window locks. By the time we'd finished, we found two of the windows were accessible from the outside, and he promised to come back the following day to make sure the hardware was updated so I would feel safe in my new home.

After that, I made myself a cup of Sleepytime tea and then fell into bed. I was officially exhausted. I couldn't remember the last time I did that much manual labor. The kitten — who I had yet to name — climbed the blanket hanging off the side of the bed and made himself at home in the nook between my ear and shoulder. I heard him purring in my ear when I drifted off. It was a soothing sound ... until it stopped and my eyes immediately popped open.

My internal clock told me I'd been down for hours. It was well past twilight, the only light in the room coming from the moon through the window. It was a crescent moon, so it didn't offer much illumination.

The first thing I thought about was the cat. He wasn't on my shoulder, as he had been when I drifted off, and I thought for sure I would've heard him try to hop from the bed due to the distance.

When I rolled to my elbows, my eyes determined as they searched the gloom, I found the kitten almost immediately. He sat on the end of the bed, his eyes rapt on the window, tail swishing back and forth as he stared at ... nothing.

Er, well, I was convinced it was nothing. I couldn't see anything. Heck, I couldn't sense anything. If someone was outside the window I would know it. There was no doubt about that.

"Here, kitty, kitty."

My back stiffened at the sound of the voice. It was low, craggy and altogether creepy. It was emanating from a spot directly on the other side of the window even though I couldn't see anyone standing there.

"Jump off the bed, kitty," the voice hissed. "Make her follow you outside. I want to get a look at her."

I frowned at the voice, annoyance coursing through me. "If you want me to come outside, perhaps you should simply ask me yourself," I challenged.

A shadow I didn't see upon first glance backed away from the window. I crawled to my knees so I could see through the glass once I moved to a spot next to the kitten. For his part, the purr monster seemed to be enamored with whatever was on the other side of the window, because he wiggled his butt and made it look as if he was about to make a jump that was far too wide for him to accomplish.

"No, you don't." I wrapped my hand around his wriggling middle and lifted him before he could fall flat on his face. "You're not going over there."

"Oh, let him come out and play," the voice taunted. "I love me a good kitten ... to eat."

The suggestion was disgusting enough that I placed the cat on the pillow and climbed out of bed. Luckily I'd thought to sleep in yoga pants, otherwise the peeper on the other side of the window would've gotten a good show.

"How about I come out and play instead?" I suggested, my temper getting the better of me. "Leave the cat alone and focus on me."

"Oh, I thought you'd never play the game."

· · ·

MOST PEOPLE WOULD'VE CALLED for help if they found themselves being taunted by a malevolent voice through the window in the middle of the night.

I'm not most people.

I was used to taking care of myself, and the only fear coming from me revolved around the cat. Should something happen, should we be separated, there would be no way for the kitten to protect itself. With that in mind, I stopped by the front door long enough to erect a protective field. The kitten, not seeing the field, ran into it headlong as it tried to escape with me ... and then sat back on its haunches and offered up a terrific wail as I took a step back.

"It's for your own good," I said, refusing to let the kitten's sad countenance sway me. "If something happens to me, Gunner will stop by to check when I haven't called in. He'll find you ... and take care of you."

The kitten only grew more baleful.

"I'm sorry. You're safer inside." I gave the animal a small wave and then straightened, turning my attention to the creeping darkness as it closed in. I was used to the city, where the buildings clung together and created a fearsome skyline. I should've felt safer here. It was open, after all. I could see my enemies coming ... yet the trees across the yard gave me pause. They beckoned and bade me to stay away at the same time.

"Are you coming?" the voice asked from the opposite direction of where I'd been looking. "Are you going to stay here and stare or come with me and ... have fun?"

"That sounds like something a guy in a van trying to pick up children would say," I complained as I stomped down the stairs. Even though I knew it wasn't the brightest move, I was confident in my abilities. I could handle whatever came ... and then some. "You should work on your material. I mean ... you've got this creepy voice in the night thing going for you. You should embrace it, find a creepy outfit to match — like, have you ever considered dressing as a clown? — and wage war on the entire town. I think that sounds like a dandy job for you."

Farther away now, the voice laughed. It was quiet, so the wind carried the sound to me. "You have no idea what you're dealing with here, do you?"

"Why don't you tell me?"

"Hawthorne Hollow isn't a normal town."

"No?" I tilted my head to the side when I thought I saw a hint of movement to the north. But the voice was coming from the west. If someone was trying to draw me out, why come at me from two directions? It seemed that an attempt was being made to distract me so someone could attack from the opposite direction. "What's abnormal about it?"

Instead of following the voice, I broke in the direction where I was certain I saw movement.

"Where are you going?"

I ignored the question and focused on a specific area, a spot protected from the moon by foliage and shadow. "Come out, come out, wherever you are," I sang out.

"Don't go over there!" The voice was full of warning. "I'm serious. That is not where you want to go."

"No? Why is that?" I was convinced my new friend was playing a game with me, and it was one I was determined to win. "Why can't I head in this direction? I think there's something over here I want to see."

The voice was succinct. "There isn't."

"Oh, but there is."

"No, there's not." He let loose a loony laugh. "You're the type who needs to find out for yourself, so have at it. Remember I warned you."

He sounded so sure I couldn't stop myself from slowing my pace. I was almost at a standstill when I caught a hint of movement again. This time, I was certain whoever was hiding in the woods had decided to come after me ... although he or she wasn't moving very fast.

"This isn't a very good plan," I called out. "I can see you. You're right there."

"That's not me," the voice countered.

"I know, but ... it's your buddy."

"It's really not."

"Right." I rolled my eyes as I prepared for whatever attack was about to come. "You just happened to show up at the exact same time. I believe that."

The voice was closer when it spoke again and I couldn't stop myself from looking toward the moon when a hint of ethereal movement caught my attention. Whatever was there was largely transparent and floating a good ten feet above the ground.

"What the ... ?" I didn't get a chance to finish asking the obvious question because the shadow from the opposite direction was on me. Whatever it was — and I was no longer convinced it was human — moaned as hands reached for my neck.

I didn't take time to think. If I wanted to live, I had to react. On a whim, I let loose an arc of fire magic and pointed it in the direction of the creature on the ground. Whatever it was — man or beast — would recognize that fire burned and run. Seconds later, I shot a freezing blast of magic to the creature hovering in front of the moon. The way it was laughing set my teeth on edge and I hoped to shut it up.

I should've thought better about combining fire and ice magic ... and in such close quarters. The outcome was something I didn't fathom, couldn't have seen no matter how hard I tried to look into the future.

That didn't mean it wasn't impressive.

I thought that right until the backlash from the fire and ice magic brushing against one another melded into one entity, snapped to attention and raced in my direction. I had only a split second to realize what was happening and throw up a shield. After that, all I could do was wait for the burst to die down ... and hope I would survive the screaming bout of mayhem that I'd plunged myself into.

"WHAT WERE YOU THINKING?"

Gunner was a furious ball of energy when he reached the yard next to my house. I didn't call him, in case you're wondering. That seemed too needy. I did call Rooster, however. He arrived within minutes. Unfortunately, he called for backup.

That's how I ended up sitting on the ground as Rooster tended to my wounds and Gunner went on a screeching diatribe.

"I didn't have time to think," I replied calmly, refusing to allow Gunner's anger to set the tone of the evening. "I knew there were two forces. I simply didn't realize the first was a ghost. I would've ignored him if I had."

Gunner exhaled on an exasperated sigh as he turned his attention to the wispy man floating in circles above our heads.

"This is the worst thing that has ever happened to me," the ghost explained. "I mean ... really. Here I was, minding my own business, when she made me solid and then set me on fire. I mean ... how do you explain that?"

Rooster, amused by the whole scene, cocked his head and stared at the buzzing ghost. "Since when have you ever minded your own business, Tim?"

The ghost huffed out an exaggerated groan. "Um ... always. I always mind my own business. That's who I am."

"That's funny because my father says you were the local pervert," Gunner challenged, his anger shifting from me to the ghost. "You were known around town as the creepy guy who stared in windows and always carried a sock."

It took me a moment to grasp what he was insinuating. "Oh, gross!"

Rooster chuckled as he slapped a bandage on my arm. "You're burned and slashed here, missy. I think you're lucky to have got out of this as lightly as you did, though."

"Lightly?" Gunner was back to glaring at me. "How do you consider this light? Look around." He gestured wildly, his hands windmilling over his head. "There're big dead spots on the lawn because she almost set the whole place on fire."

Rooster exhaled heavily as he ripped off a piece of medical tape. "But she didn't burn the whole place."

"She almost set a ghost on fire!"

"Which is darned impressive, if you ask me." Rooster winked, letting me know he was having a good time, and then fixed Gunner with a patient look. "What do you want, man? She went outside to check out a noise. That's what we do."

"Everyone who has ever watched a horror movie knows that it's stupid to go outside," he complained. "I mean ... everyone. Have you not watched *Scream*?"

"You're showing your age," I chided. "*Scream* is so twenty years ago."

"I'm going to show you my age," Gunner muttered, causing me to grin. Despite the fear that momentarily assailed me right after the spells collided, I was feeling pretty good about myself. "Can we go back to the perverted ghost? Are you saying he was the sort of guy who stared into women's homes?"

"He was the sort of guy who stared into homes and whacked off," Rooster corrected. "He was caught by a father who found him outside his teenage daughter's room and killed. It was not a pleasant death."

"I can't really work up much sympathy for him," I said, lifting my eyes to the buzzing ghost. "You're really gross, dude. You should be thankful I wasn't the one who caught you back in the day. I would've made it hurt."

"Who said it didn't hurt?" Tim shot back.

Something occurred to me, and it was almost more than I could bear. "You have a Peeping Tim instead of a Peeping Tom. That is so ... priceless."

"Yes, it's hilarious to know we had a sexual predator who managed to remain behind and keep up his antics as a ghost," Gunner drawled.

I sobered and checked my shirt to make sure it was covering everything. I hadn't bothered sleeping in a bra, so I felt a bit on display. "I guess I should get some curtains for the cabin, huh? I don't understand why the chick who stayed here before me didn't want to shut Peeping Tim out."

Rooster and Gunner exchanged a quick look that wasn't lost on me. Finally, Rooster cleared his throat and forced a smile. "I'll make sure we get curtains here tomorrow no matter what."

"Oh, that's no fun," Tim complained. "What am I going to do if she gets curtains? That means everyone in town will have closed me out."

"You could always not peep," Gunner suggested.

"Who wants to live a life that doesn't include peeping?"

"Since I can't answer that question, I'm going to move on," Gunner replied, shifting closer to the heap of flesh on the ground and hunkering down. "We need to talk about what happened here. That's much more interesting than the colliding spells and perverted ghost."

That was a matter of opinion, but from his perspective I could see why he believed it. "I can't be sure, but right before I hit it with the magic I think I saw its eyes. They were white — like milky white — and they were tinged with red. It reminds me of this horror movie I saw a long time ago ... and that movie didn't exactly have a happy ending."

Rooster snorted as he affixed the last piece of tape to my bandage and then stood, extending a hand to pull me to my feet. "Yeah, well, I'm pretty sure that we're dealing with a garden variety zombie."

My stomach twisted. "You say that in a blasé way. Down in the city, a zombie outbreak is pretty much the worst thing we have to deal with."

"That's because everyone is on top of each other," Rooster replied without hesitation. "Up here, it's not great but it's not as bad either. We can usually nip these things in the bud before they get out of control thanks to the distance between houses. We never lose more than a few people to an outbreak."

That was something of a relief. Still ... . "I could feel a shallow heartbeat," I offered, shifting from one foot to the other. "I don't think it was a zombie."

"It looks like a zombie," Rooster argued.

"It's not," Gunner said, dusting off his hands as he stood. "She's right. It's slightly different. I think it has a lot in common with a zombie, but it's definitely something different."

"Okay, you've snagged my interest," Rooster drawled. "What are we dealing with?"

"I don't know, but I think it would be in everybody's best interests if we find out. If this truly is something new, then we need to get ahead of it."

I couldn't disagree with that ... even though I wanted to find a reason to pick a fight with him. I was still unsettled from my earlier battle. Thankfully Tim was around to direct the conversation to something inane before we began wallowing in somber reflection.

"What about me?" the ghost whimpered. "I'm out of people to look at. This is just the worst. I truly hate you guys."

"There, there." Rooster mimed making a sympathetic motion with his hand. "We'll figure a way for you to survive your tribulations as well."

Tim didn't look convinced. "How? You kicked me out of the high school locker room. My life hasn't been the same since the Great Cheerleader Drought of 2015."

I wanted to punch him. "Seriously? Why is he hanging around?"

"It's a long story," Gunner replied, his expression hard to read as he stared at the body. "We have bigger things to worry about. Most importantly, we need to figure out what this is. I don't like it one bit."

That was the one thing we could agree on.

NINE

*R*ooster suggested I spend the night in his spare room, but I politely declined. He was a nice guy, but I found the notion uncomfortable. He called for a clean-up team to remove the body, offered to take me in one more time, and then took off somewhere close to four in the morning.

Gunner left at the same time, promised he would be back in the morning with information, and then ordered me to engage the locks we'd changed out that very afternoon. Even though I was exhausted, every muscle in my body aching, I still wanted to pick a fight with him. Only the shadows under his eyes — bruises I'm sure marked my face, too — held me back.

I thought I wouldn't be able to sleep, that the things I saw would darken my dreams, but I passed out right away, the kitten sleeping on my shoulder. When I woke, the kitten was gone, but I smelled fresh coffee. It took me a moment to collect myself, remember where I was — this was only the second time I'd woken up in this place, after all — and then point myself toward the kitchen.

I should've been surprised to see Gunner standing next to a new coffee pot, the kitten on the counter watching him work. I wasn't, though. He looked at home and confident. The fact that he'd been able to enter my home without waking me was a different concern.

"Welcome to my abode," I drawled, padding to the center of the kitchen.

He flicked his eyes to me, amused, and sipped his coffee. "Nice hair," he noted after swallowing, the curve of his lips causing me to instinctively reach up and touch the out-of-control tresses that felt as if they were pointing in a hundred different directions. "I take it you slept."

That was an understatement. I was dead to the world the second my head hit the pillow. "I managed to get a few Zs," I said. "How about you? Did you sleep at all?"

"Yeah. It's almost ten."

I was surprised by the statement. "Seriously?" I looked to the wall for confirmation and then remembered there was no clock in the cabin. "I didn't realize I'd slept so long. Sorry."

"You obviously needed the sleep." Gunner kept his eyes on the kitten, which was watching him with a keen expression. "When I came in, he was waiting by the door. It was almost as if he expected me."

"He was on my shoulder when I fell asleep," I said, moving toward the coffee pot. "Where did this come from?"

"I picked up a few things for you this morning. I figured you didn't have a coffee pot — and I looked to be right on that one — and I also bought curtains and doughnuts." He pulled a container of powdered doughnuts from a bag and grinned. "Do you want to get hopped up on some sugar and put up curtains with me?"

I was amused despite myself. "The sugar sounds great." I grabbed the box from him and then remembered the kitten hadn't eaten since the previous evening. "I have to feed him first."

Gunner shook his head. "I already handled that." He pointed toward a bowl on the floor. "I gave him some soft food and put the rest in the refrigerator, just FYI. He inhaled it. I think he's going to be a little glutton."

"Yeah?" I met the animal's steady gaze. "It's kind of weird how comfortable he's made himself with a stranger, huh? He hasn't even been here twenty-four hours."

"Sometimes you just know when something is right. Perhaps he feels that way."

"I guess." I opened the box of doughnuts. "How did you know I liked the powdered type?"

He shrugged. "I like them. They're for me. I wasn't really shopping for you."

I didn't believe that. "Then why do I suddenly have curtains?"

"I thought you wanted to keep Tim from peeping."

"Oh, I do." My expression darkened as I thought about the perverted ghost. "I can't believe you guys haven't forced him to the other side yet."

"He doesn't want to go."

"Since when does that matter?"

"He's mostly harmless."

"Perhaps if he was staring at you while you were undressing you would feel differently. Do you have any idea how much of a violation that is?"

His emerald eyes never left my face, emotions I couldn't quite identify storming his expressive orbs and leaving me flustered as I tried to regroup.

"I'm just saying that it's an invasion," I offered.

"It makes you feel like a victim, and you don't like that," Gunner surmised. "I get it. I should've been more sympathetic. Honestly, though, I didn't think he would find his way out here so quickly. He must be getting desperate. The only woman he can see naked regularly is Betty Hawker. She's an exhibitionist, so it doesn't give him the same thrill."

"I ... um ... exhibitionist?"

He nodded, his lips curving. "She doesn't own any curtains and enjoys collecting her mail in the nude. The entire town chipped in to buy her some robes, but she refuses to wear them."

"She sounds right up Tim's alley," I noted. "Why doesn't he camp out at her house?"

"He says it's not the same if he doesn't have to work for it."

My stomach twisted. "He's really gross."

"He is," Gunner acknowledged. "He's also a guy who can occasionally offer up useful information. That's why we keep him around."

I wasn't convinced. "I guess."

"Don't worry. We'll put up the curtains and you'll be okay. After that, Rooster has assigned us to work this case together. I figured we should head into town ... but you're going to need to shower before that. Your hair will frighten all the kids, and the last thing we need is people pointing and screaming."

His smile told me he was trying to be charming. My frown told him it wasn't working.

He cleared his throat and shifted from one foot to the other. "How about we eat some doughnuts and you take a shower? While you're getting ready, I'll put up the curtains in your bedroom and the bathroom. That will give you some privacy until you can put up the rest of them."

"Maybe I like the bedhead," I shot back, ignoring his offer. "Have you ever considered that?"

"I ... like the bedhead, too," he said after a beat. "It reminds me of when I was thirteen and I decided to grow my hair twice the length it is now. It was my heavy metal bedhead. That's what I called it anyway. I looked the same as you in the mornings. It makes me nostalgic."

I seriously wanted to punch him. "Do you think you're funny?"

"Most of the time."

"Well, I don't think you're funny."

"Then the next few days are going to be excruciating," he said, unruffled by my tone. "Rooster wants us to work together on this one. He thinks there's a reason the zombie showed up here."

"Maybe it was a coincidence ... and it wasn't a zombie."

"Yeah, well, we need to figure out what it was because it could be a threat. Also, we need to figure out why it was drawn here. This is a quiet area. You're the only one out here right now. That seems to indicate you were a target."

I hadn't really considered that, and now I felt like a moron. "Oh. Um ... hmm."

"Yeah, hmm." He reached out his hand. For a moment I thought he was going to make a romantic gesture and tuck a strand of hair behind my ear. Instead, he rested his hand on top of the snarled mess and grinned. "It's too bad it's not Halloween. You'd be a big hit."

I glared at him and took an exaggerated step back. "I think you and I are going to get along fabulously," I drawled. "It's going to be a partnership for the ages."

"Like Riggs and Murtaugh?"

"More like Anakin and the Jedi."

"Ah, you're a geek." Gunner looked delighted. "That's kind of fun."

"I'm not a geek."

He held up his hands to ward off my obvious annoyance. "Of course not."

"I'm not." I was insistent. "Just because I know a thing or two about *Star Wars* doesn't mean I'm a geek."

"I stand corrected." He looked serene as I drained the rest of my coffee and put the cup in the sink. "I'll handle the curtains and kitten while you're getting ready. You really should give him a name." He stroked the purring kitten. "Perhaps Spock would fit ... not that you're a geek or anything."

I was so done talking to him. "You make me want to punch something," I growled as I turned on my heel and strode toward my bedroom.

"The Borg?" he called out. "You can punch the Borg. They're horrible. You know who the Borg are, right? Oh, what am I saying? You're a geek. You know who the Borg are."

"I'm going to punch you," I warned.

"Make love not war," he countered, lifting his hand and contorting it in such a way that his ring finger and pinkie clung together at the same time his index and middle fingers formed a solid line. "Live long and prosper."

"Yup. I'm definitely going to punch you before this is all over."

"Resistance is futile!"

Ugh. I could feel the beginnings of a headache. It was going to be a ridiculously long day.

GUNNER FINISHED THE CURTAINS as I exited the spare room at the back of the cabin. It was more a closet than a room, and it had no window, which allowed me to change clothes without prying eyes as he tackled the window treatments in the main room.

I was relieved when I found the bedroom bathed in darkness. "That's much better." I ran my fingers over the simple drapes and sighed. "Much better. I can change and not worry about anyone looking in."

Gunner was obviously amused. "I think that must be a chick thing. Most guys I know would be perfectly happy to have a woman watch them undress."

"I had a foster brother who liked to watch me undress when I was fourteen," I mused, more to myself than him. "He was arrested for raping and killing a working girl a few months after. He claimed he thought the woman was twenty-four and taking advantage of him because he was only sixteen. Turns out she was sixteen, too."

Gunner stilled. "I am so sorry." His face flushed with fury. "I was just teasing you. I didn't think. I ... shouldn't have said that."

I fought to contain my amusement ... and failed. "I know you were teasing me. Don't get crazy or anything."

"Wait ... did you make up that story?"

He looked so hopeful I thought about lying. "No. It was true. The good news is that I had plenty of good foster brothers ... and sisters, too. He was simply one of the bad ones. The good far outweighed the bad."

"Are you still in touch with them? The good ones, I mean."

"No. Once you switch homes, it's almost impossible to keep up with the others. Still, I have fond memories of them."

He exhaled heavily. "Yeah, that doesn't make me feel better. I shouldn't have said what I said. It wasn't right."

"Hey, you brought me doughnuts. We'll call it even."

"No. I'll find a way to make it up to you that doesn't involve food."

"You already put up curtains ... and bought them."

"That was to make up for yelling at you over the Raisin situation when you couldn't possibly know she was manipulating you."

"Oh." I pursed my lips. "Well ... we'll definitely have to come up with a way for you to make the current foot-in-mouth moment up to me then. There's a whole cabin that needs refurbishing. I'm sure we'll figure something out."

"You're enjoying this," he grumbled, following me outside. He used his toe to nudge the kitten to the other side of the door and ignored its plaintive wails as he shut and locked the ball of fluff inside. "That's kind of mean."

"So is making fun of my peeping trauma."

The sigh he let loose was long and drawn out. "Okay. I suggest we start this morning over and forget the stupid things we've both said."

"Sure. Let's do that." I flashed a winning smile. "Where are we going?"

"The cemetery."

"Why?"

"Because the zombie that showed up last night came from there. We identified the body. It's Herbert Jones. He died three weeks ago."

I instantly sobered. "No joke?"

"No joke."

"But ... how?"

"That's the question of the day."

RUPERT PORTMAN HAD SERVED as the caretaker of all three of Hawthorne Hollow's cemeteries for the past thirty years. He was old, wiry and cantankerous. The second he saw Gunner approaching he made a face and turned on his heel.

"I don't want anything to do with the cops," he called out, vigorously shaking his head. "No, *sirree*. I hate the cops."

Under most circumstances, I would have to agree with him. Gunner wasn't a cop, though, so I was confused. "Why does he think you're a cop?" I slid a sidelong look to Gunner and found his cheeks flushed with color. "Wait ... are you a cop on the side? I thought you worked at the lumberyard in your spare time."

"I do work at the lumberyard," he replied, tension lining his handsome features. "He simply thinks I'm a cop because my father is the chief. He gets confused."

"He sounds like a great guy to have in control of the cemeteries," I noted. "What happens if he confuses names and faces when someone is supposed to be interred?"

Gunner ignored the question. "Rupert, we're not here to give you grief about that field of ... oregano ... that you keep behind the outbuilding," he called out. "I don't care about that in the least."

Rupert turned quickly, his eyes flashing. "I have no idea what you're talking about. If anyone says otherwise, they're lying. I ... you ... um ... ."

Gunner chuckled. "He's a bit paranoid," he explained. "My father has threatened to arrest him multiple times for the oregano. It's ridiculous."

I could see that. In Detroit, "oregano" was often grown in pots on rooftops, and the cops never bothered to issue citations. No one cared as long as meth wasn't being cooked. That seemed to be the new line no one wanted to cross.

"We definitely don't care about the oregano," I called out. "We're here for another reason."

Rupert wrinkled his nose, suspicion flitting through his eyes. "And what reason is that?"

"Herbert Jones," Gunner replied without hesitation. "He died a few weeks ago."

"I know." Rupert straightened. "He had an aortic tear. No one realized he was sick. One minute he was here and the next he was gone. It's sad, but the best way to go."

His response was dry, matter-of-fact. I was guessing Rupert wasn't exactly known for his humor.

"It is sad," Gunner agreed. "It's very sad. The thing is ... um ... is it possible that Herbert's body hasn't been interred yet?"

"No. Absolutely not." Rupert was vehement as he shook his head. "He was put to rest three days after his death. They had a graveside service and lowered him in right away. I was there when the casket was locked for the final time."

"Locked?" I furrowed my brow. "Why would you lock a casket?"

"That's actually normal," Gunner replied. "Contrary to popular belief, it's not to keep out grave robbers. Since the advent of burial vaults, grave robbing hasn't really been a thing. It's to keep out the elements so the body doesn't ... rot as fast."

I made a face. "Thank you for that lovely visual."

"It's payback for the story about your former peeping foster brother." He flicked my ear before focusing on Rupert. "Is there any way Herbert could've gotten out of his casket?"

"Gotten out?" Rupert drew his eyebrows together, confused. "He's dead. How would he get out?"

That was the question of the day and I was looking forward to seeing how Gunner would respond.

"There's simply a rumor going around," he replied calmly. "Someone swears up and down that they saw him wandering the streets the other day. I knew it was impossible — you're nothing if not diligent and dedicated to your job — but my father wanted me to ask."

"Your father only wanted you to ask because he's afraid of looking like a ninny," Rupert countered knowingly. "He wanted to make you look like a fool."

"Maybe," Gunner conceded. "Still, Scout is new to town and I wanted to take her on a tour. This gave me a reason to stop here ... and see you."

"It will certainly be a bright spot of my day," I offered, smiling.

Rupert winked at me in such a manner I couldn't stop from grimacing. "I'm the bright spot in a lot of people's days. Still, there's no way Herbert isn't in his casket. I locked him in myself. And he was most certainly dead."

"And you've been by his grave?' Gunner pressed. "The earth isn't disturbed or anything?"

"Of course not. I think I would notice if the ground was disturbed."

Rupert was very clearly obsessed with "oregano" and avoiding the cops, so I wasn't convinced that was true. Still, Gunner knew the situation better. It was probably best to let him handle things ... for now.

"Okay then." Gunner lightly rested his hand on my back and prodded me toward the parking lot. "Thanks for your time, Rupert. You can go back to what you were doing."

"Oh, well, thank you for your permission." Rupert's agitated expression didn't fade, but he looked relieved to be dismissed so quickly.

I waited until we were out of earshot to ask the obvious question. "That's it? You're simply going to believe him?"

"Of course not. There's nothing we can do during daylight hours, though. If someone is messing with the graves they're not doing it when just anyone could walk up on them. This sort of thing takes the cover of darkness."

"Does that mean we're coming back after dark?"

"What do you think?"

I groaned at his charming smile. "I think you're having far too much fun with this assignment."

He sobered. "'Fun' isn't the word I would use. Still, it can't hurt to come back. Something doesn't feel right here."

"What was your first clue?"

"Rupert," he answered simply. "I know for a fact he doesn't check on the graves daily. He gets by because no one else wants this job."

"So?"

"So he was firm that no one and nothing had touched Herbert's grave. How could he know that unless he decided to check for himself?"

That was a very good question. "So, that means we need to check."

"You're catching on quickly."

Sometimes it didn't feel that way.

TEN

"Where's our next stop?" I asked as I grabbed my helmet from my bike seat and watched Gunner. "If we can't come back to the cemetery until later ... ?"

"That doesn't mean we're out of options," Gunner replied. "We need information about Herbert's body. That means talking to the other person who had access after his death."

"I'm almost afraid to ask," I drawled. "Who has access to dead bodies around here?"

"The mortician."

"Oh." I was momentarily taken aback. "I didn't even think about that. Of course the mortician would have access to a body. Where is the funeral home?" I pictured what Hawthorne Hollow called a Main Street. "There's no funeral parlor down there."

"No, but there is one out on the highway. It serves three towns, not just one."

"I guess that makes sense. Hawthorne Hollow can't possibly have enough people to keep a funeral parlor busy."

"You might be surprised."

I waited for him to expound. When he didn't, I merely shot him an exasperated look. "So ... are we going to the funeral parlor or not?"

He smirked. "You're not big on patience, are you?"

"Not even a little," I agreed. "People say patience is a virtue. I find it's simply a way to delay things. I don't like delay."

"Sometimes waiting is its own reward," he teased, his eyes filling with mirth.

Something about the way he delivered the sentence had me wondering if he was flirting with me. The mere thought was enough to cause my cheeks to burn and stomach to churn. I didn't come to Hawthorne Hollow for this ... and I most certainly had no intention of staying. Of course, he might not have been flirting. He could simply have been sharing a nugget of wisdom that he happened to believe in. Sure, it was a nugget that you could find in any fortune cookie, but that didn't mean he didn't believe it.

Wait ... what were we talking about again?

"Earth to Scout." He mimed knocking on my temple to get my attention, his eyes lighting with interest as I jerked in surprise. "Where did your head go just now?"

"Um ... it's attached to my body. Where would it go?" The annoyance I felt was directed inward instead of at him, although he didn't need to know that. "I don't even know what you're talking about."

He didn't look convinced. "Uh-huh." He gathered his helmet from his motorcycle — I was glad to see it wasn't gaudy with large flames or some big-breasted woman adorning the side panels — and tugged it over his head. "Follow me out to the highway. It's about a twenty-minute drive. The road is mostly clear, but fairly curvy. I'm sure you can keep up."

Oh, now he was just messing with me. "Maybe you should be the one trying to keep up with me," I challenged. "Have you considered that?"

He snickered. "No. You don't know where we're going."

"Well ... I could instinctively figure it out. You'd be impressed if I did that."

"I'd be more impressed if you simply looked at me as your partner in this instead of your competition."

Crap. He picked up on that. It usually takes people days to uncover the fact that I like to win at all costs. Well, he would just have to deal with it. Or I would have to lie and divert. Yeah, that was an even better idea.

"Can we just get going? The faster we figure out what's going on with this dead guy, the faster I can return home and finish putting up the curtains to keep Peeping Tim out."

"And spend time with your cat," Gunner added, preparing to kick-start his bike. It didn't surprise me that he was old school on that front. Me? I was fine with an electric start. Purists called it sacrilege, but I didn't always have the physical strength for a kick-start engine. The first bike I had was a kick-start, so I was nostalgic at times, but in the grand scheme of things — especially if you were ever in a hurry or running for your life from a monster — electric start engines were far more practical.

"You really should give him a name," he continued. "You're a geek, so how about Who? You know, like after *Doctor Who*?"

He was a laugh a second, this guy. "I'm starting to think you're the geek given all your pop culture knowledge." I tugged my helmet over my head. "Maybe you're the one who should name him."

"No, he's yours. He wants you to name him."

"Maybe I've never named anything before."

He stilled. "Never? You never had a pet?"

"You can't have pets in a group home."

"I know, but ... ." He trailed off, uncertain. "Then you should give it some serious thought," he said after a beat, recovering. "You don't want the kitten to feel slighted. He might try to murder you in your sleep or something. He'll decapitate mice and put them in your bed as payback."

I scowled. "You're definitely the geek."

"I am," he agreed. "You'll get used to it."

Part of me didn't believe I would be around long enough for that to happen. The other part hoped that was true. There was something about him that felt warm and welcoming ... but I had no idea if I would feel the same way in several days.

. . .

THE DUNCAN AND SWAN FUNERAL Home sat on a prime piece of land in the middle of the highway that separated Hawthorne Hollow from Charlevoix. The lake glistened under the sunlight as we churned through road, and I couldn't stop myself from staring in that direction, occasionally mesmerized by the shiny surface.

Gunner was clearly familiar with the terrain, because he stared at the water often, never once panicking that he would somehow miss the turnoff to the funeral home. And, when we arrived I understood why he wasn't worried. The structure in front of us was huge ... and unbelievably gaudy.

"Wow!" I rolled my neck as I removed my helmet and peered at what could only be described as a mansion in the middle of nowhere. "This place is ... huge."

"It's big," Gunner agreed, dropping his helmet so it hung from his handlebars and unbuttoning his leather coat. Most people would find the idea of a biker wearing a leather jacket to be cliché, but I found the figure Gunner cut in the tight fabric appealing ... although I was loath to admit it. "It used to belong to an automotive family back in the forties. Not the Fords or anything, but distributors. They were known as the richest people in the area."

"Oh, yeah?" I pulled off my gloves and shoved them into the compartment under the seat. "What happened to them?"

"Legend has it they were cut off from the town during a storm and angry residents took their revenge in a unique fashion."

My forehead wrinkled as I considered the statement. "I don't understand."

"That's because you're missing part of the story," he teased. "The storm was one of those things touted as a massive event. You know, storm of the century and all that. It was basically an inland hurricane."

"I don't remember talk of a storm like that," I argued, racking my memory. "How can you have a hurricane so far inland?"

"I said it was basically an inland hurricane. It wasn't really. It was ... something else."

"Something magical?"

"That's the rumor. Obviously, it was before my time. This was in the sixties. It was even before my father's time. My grandfather, though, swore up and down that the storm descended on the area as a form of payback from a local coven. The residents knew the storm was coming.

"The family who owned this house had plenty of room to offer those in danger refuge from the elements, but they didn't," he continued. "The townsfolk cursed them. When the storm hit, everyone in the area buckled down for days. It was terrible, and many people died."

"Obviously something happened to the people in the house," I noted, jerking my thumb in the direction of three-story monstrosity. "Otherwise you wouldn't have taken the time to tell the story."

"The house was empty when rescue personnel arrived," Gunner replied. "The inhabitants were gone. We're talking three grown men — not including the staff — and three grown women. All of them disappeared during the storm."

"Were any of them ever found?"

"No." He dragged a hand through his hair to order it. "People looked for weeks. A reward was offered for information leading to the discovery of their bodies. I mean ... no one thought they survived. It seemed obvious something terrible occurred."

"Nothing? Not even stories about what happened to them?"

"There were stories, of course, but I'm not sure I believe any of them." He gestured toward the front door. "Either way, they disappeared. Another family moved into the house about two years later, but they soon left because they said the house was haunted."

I arched an eyebrow. "Do you think the house is haunted?"

He shrugged. "I've been in here a good hundred times over the years. I've never seen a ghost."

That didn't necessarily mean anything. "Perhaps the ghosts don't want you to see them."

"Perhaps. That's why I'm warning you. As a hedge witch, you're more likely to see things that others might've missed."

I understood his concern. "I'll be fine. I've seen more than my fair share of ghosts."

"I don't doubt that." He smiled. "I just wanted to make you aware of the story in case you see something once we cross the threshold."

"I appreciate your concern." We fell into step with one another, something occurring to me as we approached the front door. "Just out of curiosity, why didn't the family allow those in need to hide in the house? There was clearly enough room."

"They said that it wasn't their problem."

"So they turned their backs on the community. That's essentially what you're saying."

"Mostly," he confirmed. "They also put themselves higher than those who worked for them. They had a plant about twenty miles away. It was the biggest job provider in the area when things went down."

"Did the plant survive?"

"No."

"Then how did the community? I mean ... this isn't an area that has a huge industrial base. If the entire economy was based on that one plant, how did the community survive?"

"That's a good question. I honestly don't know."

BART DUNCAN GREETED US with a bright smile and sympathetic eyes. He was clearly used to dealing with the bereaved. He immediately offered us water and comfortable chairs.

"I hadn't realized anyone was lost last evening," he said, his voice gentle. "Was it your grandmother, Graham?"

I'd almost forgotten Gunner's real name, so at first, I searched the room for signs of his father. Then reality set in and I had to bite back a laugh at the dark look on Gunner's face.

"Don't call me that," he complained, wagging his finger. "You're only doing that because I stole Sheryl Katz from you sophomore year and you feel the need to get back at me."

Bart chuckled. "I wondered if you'd realize what I was doing. I saw your grandmother this morning. She was ... her usual self. That's how

I knew you weren't here on personal business. Although ... ." He trailed off as his eyes drifted to me.

"This is Scout," Gunner offered, leaning back in his seat and extending his legs. "She's new with my group."

"Really?" Intrigued, Bart looked me up and down. "You have the right appearance to fit in with that crowd. Although ... you look city rather than country. You fit in and yet you're somehow exotic. I get why you've been spending so much time with her, Gunner. She's a welcome addition to the town."

Gunner scowled. "Who told you I've been spending time with her for any reason other than a professional one?"

"I believe it would be best if I didn't answer that. I don't want to ruin a friendship."

"Brandon." He growled. "He won't shut up. He's got very specific ideas, which are ridiculous."

Bart's gaze caught mine for a long beat and then he smiled. "I think maybe Brandon knows what he's talking about, but now isn't the time. What are you doing here? If you're not in need of my services you must have something else on your mind."

"I want to talk about Herbert Jones."

Bart's eyebrows migrated up his forehead. "Herbert? I thought for sure you were here about Hal. I was going to make you work for it a bit longer."

"What about Hal?" Gunner asked, wrinkling his nose. "I thought the state police still had the body because of the nature of his death."

"They do, but Father Bram has been kicking up a storm about it." Bart was clearly comfortable with gossip. He didn't bother to temper his voice, instead adjusting his suit jacket so it lay smoothly as he continued without glancing around to make sure no one was eavesdropping. "The state police have some special medical examiner going over the body. Father Bram is threatening to take them to court if they don't turn it over right away."

I was confused. "Why would Father Bram have jurisdiction over the body?"

Bart shrugged. "He claims that Hal was part of the congregation, which makes him family. He's demanding the state police relinquish the body to his care."

"What do you have to do with that?" Gunner asked. "I was under the impression you didn't want anything to do with All Souls Church after the last time they tried to stiff you on a bill."

"Oh, I most definitely want nothing to do with that church," Bart confirmed. "I find Father Bram obnoxious and weird. But I didn't have much of a choice once my sister stuck her nose into things and demanded I help."

I was still catching up ... and I hated being behind. "Your sister?"

Bart bobbed his head. "Cecily. She's a bit of a ... nut. I know it sounds horrible for me to say that, but she is. My parents let her run wild as a child and now she's crazy. They're gone, but someone has to keep an eye on her. I'm basically the only one who can, so I'm often the one left to deal with her antics."

"You're Cecily's brother?" I took a moment to wrap my head around the revelation. "I met her at the church yesterday when I stopped to ask questions. She threw dirt on me. Er, well, I guess it was dust. It was gross all the same. Apparently she didn't think I was pure enough to cross the threshold."

"Don't take that personally," Bart admonished. "She doesn't know what she's doing and saying half the time. I don't mean that as an excuse. She honestly doesn't know. Father Bram doesn't help things, because he encourages her nuttiness."

I looked to Gunner for help and found him watching me with contemplative eyes. "What?"

"I forgot you went to the church yesterday," he noted. "We didn't much talk about that with everything else going on. Did you find anything of interest?"

I shook my head. "No. Father Bram is kind of a creeper ... and not the sort who peeks through your bedroom window. He gives off a bad vibe."

"He certainly does," Bart agreed. "He's a kook. Still, when Cecily called and asked me to help, I was curious enough to place a call to the medical examiner's office. I really had no intention of inserting myself into the situation, but the secretary there is the chatty sort and she said that Father Bram was threatening to bring down hellfire and destruction on the entire office if they didn't back off."

"That seems a rather extreme reaction," I noted. "When I stopped by, Father Bram acted surprised when I told him about Hal's death."

"You say 'acted,'" Gunner noted. "Do you think he was trying to put on a show?"

"Honestly? Yeah. I simply can't decide what show he was putting on. He was all over the place."

"He's not exactly known for being stable," Gunner said. "The gossip about Hal is definitely interesting and requires more thought. We're more interested in hearing about Herbert, though. You handled his arrangements, too, right?"

Bart immediately shook his head.

"You didn't?" Gunner rubbed his hands over his knees, confused. "I thought for sure you were in charge of that ceremony."

"Probably because I'm in charge of ninety percent of the ceremonies in this region," Bart countered. "I wasn't asked to be involved in that one, though. You know I had a falling out with All Souls more than a year ago. I told Father Bram then that I wouldn't handle services for his congregation because it was too stressful. I only agreed to place a call about Hal because Cecily wouldn't shut up about it."

"I guess I forgot that Herbert was part of the church," Gunner mused, his gaze thoughtful when it snagged with mine. "I think he was even a chalice bearer, if I'm not mistaken."

"Is that code for something?" I asked, confused. "Does that mean he walked around holding a cup?"

"Basically." Gunner extended his fingers in an odd stretching motion that I'd never seen before. He seemed eager for the first time since we'd left the cabin. "I guess we need to take another look at the church and the people who participate in its rituals."

"Go ahead and watch Cecily," Bart offered. "If you catch her doing something weird, tell me. We've been trying to have her locked up for years."

He seemed awful blasé for a guy who was trying to get his sister involuntarily committed.

"Aren't you worried they'll hurt her? I mean, if this Father Bram isn't on the up and up, she could be in danger."

"She could be," Bart confirmed. "The thing is ... you can only do so much for a person. You can't make him or her accept help. My sister is the sort who refuses to accept help. I can't live my life worrying about her. At a certain point, she has to be the one who takes responsibility for her actions."

"I guess." I glanced at Gunner. "So, where do we go next?"

"The church. That's our only thread tying both Herbert and Hal together. There has to be a reason for that."

"Okay, but I don't want to be stuck alone with Father Bram again. He gives me the creeps."

"I'm fairly certain everyone in town feels that way," Bart said. "The guy is even crazier than my sister. Steer clear of him if you can."

That sounded like good advice.

ELEVEN

Spying on motorcycles isn't nearly as easy as playing *Mission: Impossible* games with a vehicle at your disposal. I voiced that concern before leaving the funeral home's parking lot. Gunner suggested borrowing one of the trucks from the lumberyard, but I wasn't comfortable with the idea.

"Why?" He folded his arms over his chest and eyed me. "I don't see what the big deal is."

Of course he didn't. "If we pick up the truck, we'll have to answer questions."

"What questions?"

"About what we're doing."

"We'll simply say we're on a private secret mission," he suggested, grinning. "I'm sure that will stop people from asking questions right away."

I glared at him. "We'll also have to explain what we're doing together."

He arched an eyebrow. "Oh, so you don't want Brandon thinking we're going to do something dirty in his truck. I get it."

"I didn't say that," I countered.

"You're thinking it." He tapped the side of his head for emphasis.

"That's some strategic planning there. The last thing we want is Brandon assuming we're doing something dirty."

"I didn't say dirty!" I snapped. "Why do you keep going back to that word?"

"Because you're thinking dirty thoughts," he shot back. "Don't worry about it. I get it. You're hot for me. There's nothing to be ashamed about." He rubbed my shoulder, as if offering solace. "I mean … I'm a handsome guy. People are all the time telling me they're hot for me. I'm used to it. You don't have to be ashamed."

I wanted to wrap my hands around his neck and give it a good squeeze. "I am not hot for you."

"Sure you are. Otherwise, why would you care what other people think? I mean … unless it's true, that is. Most people don't get worked up about something that isn't true."

He was baiting me. We both knew it. But I couldn't back out gracefully. He'd manufactured a situation that was going to make me look like an idiot regardless. There was no way for me to save face.

"Let's just head over to the church, huh?" I gritted out, clenching and unclenching my hands into fists at my sides. "We're wasting time sitting here. We should head over there and see if we can find out why people are dying … and apparently rising from the dead. That seems a smarter course of action than what we're doing here."

Gunner's smile stretched all the way across his face. "That sounds like a fabulous idea. By the way, I'm having drinks with Brandon this weekend. I'll make sure he knows we're absolutely not doing anything in any of his vehicles – dirty or otherwise – to set your mind at ease."

"Why are you still talking?" I complained, sliding onto my bike. "I mean … do you do it simply because you like the sound of your own voice?"

"I think the more important question is, do you like the sound of my voice? Does it make you want to do dirty things?"

"I can't believe we're still having this discussion," I lamented.

"That makes two of us. It's probably the dirty thoughts. I, for one, know that I can never shake the dirty thoughts once they come. I'm a slave to my hormones."

"Coming here was the worst decision of my life," I complained.

"Did you have dirty thoughts about people in Detroit? You must have. Wait ... am I special? Oh, that's kind of sweet. She has dirty thoughts about me, folks." He pointed, as if playing to an audience, even though we were the only people in the parking lot. "Her mind is one big dirty thought."

"Stop talking to me right now!"

"I will, but only because I'm afraid your dirty thoughts will start spewing out of your mouth. Nobody wants to hear that."

"I just ... ." I let loose a strangled cry and stared at the sky as he chuckled. "You're having far too much fun at my expense."

"True, but if you have to figure out why people are rising from the dead, at least try doing it with a smile on your face. That's my motto."

"Which you just made up."

"At least it's not a dirty motto."

"Yup. I walked right into that one."

"You really did."

WE PARKED TWO STREETS from the church and hid our bikes in the woods. I wasn't keen on leaving my most important possession behind, but I didn't see where we had many options. The bikes weren't quiet. People would undoubtedly notice us. Unfortunately, Gunner's idea of hiding and mine were vastly different.

"I can't believe I let you talk me into this," I groused, crouching low beneath the boughs of a willow tree to get a better look at the church. "Seriously. It's gross and dirty in here."

Gunner chuckled as he stretched out on his legs and leaned back on his hands. Apparently our current predicament – hiding under an absolutely huge tree and whispering so people wouldn't notice us – didn't bother him at all.

"I take it you're not an outdoor girl," he supplied.

That sounded like an insult, although it was most certainly the truth. "I've been outdoors plenty of times," I argued. "That's how I get from air-conditioned spot to air-conditioned spot in the summer."

"Malls, right?"

I scorched him with the darkest look in my repertoire. "Oh, grow up. Malls are basically a thing of the past thanks to online shopping. Most malls will be something else entirely in ten years. Besides, do I really look like a mall person?"

He shrugged. "Kind of. I'm fairly interested in your take on malls, though. Why are they going extinct?"

"They can't sustain in the current environment. People would rather shop online than risk having to put on real pants and brave annoying people. That means that stores can't afford to pay rent in the malls, and without rent the malls themselves will not survive."

"Wow. That is a … really weird thing to know." He smiled in such a way I went warm all over, which made me want to smack myself, because I never reacted this way when it came to men … no matter how attractive. "I guess you're more than a pretty face."

Of course he picked the most annoying thing in the world to say. I mean … wait, did he say I was pretty? I narrowed my eyes. "We're here for a job," I reminded him, tilting my head toward the church. "We're supposed to be watching the congregation, although I have no idea why. We're not going to find answers from a distance."

"Oh, that was almost poetic." He flicked the end of my nose – a move I'm certain he realized would irritate me to the very tips of my toes – and then focused on the yard in front of the church. "That's what we're looking for."

I followed his gaze, frowning when I caught sight of Cecily. She looked to be having a disagreement with another woman, and whatever they were fighting about appeared to be extreme. "Do you know who she's talking to?"

Gunner nodded, his expression hard to read. "Lindsay Boyles. I went to high school with her."

I studied his profile, uncertain. "You seem sad. Is she the one who got away?"

"What?" He quickly shook off the melancholy he had momentarily lost himself in and chuckled. "No. We never dated. She wasn't my type, although she did follow me around for a bit in tenth grade."

I could see that. "I'm guessing you were popular in high school, huh? Quarterback, good grades, constantly had people fighting over you, that sort of thing."

"I was a defensive player," he corrected. "A cornerback, if you must know. My grades were okay. If I fell below a B, my father melted down and threatened me, so it was simply easier to keep them up. As for girls throwing themselves at me, it's been known to happen." His smile was mischievous. "It still happens."

"You're so full of yourself," I muttered, shaking my head. "I'm surprised you don't fall down more under the weight of your ego."

"Oh, like you don't have a huge ego," he teased. "Are you telling me you never went to a high school dance?"

I met his gaze evenly. "We had curfews at the group home. We were allowed to have jobs, but no matter what, we couldn't stay out past ten. There really was no point in going to a dance when you were forced to leave early.

"Besides that, dances were never my thing," I continued. "I'm rhythmically challenged and feel as if my feet are too big for my body when I try to move in time with another human being."

His smile faded. "You know what sucks?"

"No, but I'm sure you're going to tell me."

"I can't even tease you most of the time because everything that I throw at you somehow gets tossed back in my face in a really unappealing way."

"Well, I'm sorry I was abandoned as a child," I offered. "If I could change things, I would. Since I can't ... well ... I hope you get over your pain."

"That right there." He jabbed a finger at me. "That is very annoying. You're going to make it so I have to think before I speak. You have no idea how much I hate that."

"I have some idea. I hate thinking before I speak, too."

"Not as much as me."

"Well ... you could always keep doing what you're doing," I suggested. "My feelings are very rarely hurt. You don't have to change who you are. I can take it."

"Yeah?" He leaned forward so we were staring into each other's eyes. I didn't back down because I hated looking weak, but my heart skipped a beat when he invaded my personal space. "I can't take it. I like to be as polite as possible."

"Because that's what your father taught you?"

"Because my mother taught me that manners were important before she was taken away," he replied. "She wasn't perfect, but that was the one thing she said to me that I took to heart."

"Because you wanted something to hold onto."

"Because ... I like being polite when I can manage it," he corrected, refusing to back down. "You've had a hard life."

"Yours hasn't exactly been gingerbread cookies and hot chocolate."

"I have no idea what that means, but I'll agree because it seems prudent. You've had a hard life. I don't want to make you feel bad about any of it. If I say things sometimes ... it's simply because I don't think before I speak."

"Well, the same can be said for me. It's never my intention to be rude ... at least unless I'm really trying to be rude. That's rare, though, and almost always warranted."

He chuckled. "Well, I'm glad we got that straight." He maintained his gaze for several seconds before turning back to the church. "Cecily doesn't look to be leaving anytime soon. I think we're going to be clear for the foreseeable future."

"Clear for what?"

His smile was back. "You'll see."

IF GUNNER THOUGHT HE WAS going to shock me by trying to break into Cecily's house, he was about to be disappointed.

"Just give me a second with the lock," he instructed, digging into his pocket and coming back with his wallet. "I have a credit card and I know exactly what to do."

I thought about pointing out that he was working with the sort of lock that would defy credit card intervention, but he was so sure of himself I decided to let him fail on his own timetable. "Knock yourself out."

Cecily had an older home, and the front porch was so big it ran the complete length of the house from east to west. I moved to the west as Gunner worked on the lock, my eyes going to the maple tree in the center of the lawn as he muttered under his breath.

"Son of a … !" Slowly, I turned to find him on his hands and knees, his fingers under the door.

"What are you doing?" I asked, amused.

"I seem to have dropped my credit card," he admitted. Even on his hands and knees, his hair hanging to one side and his face red with embarrassment, he was ridiculously attractive. It was annoying.

"Under the door?"

"Yeah, well … it slipped."

"Uh-huh." I thought about torturing him a bit longer – he was a know-it-all, after all – but I couldn't take it. He was obviously feeling self-conscious. I felt the discomfort rolling off him in waves. "It just so happens I can get us into that house," I finally said.

His expression turned from agitated to suspicious. "You can get us into this house?"

"I can."

"How? Wait … are you going to use magic?" He straightened and glanced back at the door. "I don't think fire is the appropriate response for this predicament."

My lips curved down. "Fire isn't my go-to magic of choice."

"I've seen you respond magically twice and both times it was with fire. Even last night, when your attention was split, one of the ways you responded was with fire … and it wasn't a pretty outcome."

Now he was just being petty. "Fine. I won't help you get your credit card back. Is that what you want?"

"No. That wouldn't be my first choice. I'm not a big fan of setting Cecily's house on fire either."

"I have no intention of setting the house on fire." My agitation came out to play as I showed my teeth and shoved him aside. "I can get into the house another way. While I'm doing that, I need you to take a look at that tree. I think there's something off about it."

He glanced between the tree and me, confused. "You think there's something off about the tree?"

"I do."

"Well ... ." He took a step in that direction and then stopped himself before he could go too far. "How are you going to get into the house?"

Instead of answering, I dug in my pocket and retrieved an aged lock pick set. Gunner's eyes went wide when he realized what I was holding. "Seriously?"

I nodded. "You learn interesting tricks when you're shuttled from one home to another," I offered. "One of my foster fathers was a high-end art thief. He taught me the tricks of his trade."

"Really?"

I thought about dragging things out, but it seemed mean. "No. I made that one up. One of my foster brothers did earn extra money on the side breaking into the school to change people's grades. He taught me how to get past most locks ... and then he got caught on camera and arrested. He left his lock pick set behind and I continued practicing with it for a few years."

"So, you can really break into the house without anyone being the wiser?"

"I really can." I dropped to my knee in front of the door. "While I'm doing this, I need you to look at the tree. I wasn't joking about it being weird."

"I don't understand." He forced his eyes back in that direction. "It's just a tree. It looks like a normal tree."

"Not if you go to the far corner and look at it from that direction."

"Okay. I'll play." He strode across the porch, not stopping until he hit the corner I'd indicated. Once there, he stared hard at the tree. I didn't miss the moment he realized exactly what I was talking about because I heard him suck in a breath at the same moment the lock tumbled. "There are runes carved into this tree."

"There are," I agreed. "I can't quite make all of them out. I don't think they're friendly runes, though."

"Definitely not." He stroked his chin. "Why would Cecily have runes carved into her tree? I mean ... she makes a big deal out of being religious."

"I have no idea, but it's troubling."

"Definitely. You need to get that door open so we can see if there are more troubling things inside."

As if on cue, I pushed open the door. "Your wish is my command."

"That would've been sexier if you weren't making me look like a fool when you said it."

"You can't have everything."

TWELVE

$\mathcal{W}$e spent as long as we dared inside Cecily's house (which wasn't nearly as long as I would've liked). Gunner snapped photos of the tree with his phone while I searched the woman's office for signs that she was ... well, I have no idea. I wasn't even sure what we were looking for. Something out of the ordinary was my guess, but I had no idea what was considered out of the ordinary in this town.

Once we were finished, we left the house and disappeared through the woods. It was good timing, because I heard a vehicle on the road just as Gunner dragged me into the woods. We stood perfectly still, shoulder to shoulder, and watched as Cecily pulled into her driveway. She seemed lost, in her own little world, and didn't as much as glance in our direction as she climbed the porch steps and disappeared from our view.

"Oh, crap," Gunner muttered, shaking his head. "I forgot to grab my credit card. We're going to be caught. Good luck explaining that to my father."

I could've left him twisting a few minutes longer, but it seemed unnecessary. Instead, I produced his credit card from my pocket and handed it to him. "You're kind of a bad criminal," I noted as he snatched the plastic and shoved it in his wallet. "You need to think about things like this going forward."

"We can't all be masterminds when it comes to breaking the law," he drawled, shaking his head. "That does beg a question, though. Why are you so good at this?"

I smirked. "Are you asking if I'm a criminal?"

"I'm asking ... why you're so good at this." He seemed uncomfortable and yet determined to ask the question.

"Breaking into buildings to hunt monsters is a regular occurrence in Detroit," I explained. "When you have that many abandoned buildings, it leaves a lot of places for creatures of the night to take refuge. We don't often have time to figure out who owns a building and how to legally gain entrance."

"Oh." He almost looked relieved as he exhaled heavily. "I didn't think about that. It makes sense."

I was amused. "I'm not nearly as bad a person as you think. Just because I didn't grow up in a 'traditional' home doesn't mean I'm evil." I used the appropriate air quotes even though my annoyance was threatening to come out and play. He had a prurient streak that grated.

"I wasn't trying to insult you," he protested. "Don't think that."

"Yeah, well ... I'm used to people judging me for my childhood. You don't have to worry about being the first ... or the last, for that matter. I no longer take it personally." Well, *mostly*, I silently added. In truth, I tried not to take it personally. There were times I simply couldn't let it go. I blew out a weighted sigh and turned toward where our bikes were hidden. "Where next?"

"Wait a second." Gunner grabbed my arm and stopped me from stalking away. "I'm getting sick and tired of saying things that offend you," he groused.

"I'm sorry I'm so easily offended," I deadpanned. "From now on, I'll try to take it like a man."

He scowled. "You're not making things easy for me."

"I didn't realize that was my job."

"I didn't say it was your job." Frustrated, he released me and dragged a hand through his hair. "I'm trying here. I know I was less than hospitable when you first showed up — and that's on me because I should've been nicer — but I'm trying to make amends. You won't let me."

He had a point, which I was loath to admit. "I ... you ... ."

"Oh, you're speechless. I'll have to make a note of this in my calendar so we can celebrate." He cracked a genuine smile. "It's surely a Hawthorne Hollow miracle."

I regrouped quickly. "I'll try to refrain from jumping all over you."

His smile was quick and sly. "Well, let's not be hasty. What kind of jumping did you have in mind?"

I glared at him. "You're kind of a pig."

"I have a reputation to maintain."

"How awesome for you. What sort of hit will your reputation take if we're caught spying on the town kook?"

He sobered. "Good point. Let's get out of here. I want to take a better look at the photos and make a plan."

"Fine. Where do you suggest we go to do that?"

"How do you feel about chili?"

Was that a trick question? "I ... what?"

He chuckled. "Come on. You're right about us needing to get away from here. I still need to think, and I know just the place to do it."

MABLE'S COUNTRY TABLE WAS exactly what you'd expect; quaint, cutesy and full of locals. All conversation stopped when Gunner and I walked through the door. Then the squealing began and it took everything I had not to cover my ears and roll my eyes.

"Gunner, I can't believe you're here!" A blonde with a narrow waist, shorts that showed off legs that seemed to go on for miles and a rather impressive rack threw her arms around his neck. She wore an apron with bulging pockets, which made me think she was a worker.

"Let me guess," I drawled, annoyance creeping over me. "You must be Mable?"

The young woman — who barely looked old enough to drink —

sent me a derisive look as she clasped Gunner tighter. "Mindy," she corrected. "Mable is my mother."

"And Mable thinks you should get back to work," a harsh voice barked from behind the counter.

When I turned, I found a woman in her fifties watching the scene with unveiled interest. She looked like the blonde, only older ... and harder. She'd clearly lived well over the years, but she didn't look happy about it right now.

"Hello, Mable." Gunner extricated himself from Mindy and crossed the room, pulling the cantankerous older woman into a hug even though she clearly didn't want it. "It's been far too long."

"You were in here last week," Mable argued, making a face as she pulled away from Gunner's exuberant embrace. "You were just as goofy then as you are now."

"Maybe you bring it out in me." He winked at her before gesturing toward me. "This is Scout. She's new in town."

"Hello." I offered her a lame wave. I felt a horde of eyes on me from every corner of the restaurant, but I remained calm. "It's nice to meet you."

"It's nice to meet me?" Mable didn't look convinced. "Well, you'll change your mind on that soon enough. Until then, have a seat over there." She inclined her chin toward a corner booth. "I'll send someone over to take your order in a few minutes."

"I'll be taking your order," Mindy supplied, moving closer to Gunner. The looks she shot him could've cooked pancakes on a hot sidewalk. He didn't return the covetous gazes, though, which I found interesting.

"I'll send someone over," Mable repeated. "It might be me. You never know." She pinned her daughter with a dark look. "I believe you have other tables to take care of, if I'm not mistaken."

Mindy turned sulky. "I was just talking to him."

"And now you're not."

Gunner took advantage of the distraction and prodded me toward the corner booth. He seemed amused by the turn of events, which only confused me more.

"Is Mindy your girlfriend?" I asked as I sat across from him.

"Absolutely not." He grabbed a menu from the display at the end of the table and handed it to me. "I'm extremely fond of Mable. Mindy is ... another story."

That was interesting. "She has a thing for you," I pointed out.

"I've noticed. That doesn't mean I reciprocate those feelings."

I glanced around the restaurant and found at least five sets of eyes focused on us. All of them were female. "I'm starting to think a lot of people in this town have a thing for you."

Gunner looked up from the menu and followed my gaze, his lips curving when he realized what I was talking about. "Yes, well, I'm Hawthorne Hollow's favorite son."

He seemed to bask in the position. "Why are you so fond of Mable?"

"She's always listened to my crap," he replied without hesitation. "When I was a kid, right after my mother was taken away, I came in here for something to eat. I was upset. Mable had a reputation for only caring about herself, but she sat with me for hours and listened to what I had to say.

"I didn't have a mother of my own any longer," he continued. "She was a great surrogate. Heck, she was better than the mother I grew up with. She listened for a long time, explained that I would always remember and never really get over it, and then insisted I move on."

I was impressed. "Most adults lie to you about things like that," I mused. "I can't tell you how many times I got moved from a foster home, told that I would find a better foster home and there was nothing to worry about. It was never true ... although, honestly, some foster homes were better than others."

"And yet you were never adopted," he mused, leaning back in his seat. "Why do you think that is?"

"Maybe I have a personality that's impossible to love." I'd considered that more than once and I wasn't feeling sorry for myself when I suggested it. I figured it was a very real probability. "You'll have to ask them why they didn't want to keep me."

Gunner narrowed his expressive eyes. "That's not what I meant ...

and I very much doubt that's why you weren't adopted. Your personality isn't exactly a bowl of ice cream most days, but I'd wager that's because you spent so many years protecting yourself," he countered. "You were young when you were abandoned, right?"

"I don't know exactly how old," I replied. "Four or five."

"That's young enough for people to want to take you on. I find it interesting that people kept sending you back."

"Yes, it was totally interesting," I deadpanned. "Not painful at all."

"You're missing the point." He was somber as he held my gaze. "You were a small child. Infants are coveted, but so are kids under a certain age. You should've been adopted ... and fast. You weren't. I don't think that's a coincidence."

"Oh, really? What do you think it was?"

"Magic." His answer was short, perfunctory, and it threw me for a loop.

"Excuse me?" My eyebrows flew up my forehead. "You think someone cast a spell so I wouldn't be adopted?"

He shrugged. "I don't know. Maybe that wasn't the ultimate goal of the spell. Maybe whoever cast it wanted something else, like to hide you or something, and the end result was that you couldn't be adopted. I can't say for certain. I simply find it weird that you weren't adopted."

I rested my palms on the tabletop, unsure how to respond. Part of me was intrigued by the supposition. The other part was annoyed that he insisted on sticking his nose into my business. Finally, I merely shook my head.

"It doesn't matter," I said, calm. "It's in the past. I can't change it, so it is what it is. I understand why you're attached to Mable. Finding an adult who tells you the truth as a kid is like winning the lottery.

"That doesn't change the fact that her daughter wants to grease you up with butter and rub herself over you like a piece of popcorn," I continued, smirking when he barked out a laugh. "I was simply curious about how that worked."

"Mindy has had a crush on me for a very long time," Gunner replied, wisely opting to drop the discussion of my adoption woes. "It was cute when she was seven ... and even thirteen. The older she gets, the more uncomfortable I get."

"You could tell her to knock it off."

"I did that when she was seventeen. It resulted in tears."

"Well ... that's difficult, but she's an adult now. She needs to suck it up and find a guy who's age-appropriate."

Gunner's eyes filled with mirth as he regarded me. "How can you be certain I'm not age-appropriate? Women mature faster than men. We might be on the same level, for all you know."

That was certainly a possibility. "I ... ." I had no idea where to go next with the conversation, so I was relieved when the bell over the door jangled to signify someone was entering the restaurant. I was surprised — and thankful — when I recognized Brandon. He took a moment to survey the diner and then headed in our direction.

"Your buddy is here," I noted, moving over when Brandon positioned himself at my side of the booth. "Maybe he'll be able to explain why you're not age-appropriate for Mindy."

"Who isn't age-appropriate for whom?" Brandon asked, a charming smile flitting across his face as he winked at me. "Thank you for allowing me to sit next to you. I'll be the center of town gossip for days once this gets out. You can kiss me right here if you really want to see things run off the rails."

I made a face as he tapped his cheek. "What?"

"Ignore him," Gunner instructed. "He's just trying to get a rise out of you. That's what he does."

"On the contrary," Brandon countered. "I find Scout intriguing and delightful ... and only half of that is because of her name. I love *To Kill a Mockingbird*."

Once I found out my name originated from a book, I decided to read it when I was still in elementary school. I didn't understand it then, but I kept reading it once a year after that. By the time I hit adulthood, the book had grown to be important to me ... even if I didn't always understand why the name was so fitting.

"It's a good book," I agreed. "That's not my real name, though. I don't know my real name."

"It's your real name," Gunner countered. "It doesn't matter what name you were born with. This is your name now. Even if you suddenly found out your birth name, do you think you would go back to using it?"

That was a fair question. "No," I replied after a moment's contemplation. "I guess you're right."

"I'm always right," he agreed before turning his attention to Brandon. "What's up with you?"

"I'm here for lunch," Brandon supplied. "I want some of Mable's world-famous chili. What about you guys? Where have you been?"

"Tracking down answers on Hal Crosby and Herbert Jones. I don't suppose you know if they had any connections, do you?"

"All Souls Church."

"We're aware of that connection." Gunner wrinkled his nose. "I was hoping you knew of another connection."

"Not that I can think of off the bat. Herbert spent all his time with the church members. I mean ... he was devoted. Hal was equally devoted at the start but lost interest over time. I think he had other things on his mind, if you know what I mean."

Brandon winked, clearly enjoying himself. Gunner, however, was obviously confused, because he wrinkled his forehead and leaned forward. "What other things?" he asked, confused.

"You know ... things."

"I don't know."

Brandon let loose an exaggerated sigh. "And here I thought you were up on all the town gossip," he muttered. "You disappoint me."

"Just spill."

"Mama Moon," Brandon offered. "Rumor is that Hal was seeing Mama Moon up until a few weeks ago. I wasn't sure the rumors were true until I saw them together one day. They were obviously sneaking around, because it was before seven and Hal was leaving her house."

"You're kidding." Gunner was flabbergasted. "I can't believe Mama Moon was seeing Hal. That's just so ... ridiculous. They have nothing in common."

I was behind, and I hated being behind. "Who is Mama Moon?"

Brandon sent me a pitying look. "She's the town loon."

"I thought Cecily was the town loon."

"Cecily Duncan?" Brandon snorted. "She's more of a little loon. Mama Moon is the big loon."

I turned to Gunner for further explanation.

"It's a long story," he hedged.

"We appear to have plenty of time."

"I guess." He fanned his menu in front of his face. "No matter how I tell the story, she's going to come off looking like a loon. You should prepare yourself for that."

I was confused. "Why should I care?"

"Because she's the original Spells Angel in this area ... and she's basically thirty pounds of crazy in a five-pound bag. I mean ... she's nuts, and I don't throw that term around lightly."

Ah, well, now things were getting interesting. "Tell me about her."

"Just remember ... you asked. You can't put this particular genie back in the bottle."

THIRTEEN

*T*he story of Mama Moon was fantastical ... and unbelievable.

"Get out!" I shook my head as I wiped the corners of my mouth with a napkin. "There's no way that's true."

It took Gunner and Brandon the better part of an hour to tell the tale, so we were finishing lunch by the time they wrapped up.

"It's totally true," Brandon enthused, sliding his arm along the back of the booth. "Mama Moon is a legend around these parts."

"He's full of crap, right?" I focused on Gunner, who seemed to be staring at a specific spot over my shoulder. When I turned to look I couldn't find anything that warranted his interest. "What are you looking at?"

"What?" Gunner shook his head to dislodge whatever thoughts he was mired in. "It's nothing. I ... it's nothing."

I waited for him to answer my question. When he didn't, I pressed him harder. "Mama Moon," I supplied. "Brandon is exaggerating about her, right?"

"Brandon never exaggerates about anything," Brandon countered, referring to himself in the third person. Generally I would've found that annoying, but there was something lovable about the guy ... in an out-of-control-teenage-boy-under-the-thrall-of-rampant-hormones way.

"I don't believe that." I smiled at him to take the sting out of my words before focusing on Gunner. "Seriously, he has to be exaggerating."

Gunner, his eyes narrowed, shook his head. "He's not exaggerating, but ... he does have a penchant for stretching the truth. You should know, he brags about things he's never even done ... especially when it comes to fishing."

"Oh, here we go," Brandon groused. "He's just trying to make me look bad in front of you." He waggled a finger for emphasis. "Don't think I don't know what you're doing."

"And I know what you're doing," Gunner shot back. "It won't work. We need to decide how we're going to approach Mama Moon. She's what's important right now, mostly because she has information we might be able to take advantage of."

I tilted my head to the side, considering. "You said she's a fortune teller," I noted. "What building does she work out of? I don't remember seeing a fortune teller sign on the main drag."

"Contrary to popular belief, not everything is located on the main drag ... and that includes Mama Moon," Gunner explained. "She's got a place out on Plum Cove Drive. It's close to the dive bar out there."

"There's a dive bar?" Now I was officially intrigued. "Why didn't tell me about the dive bar?"

"You don't want to go there."

I took offense to that remark. "You don't know. I enjoy a good dive bar. They're a breath of fresh air in Detroit, where everything old is new again and you need a theme if you want to go out and have a drink."

"Of course. That's perfectly reasonable." Gunner shook his head. "This dive bar is full of people who have lost hope and want to drink to the point of forgetting. They're not a fun crowd."

I got what he was saying, but I didn't appreciate him telling me what I would and would not like. "Yes, well, I expect I'll be stopping in regardless at some point. Go back to Mama Moon. She can't be as crazy as you say."

"She is."

"She's really been married nine times?"

"That's what she says."

"And she has a bear for a best friend?"

He smirked. "I've seen Barney with my own eyes. He doesn't walk on a leash or anything, but he does follow her around. Legend has it she rescued him from a trap when he was a cub, and he's been glued to her side ever since."

That was ridiculous. "And what about the story you told me about her actually flying a broom over the town on Halloween? That has to be made up."

"I saw it with my own eyes. I was eight at the time."

"Yeah, but ... ." I trailed off. "She sounds entertaining."

"You'll get the chance to find out for yourself," he said. "That's our next stop." He tapped the side of my plate. "Finish your chili."

"It's only two bites. I'm done."

"Finish it."

I made a face. "It's cold. I mean ... the chili was good, but it's cold now. I'm fine."

Gunner glanced around and then lowered his voice. "Finish it or Mable will make a scene."

"You don't want Mable to make a scene," Brandon added.

"Definitely not," Gunner agreed. "Just ... eat it."

I stared at him for a long beat. "Are you serious?"

"Deadly."

"Fine." I heaved out a sigh and scooped up the last of the chili. "The more time I spend in this town, the weirder you all start to look."

"We'll take that as a compliment," Brandon said.

"It wasn't meant as one."

"You'll learn to love us." He squeezed my shoulder and smiled serenely at Gunner, who returned the expression with a dark glare. "Oh, you look glum. Tell Brandon what's troubling you."

"I hate it when you refer to yourself in the third person," Gunner fired back.

"You need to get over that. Brandon likes talking about himself that way."

"Ugh." Gunner made a disgusted sound deep in his throat and focused on me. "Finish that so we can get out of here. I can't take much more of this."

He wasn't the only one.

MAMA MOON'S fortune-telling business was conducted in a building that defied explanation. The roof was purple, the walls pink, and the neon sign in the window green. It made for a disturbing ambiance.

"Well, this is ... fun." I rested my helmet on my bike seat as I stretched my back. The road leading to the fortune teller's home turf was bumpier than I'd expected. "I like her signs." I read them out loud. "Psychic parking only. Violators will be cursed. Talk to the hand ... with an actual psychic hand. If door does not open, do not enter."

Gunner chuckled. "She's a peculiar soul."

I slid my eyes to him. "How well do you know her?"

"Well enough that I'm uncomfortable having to talk to her about this," he answered. "She's not exactly my favorite person."

I could see that. "Well, I don't see where we have a choice." I took the practical approach and moved toward the door. "I'll do the talking if you're uncomfortable. I've got everything under control. I ... ." I broke off when I got a closer look at the small sticker on the front window. It read, "Don't eat yellow snow."

Gunner moved behind me and chuckled. "Yeah. Mama Moon is ... there are no words."

"Now I'm doubly looking forward to meeting her."

"Remember you're the one who said that, because odds are you're going to change your mind."

. . .

WIND CHIMES JANGLED ABOVE the door as I pushed it open. They let loose a magical sound that would've been soothing under different circumstances. I'd been prepared for the worst in this particular case, so nothing could ease my nerves ... especially the woman sitting on a round sofa in the center of the room, her feet propped on a stool as she popped candy into her mouth.

"What the ... ?"

Gunner snorted as I absorbed the sight. Mama Moon wore an oversized blue dress that made her look as if she was drowning in yards of rayon, and a turban that wasn't tight enough so it allowed tufts of gray hair to poke from beneath the ill-fitting band nestled around her forehead. Her makeup was garish, her features unnaturally pale and the smile she graced us with was right out of a Batman movie.

"Hello, young lady. I've been expecting you."

I kept quiet and tried not to focus on the fact that she'd missed her lips when applying her lipstick. "Hello."

"You've been expecting her?" Gunner was more at ease with Mama Moon, and he grabbed a chair from the table in the corner and handed it to me before going back to claim a second seat. "Why have you been expecting her?"

"The spirits are roiled," she replied, her eyes heavy as they looked me up and down. "She's been expected in this area for quite some time. Her coming is like a fulfilled promise. Finally, you're where you belong."

Instinctively, I understood she was playing a part. People fell for her nonsense, believed she had divine insight and could point them in the proper direction to make their dreams come true. I knew better. At least I thought I knew better. I expected to come face to face with a con woman — and I was fairly certain I had — but there was an energy zipping around the room that I couldn't quite identify. It wasn't magic, at least as I knew it, but it was ... something.

"You know me?" I forced a smile that I knew didn't make it all the way to my eyes. "How so?"

"Not you," she corrected. "I know your tribe."

"My tribe? I didn't realize I had a tribe."

"You lost them when you were young. So young that you have trouble remembering them. That's not because of your age, though. They cast a memory spell on you as a form of protection."

She was so matter-of-fact it set my teeth on edge. "I ... you ... um ... ." I was at a loss, unsure what to say. Thankfully, Gunner decided to take control of the conversation. He seemed more agitated than me by the revelation.

"If you know something, now would be the time to tell us," he prodded. "If you don't, stop playing games. We're not here to feed your ego."

If Mama Moon was offended by the statement she didn't show it. "Oh, Graham Jr., you're always such a pill. Have you ever asked yourself why you manage to suck all the fun out of life? You're like what's left of a grapefruit when all the good stuff has been eaten."

"I didn't know there was any good stuff in a grapefruit," I muttered absently, causing her to chuckle.

"Good point." She beamed at me. "As for what I said, Graham is right. Now is not the time to discuss that. There will come a time in the future when we will have no choice but to discuss the past ... but not now. You're here for another reason."

"We are," Gunner confirmed. "We want to talk about Hal Crosby. It's come to our attention you were dating him."

"I was," Mama Moon confirmed, bobbing her head. "It was a long time ago."

"I was told you were with him a few weeks ago," Gunner countered.

"That's a long time to a woman well past her prime and on the down side of her life," Mama Moon noted. "Still, if you want a definitive outline of the time we spent together, I can't help you. When you get older like me, everything melds together. I don't know how to explain it."

"Well, you still must have an idea of how long you were together." Gunner refused to back down. It was obvious he didn't like Mama

Moon. I had a feeling she was used to that and didn't hold it against him. The things she said about me, though, were fueling his current path through annoyance and doubt. He was angry on my behalf, which I found sweet ... and confusing.

"We were together as long as our hearts asked us to be together," she replied calmly. "They were in charge of our destinies."

"Oh, cut the crap." Gunner swore viciously under his breath. "I know you get a charge from talking in circles — and on a normal day I might be content to listen to your nonsense as long as I had nothing better to do — but this is serious. Hal is dead."

I watched Mama Moon, gauged her for a reaction. She didn't seem surprised ... although she didn't appear worked up either.

"Did you know he was dead?" I asked, my voice much quieter than I expected.

Slowly, Mama Moon dragged her eyes from Gunner to me.

"I knew," she said after a beat. "I didn't feel the exact moment he shuffled off the mortal coil. I'm still asking myself why, because I should've been privy to that information. But I knew he was dead. One minute he was there and the next he was ... *poof*. He was gone, and the world became a sadder place without him."

She almost seemed sad, which made me feel for her. I was suspicious about her motivations, though, so I held myself in check. "He was part of All Souls Church. Are you familiar with them?"

She let loose a hollow laugh as she straightened. "I'm familiar with them. They're not exactly what I would call upstanding citizens. They would refer to themselves in that manner, but the rest of us don't feel that way."

"Did they give you grief for dating Hal?" Gunner asked, his voice free of recrimination. "I've seen them in action before. They're pretty adamant about church members dating other church members."

"They are," Mama Moon agreed. "I don't think they realized that we were dating at the start. Hal was careful to keep me separate from them. I was fine with that, mind you. I've never trusted that group."

"I'm betting they'd say the same about you," Gunner interjected.

"Oh, I'm certain they would," she agreed. "They've always disliked me, and I them. It's one thing to cling to the life you know and another to shun the life you haven't taken the time to investigate. The people at that church are the absolute worst."

"What about zombies?" I asked, going for broke. "Have you heard anything about them trying to create zombies?"

"Zombies?" Mama Moon arched an eyebrow as her lips curved. "I don't think they're sophisticated enough to work magic like that. In fact, I'm almost positive they don't believe in magic."

"I've heard things about them throughout the years," Gunner countered. "This isn't the first time something weird that has happened has been associated with them. We're not sure what we saw in the woods was a zombie, but it had a lot of the same characteristics ... including a familiar face."

"A familiar face? Really?" She wrinkled her forehead and briefly closed her eyes. "Hmm. I can't see beyond the veil. What familiar face are you talking about?"

I braved a glance in Gunner's direction, expecting to find him laughing ... or at least scowling. Instead, he looked intent. "Herbert Jones."

"Another member of the group." Her eyes never opening, Mama Moon pursed her lips. "I don't know what they're doing," she said finally, sighing. "Whatever it is, they've got their intentions on lock-down. I'm guessing that they're purposely clouding the channels so I can't figure out what they're up to."

"Or *they're* not up to anything," I countered. "I don't necessarily believe that entire group is to blame for whatever is going on. It's much more likely that only one person is involved and he or she happens to be a member of the church."

"That seems a very practical notion," Mama Moon agreed. "But I'm not sure I agree with you. That church has always been peculiar. I've never trusted Father Bram. He's ... slimy."

"Is that your psychic powers talking?" I asked.

"That's my personal intuition talking," she countered. "I might not know everything about that group. but I know enough to recognize I want nothing to do with them. You should feel the same way. They can bring you nothing but trouble."

"Yeah, well, I'll take your opinion into consideration." I got to my feet and looked at Gunner. "This was a waste of time. I ... ." Whatever I was going to say died on my lips when Mama Moon grabbed my hand.

I was never okay with people invading my personal space — I had a thing about hands going places they weren't meant to go — but this was even more invasive.

"What the ... ?"

"Let her go," Gunner ordered, hopping to his feet. "What are you doing?"

"Just taking a look," Mama Moon replied, gripping me tighter. "I just ... I ... that is amazing."

"Let her go!" Gunner tried to wrench Mama Moon's fingers from my wrist, but he didn't have the strength. Mama Moon's mouth dropped open in amazement as a magical burst of energy coursed through me.

"Look at that," she enthused, her eyes going wide as saucers. "Look at that!"

"Look at what?" Gunner was beside himself.

At the same moment he asked the question, a bolt of magic I didn't realize was building inside of me broke free and careened into Mama Moon. It knocked her back, forcing her to give up the hold she had on my wrist. The blow was so strong she tumbled off the side of the round couch and hit the floor with a terrific thud.

When she managed to regain control of herself and look in our direction, the turban was askew and hanging from a few clips as she stared at us, dazed.

"Now that right there was impressive," she murmured, her voice dreamy. "I've never seen a barrier spell like that. You, my dear, are something special. Where exactly did you come from? No, seriously. Where are your people? I would very much like to meet them."

I didn't have an answer, so I merely stared at my hands, my mind busy as I thought about the burst of magic. I had no idea where it came from. I certainly hadn't summoned it. So, why did it pick now to appear? And what exactly was it protecting?

I had no answers ... no idea if I honestly wanted to learn the truth. This was more than I expected and it made me want to turn tail and run.

FOURTEEN

"*A*re you okay?"

Gunner knelt in front of me, his face etched with concern. I sucked in a breath to calm myself ... and then another ... and then another. No matter how hard I tried, my heart continued to pound and my mind refused to clear.

"Scout." Gunner lowered his voice and leaned forward, cupping my chin and forcing me to look at him. "Are you okay?"

He looked genuinely concerned, fearful even. That was enough to send me careening back to reality.

"I'm fine." I swallowed hard and frowned at how squeaky my voice sounded. I cleared my throat and tried again. "I'm fine." This time I sounded stronger. I didn't feel it, but I sounded okay, which is all that mattered.

"You don't look fine." He pushed my hair away from my face and scowled at Mama Moon. "What did you do to her?"

"I tried to see the part of her that's hidden," Mama Moon replied, her tone dull and unfocused. "I knew it was there. You could see it shimmering under the surface. But it's untouchable."

"What is she talking about?" I asked, confused.

"I don't know." Gunner appeared troubled as he continuously

moved his hand over my hair. I didn't know if the motion was meant to soothe me or him. "I don't ... what did you feel when she touched you?"

I shrugged. "I don't know. I ... felt invaded. I didn't want her to touch me."

"So, you sent that bolt of energy out to get her." He looked hopeful. "You were cognizant of what you were doing, right?"

Well, not so much. "Not exactly," I hedged, shifting on my chair. "I don't know what happened. I don't think I did that. I think she did."

"No, that definitely came from you." He pressed the back of his hand to my forehead. "You're warm. That wasn't the normal fire magic you tend to rely on. That was something else. It came from somewhere else."

"If it didn't come from me, it had to come from her." That had to be true. It was the only thing that made sense. "She did it. She's putting on a show."

He slid his eyes to Mama Moon, who had about as much color as a Hanes T-shirt, and shook his head. "I don't think so. It's not important right now. We need to get you out of here."

"Sure." I stood on unsteady feet, something in the back of my mind registering that I was a bit hazy and probably should take things slow. "I'll meet you out front." I spun on my heel and headed toward the door, causing Gunner to hiss something unintelligible.

"I'll want to talk about this later," Gunner warned. I heard him getting closer to me, which was good, because my fingers didn't want to work correctly and I couldn't turn the doorknob. "You are going to tell me what just happened."

"I don't know what happened." Mama Moon sounded as hazy as I felt. "She's warded."

"You can't ward a person," he barked.

"Someone warded her. Whatever she is, someone wanted to protect the secret. She is utterly fascinating."

"She's a person." Gunner put his hand on my hip and frowned when he realized what I was trying to do. "She's confused and slow right now, but she's still a person. This isn't over. I'll be back for more information."

I HAD NO IDEA HOW I got home.

I woke on my bed, the kitten positioned on my chest so I was staring directly into his bi-colored eyes the moment my eyes snapped open. My back ached thanks to the position I'd fallen asleep in, my neck cranked a bit to the right, and my stomach growled as if I'd gone days without food. A quick look at the window told me that at most it had been hours. The sunlight was still bright through the window, so it couldn't possibly be that late.

Gently, I dislodged the kitten. He protested slightly, nipping my fingers as I carefully placed him on the mattress. I felt disjointed as I walked through the cabin, muddled, but I slowly began recovering my faculties as I picked my way through the rooms, ultimately landing on the front porch.

I found Gunner sitting on the ground with a screwdriver and a chair I didn't recognize. It looked to be a glider, one meant for a front porch instead of indoors, and he was focused on it as I tried to absorb the rest of the scene.

"How did you get me and my bike back here?" I asked after a moment's contemplation.

He slid his eyes to me and smiled. "I called for backup. I wasn't keen on getting Brandon involved, but I didn't have much choice. He has a truck big enough for both our bikes, and I couldn't very well leave you there."

"Yeah, well ... ." Weary, I sank to a sitting position on the top step. "What happened again?"

He chuckled, but remained focused on the chair. "You passed out. Mama Moon tried to invade your head and somehow you kept her out ... and in fantastic fashion. Whatever you did to her was powerful. I have a feeling she's still recovering, too."

I vaguely remembered that, although the flashes flitting through my brain felt as if they were from a movie I'd watched twenty years ago instead of a real-life event that had just transpired. "She said I was protected."

"She did," he confirmed, his eyes thoughtful as they snagged with mine. "She said that someone put a barrier spell in your head and that you were warded."

"You said it's impossible to ward a person," I remembered. "That's essentially true."

"Essentially," he agreed. "Still, she was adamant."

"She's a kook, though. I mean ... she's nuts."

He made a frustrated sound in the back of his throat and shifted to face me. He didn't drop the screwdriver, but forward momentum on the chair was lost. "She's nutty," he agreed after a beat. "But she's not nuts. I told you, she was the first person in the area recruited into Spells Angels."

"That doesn't necessarily mean anything," I argued. "Just because she was once one of us ... ." I trailed off.

"I know it's difficult to believe, but she was once well-respected in this area," he offered. "She was powerful and fought the good fight."

"Then why did she leave the group?"

"I don't know." He was earnest as he studied my face. "Even before she left the group — which happened when I was a kid — she had a reputation for being eccentric. She was known as flamboyant, blunt and a heckuva a good time."

"So, what happened?" I rested my chin in my hand and focused on him. "How did she go from being respected to the town joke? Something had to happen to shift perception."

He absently scratched his cheek. "When I was in middle school, Mama Moon was still in charge of this chapter of Spells Angels. At the time, I didn't know what the group was.

"I mean ... I knew the members hung out together at the Cauldron as a group," he continued. "I knew my father was always agitated because he couldn't figure out what they were doing in the woods at all hours. He thought there was some naked dancing or something going on, because he heard that was a thing with witches. There was some cop in Hemlock Cove who swore he saw it happening there, and the story spread like wildfire."

I was intrigued. "You're not a witch."

He smiled. "No."

"I realized that from the start, but I never thought to ask. We have a lot of different paranormal types in our group in Detroit, but everyone kind of congregates together. The shifters hang with the other shifters by the sports complexes. The witches spend a lot of time on the Ambassador Bridge. The gargoyles head for the old buildings along the Cass Corridor because they can't kill anyone, but that doesn't mean they can't lap up blood if humans go after each other."

He smirked. "You have gargoyles? That's kind of cool. I've never seen one. We don't have them up here."

"I'm sure you don't. There's nowhere for them to hide here. It's much easier in the south."

"Yeah." He was thoughtful as he stared at me. "Do you want me to tell you what I am?"

That seemed like a loaded question. It also seemed as if I should already know. He hadn't set off any alarm bells when we'd first met. That meant I already inherently recognized his kind upon initial introduction.

Things clicked into place quickly. "You're a shifter."

"I am."

"Wolf shifter," I surmised quickly, smiling. "You're not pack, though. You're an independent."

"That's also true. My parents were pack until my mother lost her mind. Instead of helping, the pack kicked her out ... which only exacerbated things."

I didn't know much about shifters. The factions really were separated in Detroit. Once, I heard one of the witches lament that it was racist. I didn't realize what she meant at the time, though I understand now.

"Your father pulled you out of the pack when your mother got sick," I mused. "That must have been difficult for you."

"You would think so, but it really wasn't. Packs are for people with standing. My father is the chief of police, but Hawthorne Hollow is so tiny it could fit on a pin with room to spare. He could give the pack nothing, so they had no inclination to go out of their way to keep him. I don't really remember participating in many pack events when I was a kid. I'm okay with not being in a pack."

"Still, at some point you figured out what the Spells Angels are," I noted. "That had to be ... exciting. It also has to be terrifying. In a town this size, the idea of a paranormal threat taking over had to consume you."

"See, I don't think I worried about paranormal beings taking over in the same manner you did," he countered. "You've lived a different life. A lot of the things we dealt with were similar, but only on an emotional level. The nitty-gritty was different.

"I had a mother I feared, and I lost her," he continued. "You have no idea who raised you before you were five. You don't know if the people were good or evil. All you know is that you were abandoned, and I can't imagine what you've dealt with because of that.

"I wasn't abandoned, but my mother is mentally ill. She's still that way and will stay that way until she dies. Your entire history is a question mark."

"You're not making me feel good about this sharing thing," I offered, rueful.

His smile returned, lighting up his features. "I'm sorry. There really was a point to what I was saying. In your head, I had to be fearful about what the Spells Angels were doing here when I was a kid. I was the opposite, though. I was fascinated with them."

"When did you figure out what they were?"

"I think part of me always knew there was something different about them. When Mama Moon was in charge, I was slightly more fearful. She had a certain reputation."

"Oh, really?" I arched an eyebrow. "I never would've guessed."

"She wasn't that odd back then. I mean, she had her eccentricities, there's no doubt about that. But she wasn't crazy. The way she acted today, the show she put on, that's more of a recent development."

I was officially intrigued. "Do you think it's a facade she's embraced because she lost control of the group?"

"What makes you think she lost control of the group?"

"That's what you basically said without coming right out and saying it. You hemmed and hawed around the subject. I got the gist of it. Something happened when you were in middle school. You were about to tell me and then we got distracted by how similar we are."

He laughed. "You are ... something. I haven't decided if it's a good something yet, but you're definitely out there."

"I'll take that as a compliment."

"Fair enough." He nodded. "Mama Moon was in charge of the Spells Angels when Evan Greenspan went missing. He was in third grade, several years younger than me. The school was only four blocks from his house and it was a straight shot, so he walked by himself.

"One day in October, he didn't make it home," he continued. "His parents were beside themselves. No one understood what was happening. Hawthorne Hollow isn't like the big city. It's untouched in certain ways. Back then, it was also naive."

My stomach flipped as I sensed an uncomfortable story in my future.

"My father organized search parties," he continued. "I called all my friends and they called all their friends. Every able-bodied individual hit the woods looking for him. Since the Spells Angels were always in the woods, my father swallowed his pride and approached Mama Moon. He knew he needed help, because we had a lot of ground to cover.

"By then I knew what Spells Angels was, at least on a very basic level," he said, rubbing his forehead. "I knew that everyone involved had some sort of ability. I likened it to the Justice League, but with vampires and witches."

I smiled. "That sort of makes sense."

"Yeah. Anyway, Mama Moon said she would help and sent some of her people out into the woods. To this day, I'm not exactly sure what happened. I know that a lot of people were out there looking, but somehow there was an accident."

I rubbed the spot over my heart. "Evan?"

"No. Evan was never found. He disappeared in the middle of the day and nothing was ever found of him again. Er, well, I shouldn't say nothing. His backpack was discovered, shredded. People assumed a bear got him, but that never made much sense to me."

Something clicked in the back of my mind. "You said Mama Moon has a bear. I didn't see it while we were there."

"Yeah. Barney. He hangs around the woods behind her house most of the time. He's ferocious when need be — mostly when she's mouthed off to someone at the bar and they follow her home to threaten her — but he's mostly gentle. I never bought the idea that he killed Evan."

I was confused. "If people thought the bear killed Evan, why didn't they destroy it? I mean ... I've heard of that happening numerous times."

"I have, too," Gunner agreed. "It didn't happen this time, though. I don't know what happened. The townsfolk turned on Mama Moon. She was upset to the point that she started drinking ... a lot. She left the group not long after that, although there are arguments about whether she truly left or was forced out. Most people believe she was forced out."

"And you don't know why? Other than the obvious, I mean."

"No."

"And you didn't ask why?"

"No."

"Well, you're a better person than me," I said after a moment's contemplation. "That sounds like quite the story. I would've hounded her until she told me everything that happened. I mean, the woman has a pet bear ... but I'm not going to really believe that until I see it."

"I'll make sure you see it. As for Mama Moon, she carries a lot of sadness with her. She's also a kook and gets off on the town believing she's nuts. I don't know why she does the things she does, but her fate is sealed when it comes to the people of Hawthorne Hollow."

I swallowed hard before I asked the next question. I was uncomfortable with the idea of pushing things further, and yet I couldn't continue without at least trying to find answers. "Do you think it's possible she knows something about me?"

He stared for a long time before finally getting to his feet and sitting next to me. He didn't put his arm around me or offer me a knee pat as a form of solace. Instead, he merely closed the distance and offered me a bit of the warmth he seemed to have at the ready.

"I don't think she knows anything about you like you're asking," he replied finally. "I mean ... nothing specific. If you're asking if I believe it's possible she truly senses something about you, I do. I wish I could help you on that front, but I can't. She might have answers worth pursuing down the line."

"But we have other things to focus on right now," I said, rubbing my forehead. "I can't forget the bigger picture and focus on myself. That's not what we do."

"It's not," he agreed. "But you don't have to forget the bigger picture to chase your own truth. We can do both."

"Maybe I don't want to know." I faked bravado for his benefit. "I'm perfectly fine not knowing."

"I don't think you are, but I also don't think we're close to the answers you need. We're going to have to play things by ear, take things one day at a time."

"You sound like a fortune cookie."

"Yeah?" He brightened as he lightly brushed his fingers against my cheek, freezing in the moment with his face close to mine before abruptly pulling away. "That's quite a coincidence. I was thinking about ordering Chinese. How does that sound?"

"I didn't see a Chinese place downtown." I was confused. "Why did you tell me everything was downtown when it's not?"

"I told you Hawthorne Hollow was a mystery."

"I know but ... it's more than that. Chinese sounds good, though. While we're waiting for it to be delivered you can tell me about Peeping Tim. I'm dying to hear the full story on that guy."

"You're really not. Barney the Bear is more entertaining."

"What makes you think I don't want to hear about both?"

FIFTEEN

*G*unner stayed late, so late I thought he was angling for an invitation for an overnight visit. We talked about things — so many topics I thought my head might spin — and we laughed. We laughed so much my stomach hurt. When I first met him, I thought that was impossible. Apparently, I was wrong.

"That's all the windows," he said after we finished hanging curtains throughout the entire cabin. "Now Tim won't be able to see you unless you want him to see you."

"Under what circumstances would I want him to see me?"

He shrugged, noncommittal. "I don't know. You'll have to take that up with him. I don't want to involve myself in your private business. What happens with the ghost, stays with the ghost."

"Ha, ha." I flicked his ear, jolting slightly when he caught my wrist and wrapped his fingers around it. "Um ... ." I forgot what I was about to say, instead finding myself lost in his intense gaze.

"Tim is harmless," he said, shaking his head. "He's a pervert, but he can't touch you. He's a ghost ... and ghosts can't touch."

"That doesn't make it any less invasive. How would you feel if a female ghost peeped in your windows all the time?"

His grin was mischievous. "I think you just highlighted the difference between men and women."

My skin tingled where he touched me and, I'm ashamed to admit, I felt light-headed. "I don't think you would be nearly as okay with it as you pretend."

He shrugged. "I guess it depends on the woman." He shifted his head closer to mine and my mouth went dry. I wasn't sure how this was even happening, but for some reason I was perfectly happy with the notion of him kissing me.

"So, you're saying that you would be happy if a particular woman peeped on you?"

"Maybe. I ... ." Whatever he was about to say died on his lips as the kitten picked that moment to make his presence known.

He howled ... loudly. In fact, I had no idea an animal that small could make that much noise. The screech was enough to break the spell — although I'd yet to decide which one of us had woven it — and Gunner released my wrist and took an involuntary step back. He seemed as surprised as me by the turn of events.

"I should probably get going," he offered lamely as I collected myself. "We need to strategize tomorrow. I'm not sure where to go next, but ... I need to think about it."

I felt ridiculous as I backed away from him. "Right. I'll think about it, too."

"Right."

It was obvious we were both uncomfortable as he started walking toward the door. The kitten was getting underfoot, so I scooped him up and followed.

"Make sure you lock this behind me," he instructed, tapping the door handle as I watched him slip through the opening. "It won't keep everyone — or everything, for that matter — out, but it's an added layer of protection."

"You don't need to worry about me," I said quickly. "I can take care of myself. I've been doing it for a long time."

"I'm sure you have. Still, it's better to be safe."

"I'll be safe."

"Great. Well ... I'll see you in the morning." He lingered a moment, as if unsure what to do, before turning on his heel and disappearing into the darkness.

I remained where I was, the kitten clutched against my chest, and listened as he fired up his motorcycle.

"You either saved me from making an ass of myself or ruined what could've been a great night," I told the kitten. "I'll decide tomorrow which one it is."

The kitten was solemn as he looked up at me. I could almost read his thoughts.

"I wasn't going to do anything stupid." I felt defensive. "I was just ... he was there and he has a nice smile ... I ... why am I explaining myself to you anyway? You're a cat."

The kitten rubbed his head against my chest.

"Yeah, yeah, yeah," I muttered, double-checking the lock before hitting the lights. "I don't need the judgment, pal. I'm perfectly capable of making my own decisions."

The cat, of course, merely stared at me.

"I hate it when you look at me that way," I groused, striding into the bedroom. "We're going to talk about your attitude later. You've been warned."

The kitten didn't look remotely worried.

I WAS UP AND DRESSED WITH the sun the next morning. I didn't sleep well, my dreams muddled by a bevy of visuals I didn't want to lay claim to. Gunner featured in all of them, so I wasn't exactly thrilled at the idea of seeing him first thing, but my heart gave a jolt at the sound of a motorcycle pulling up outside the cabin and I couldn't stop my stomach from doing a lone somersault.

I managed to pull myself together by the time he knocked, and when I opened the door I had every intention of taking the motor-cycle by the handlebars ... so to speak. I wanted to talk about what was happening between us, get it out in the open and at least see where he stood on the issue. Pretending nothing was happening wasn't working, and I didn't want to be the sort of person who ignored an issue until it came back to bite me in the worst possible way.

When I opened the door, though, it wasn't Gunner I found waiting for me. It was Bonnie ... and I was dumbfounded.

"What are you doing here?" I blurted out before I thought better of it.

"Good morning to you, too," she said dryly, shaking her head. "I take it you're not a morning person."

I didn't believe anyone was really a morning person. I was convinced it was all an act upbeat people insisted on putting on so they could pretend to be something they weren't. No, truly. There's no way being a morning person is a real thing.

"I'm sorry," I offered, rubbing my hands over the front of my jeans as I tried to gain control of my emotions. "I didn't mean that the way it came out."

"No?" Bonnie looked amused. "How did you mean it?"

"I just ... expected someone else." I forced myself to voice the obvious. "I thought I was working with Gunner. That was the impression I got yesterday, anyway."

"That was my assumption, too," she said, blasé. "I only know that Gunner had something come up — I guess it's top secret or something because they didn't tell me what it was — and he was called away. Rooster doesn't want you working on your own because of the way the body was found, so he sent me to be your backup."

That was great. I simply had no idea what she was supposed to back me up on. "He had something come up?" I was instantly suspicious. "What?"

"I already said I don't know."

"Yeah, but ... you must have heard. Did some paranormal creature decide to build a nest in his backyard? I'm confused about when this emergency could've possibly come up."

Bonnie was taken aback. "I don't know. He doesn't run his schedule by me. You'll have to ask him."

The expression on her face told me I was overstepping ... and in a big way.

"I'm sorry," I said hurriedly, fighting to control my agitation. "I wasn't trying to be a pain. It's just ... I was confused. Gunner said he was going to brainstorm about what we should do today. I was going to do the same. I came up with nothing, so ... ."

"So, you don't know where to start looking." Bonnie relaxed and chuckled. "That makes sense. I hate it when I don't know where to start looking. I don't know what to tell you. Why don't you tell me what you've got and we'll go from there?"

"Sure. That sounds like a good idea."

I invited her in for coffee because it seemed the neighborly thing to do, introduced her to the cat and then launched into the story. I left out certain things — mostly Mama Moon's reaction to me and what happened when she put her hands on me for a reading, because that seemed private ... and kind of an overshare. When I was done, Bonnie was agape.

"Wow! Sounds like you've had a busy two days." She rubbed the back of her neck as she sipped her coffee and shot the occasional smile toward the cat. "I didn't know Mama Moon and Hal were dating. That seems an odd pairing."

"After meeting Mama Moon, I would guess that's something that can be said of every pairing she's been involved in."

"Yeah, well ... ." Bonnie pursed her lips. "Mama Moon is only going to share as much information as she feels comfortable with. She's not a giver."

"You know her?"

Bonnie shrugged. "Everyone knows her. I mean ... she's a fixture in this community. I didn't grow up in Hawthorne Hollow. I grew up a few towns over. I was familiar with Hawthorne Hollow, but only hung out here if something specific was going on ... which was rare.

"Essentially I'm saying that I didn't know the old Mama Moon, the one who was in charge of the group," she continued. "I've only ever known the kook. Rooster has glowing things to say about her and seems sad when anyone mentions how weird she's become. Gunner also has memories of her being more than she is now."

"Do you think she's capable of killing Hal?" I asked.

"Capable? Yes. Is it likely that she carried it off? I'm not so sure. I mean ... why? If she wanted to break up, all she had to do was dump him. Hal's face was missing. That seems like overkill for a simple breakup. I don't even know how that happens."

"Magic," I muttered, picturing the body in my mind's eye. "There's no way that was done with a weapon of any sort. I don't know any doctor who could've made lines that steady. That means that someone either cast a spell or used a form of magic we're not familiar with."

"Okay. How do we track that magic?"

There was only one way I could think of. "We have to go back to where the body was found," I said finally, making up my mind. "I can try casting a tracking spell from that position to follow the individual who killed Hal. It's not a given it will work — especially after so much time has passed — but we don't have many options."

"I'm good with that." Bonnie flashed a tight smile. I didn't know her well enough to read her emotions, but I was almost positive she didn't like the idea of tracking Hal's murderer. Still, she didn't put up a fight. "We can park at the bar and walk in from the back," she suggested. "It will be shorter than the initial route you took with Gunner."

"Sounds good to me. At least we have a place to start."

WE PARKED IN THE BACK of The Rusty Cauldron. It wasn't even nine and yet there were several bikes parked in the lot, including one that I recognized as Gunner's.

"I guess his important business involved a visit to the bar before lunch, huh?"

Bonnie followed my gaze and shrugged. She wasn't nearly as agitated as I felt. "I don't know. Maybe he's touching base with Rooster before doing whatever needs to be done."

It was a feasible suggestion. I didn't believe it for a second, though. Gunner wasn't on an assignment that "popped up" out of nowhere. He was avoiding me. I wasn't an idiot.

"I guess it doesn't matter." I forced a smile for her benefit and turned toward the woods behind the building. It was a good quarter-mile walk, but I was looking forward to getting some of my aggression out. "Shall we?"

Bonnie chewed her bottom lip nervously, uncertain. "Okay, but if we get attacked by a monster that can remove faces I'm totally leaving you to fight it. I just want you to be aware before we go in there. I'm not a coward or anything, but I don't want to lose my face."

That was a fair warning. "Okay. I'll handle the fight if we find a monster."

"Great." Bonnie brightened considerably. "That's a deal."

It took us only ten minutes to reach the site where Hal's body had been discarded. The police had obviously been there, because a large octagonal area was taped off, but the weather the previous two days had caused the tape to dip in places.

"Right here?" Bonnie asked, pointing.

I nodded as I glanced around, my gaze falling on the trees. I was looking for symbols, I realized, something that tied into what I saw at Cecily's house. I didn't see anything, but I couldn't shake the feeling that the symbols at Cecily's house were somehow important. I made a mental note to follow up on them.

"I'm not familiar with the town," I said, hands on hips as I swiveled. "Who hangs out in this area?"

Bonnie, who had hunkered down for a better look at the location where the body had been found, shrugged. "No one. I mean ... not really."

"There's a path," I reminded her, pointing toward the woods. "Someone has to hang out here."

"I think kids go in those woods to party sometimes," she offered. "I don't believe it's often, though, because it's so close to the road commission outpost."

I knit my eyebrows. "Road commission?" I didn't remember seeing any road commission vehicles when I was back there. "Where is that?"

She pointed east. "It's not even a quarter of a mile that way. You can't see the fence that surrounds it because of the big pile of sand."

I'd noticed the sand. It was essentially a small mountain, especially since the rest of the town was flat. I'd never considered what it was doing there. "Why do they have the big pile of sand?"

Bonnie chuckled. "You're not the only one to ask that question. I think it looks like a giant litterbox. I'm surprised we don't have an out-of-control feline population. I asked about it once; supposedly it's for filling in sinkholes and road work projects. But I've been here a few years and I've never seen it shrink or grow in size."

I stared at the sand pile for a long time and then shook my head. "That probably has nothing to do with what happened here."

"Probably," she agreed. "It's interesting to theorize about, though. However, that should probably be saved for a different time. We have other things to worry about."

"Namely a face-eating enemy that could be virtually anywhere," I supplied.

"Pretty much," she agreed. "You said you were going to cast a spell? I'm curious what sort of spell you're going to use. I'm not familiar with hedge witch spells, so I want to see what you come up with."

"It's not a hedge witch spell," I said, stretching my fingers as I prepared to unleash my magic. "This is something different."

"You said you were a hedge witch."

"I'm a hereditary witch, too," I reminded her.

"Yeah, but ... all that means is you inherited some magical ability from your ancestors."

It meant more than that, at least to me. "Well, I don't know where this spell came from, but I've used it before. I simply need to focus. Give me a second."

I pressed my eyes shut and concentrated, the magic pulsing through me. I felt it sparking out of my fingertips, but I didn't unleash it. Not yet.

I sucked in a cleansing breath, focused on exactly what I wanted to happen, and then unleashed the wave of magic while uttering one word three times in rapid succession: "*Vestigo.*"

The magic grew in strength as it scoured the ground, lighting up to illuminate footprints on the flattened earth. The blue haze that surrounded the prints was weak, but it was there, so I was taking it as a win.

Bonnie's eyes were wide when I finally turned to her. "That was ... impressive," she said finally.

"Thanks." I wiped my hands on the seat of my pants and grinned. "We should start following the trail before it dies. I don't know how much juice is in that spell."

"Sure." Bonnie tilted her head to the side and regarded me without moving. "Just one question."

"Shoot."

"What was that thing you whispered? The word, I mean."

I wrinkled my nose. "*Vestigo?* It means 'track' in Latin."

"Did you take a class to learn Latin?"

"No. I did read a few Latin books when I was a teenager."

"And you just picked it up?"

"I ... well ... kind of." I shifted from one foot to the other, uncomfortable under her scrutiny. "I've always been that way. I can read things and turn them to my advantage. It's not that big of a deal."

"It's a bigger deal than you realize, but we'll put it behind us for now," Bonnie said, inclining her head toward the woods. "Come on. We'll see where the tracks lead. I'm not nearly as worried about meeting the face-eating monster as I was before."

SIXTEEN

*T*he trip through the woods was tense, mostly because I was on alert in case a spriggan decided to hop out and try to kill me. Now that I knew they existed I was keen to see another ... and experiment with ways to kill them.

What? I like learning things. Sue me.

Bonnie was quiet at the start, but I felt her need to ask questions. Finally, I did the only thing I could and brought the conversation to her.

"If you have something you want to say ... ."

"What makes you think I have something to say?" Bonnie turned innocent. "I'm not doing anything but minding my own business."

"That's what makes me think you have something to say," I admitted. "I would rather you let it out now." I eyed a moving leaf suspiciously, but kept walking. I didn't sense danger. Sure, I hadn't sensed danger the first time a spriggan attacked, but I'd decided to blame that on the excitement of a new environment. My instincts had never let me down before.

"Okay." Bonnie licked her lips. "There's a rumor going around that you're something special, like a white witch to end all white witches. I guess I'm curious why people think that."

I was caught off guard. "What do you mean? Who is saying I'm something special?"

"That's the rumor going around."

"But ... who said it?" I thought of Gunner, the look on his face when Mama Moon started spouting nonsense after trying to invade my mind. Perhaps I'd been wrong from the start. It was entirely possible he didn't want to be around me because he was afraid I was somehow going to turn into something so powerful he would have no idea how to fight me. It might not have anything to do with the moment I thought we'd shared and everything to do with the past I couldn't remember. "It was Gunner, wasn't it?"

"No. Definitely not." Her eyes went wide. "It definitely wasn't him."

I didn't believe her. The realization that Gunner was spreading stories caused my hackles to rise. "You don't have to worry about me hurting you." I kept my eyes forward. "In fact, there's no reason for you to hang around. I've got this. I can handle it myself."

"That's not what I meant," Bonnie protested. I could practically see the frustration oozing from her pores. "I didn't mean to upset you."

"I'm not upset." I brushed the back of my hand over my forehead. "You can head back. You don't need to stick with me. I'm more than capable of taking care of myself. In fact, I prefer that. I don't need a partner."

Bonnie huffed out a sigh. "Geez. I can tell you're going to be a lot of fun. Really, I wasn't trying to upset you."

"Do I look upset?"

"Yeah." She didn't back down, for which I had to give her credit. "You look ... frazzled. I'm not telling you how to feel — mostly because I hate it when people tell me how I should feel about something — so I'm not trying to do that. But it's obvious you're worked up."

"I'm not worked up." I told myself that was true. "I'm simply ... dealing with a lot. I moved. I adopted a cat. I got attacked by a creature I've never heard of. I found a body that was missing a face. You're worked up about the face thing, too. You get that."

"I do," Bonnie confirmed. "I most definitely get that. The thing is, you were upset about something this morning and I didn't really pick up on it. My question made things worse. I'm sorry. That's the last thing I want. I was simply curious."

"About the extent of my powers?"

"Yeah." Bonnie's smile was sheepish. "You're extremely powerful. That's the rumor going around. You burned a spriggan in its tracks. No one has ever done that, at least to my knowledge. Rooster said that the body was disintegrated to the point he couldn't tell what tribe it came from."

"They have tribes?" I was dumbfounded. "They're sticks with eyes."

She chuckled. "Not everything is as it appears. Spriggans have been around for centuries. There's a reason for that. If they were as stupid as you seem to assume, I don't think that would be possible."

She had a point, but still ... . "Certain marine species have been thought to be extinct multiple times," I pointed out. "They were found centuries after they were assumed to have died out. They didn't survive because they were smart as much as people were dumb and didn't look in the right place."

"I guess you could look at it that way."

"But you don't," I muttered, shaking my head. "I don't know what to make of them. We don't have them in Detroit."

"I'm sure you have things down there that we've never heard of," she said pragmatically. "I'm more interested in the method of death. You have fire magic, which isn't a standard gift. It's believed that fire magic is only bestowed on the most powerful."

"How do you know that?" I was honestly curious. "I don't remember reading that in any of the textbooks leading up to the final test in order to garner Spells Angels certification."

"I'm something of a historian. I've read about witches throughout history. I'm not overly powerful. I mean ... I can hold my own. But compared to you .... There are times I wish I was more powerful, I'm not going to lie. It just wasn't meant to be."

For a brief moment she looked so sad it tugged on my heartstrings. "You're probably better off. Look at me. People think I'm powerful, which should earn respect, but it doesn't. It's worse. It draws fear, so they watch me with suspicion."

"If you're talking about me, I was not watching you with suspicion. I was merely asking a question. There's no reason to get your panties in a bunch."

"My panties are most certainly not in a bunch," I fired back, annoyed. "I don't even like that saying."

"Well, that doesn't change the fact that you're getting worked up. I'm not sure I understand why either. You've been here three days. There's obviously a learning curve to changing locations. It's okay to not know everything right off the bat."

Was that the way I was coming off? I didn't like that idea one bit. "I'm fine not knowing everything."

"That's not how it appears." Bonnie's tone was light and easy, but there was a seriousness about her that couldn't be denied. "I think you're worked up because you're new and you're not used to being the center of attention. Perhaps in Detroit you could fade into the background and it wasn't a big deal. That's not possible here because you're kind of like a celebrity, what with the hero worship from Raisin and killing a spriggan with fire less than an hour after arriving.

"There's no reason to let your emotions get the best of you," she continued. "We're not going to judge you for being different. In fact, we're fairly excited about you being different. We think that means we can learn from you. If that means we have to teach you a few things along the way, so much the better."

I stared at her for a long moment. "Well, that's great. I ... ." Honestly, I had no idea what I was going to say. If I was going anywhere with the rest of the conversation, I wasn't sure where. I felt put on the spot, and I wasn't entirely sure why because Bonnie had been nothing but straightforward and polite.

In truth, the people of Hawthorne Hollow had been open and welcoming. They'd been nice and willing to engage me in whatever conversation they thought might interest me. I wasn't used to that. In Detroit, you had to be careful. It wasn't wise to trust everyone.

I was about to admit that when I heard a noise that caught my attention. When I realized what I was looking at, all thought of opening up for a serious conversation with Bonnie fled.

"All Souls Church," I muttered, shaking my head. "That's ... interesting."

"Why is that interesting?" Bonnie asked, her eyes busy as she watched church members casually move between the building and parking lot. "I've always found this place weird. Like ... really weird. I'm not exactly religious outside the craft, but if I was, this is the last church I would visit."

"And why is that?" I cast her a sidelong look. "What's weird about this church?"

"What's not weird about it?" She snorted derisively. "Seriously, I don't have anything against organized religion. It's not my thing, but I don't get worked up over people worshipping. In fact, I'm a big fan of people worshipping however they choose."

"But?" I prodded.

"But this place is weird." She said it with such confidence I couldn't help but laugh. "No, seriously. If you watch those television shows about cults — which I do because I find the whole thing fascinating — All Souls could be switched out for any number of them.

"They're insulated, have a charismatic leader — at least they think so — and they shun others," she continued. "The whole thing is creepy and weird."

I had no intention of arguing with her because I felt the same way. "I met Father Bram the other day. He's a bit ... odd."

"Oh, you think?" Bonnie's eyebrows hopped as Cecily exited the church and pulled up short, the woman's eyes automatically tracking to us. "She doesn't look happy to see us, does she?"

"No." I pursed my lips. "She's really weird, too."

"I'm telling you the entire congregation is weird," Bonnie said. "They're like Waco weird."

On a whim, I raised my hand and waved at Cecily. I wasn't surprised when she scowled and refused to wave back.

"She likes you," Bonnie enthused, chuckling. "You two are going to be best friends. She's going to hug you, and gossip with you and go to Starbucks with you because, girl, she's ready to bond with you."

I didn't move my eyes from Cecily. In turn, she refused to stop staring at me. It was an interesting standoff. "Don't call me 'girl,'" I said absently.

"Would you prefer I call you 'majesty' or something?"

"No. I just hate the term 'girl.' It's demeaning. I have a name. 'Girl' is something only annoying people say. In fact, back when I first started with Spells Angels I had a roommate who called everyone 'girl.' I came to realize she thought it made her sound cool when, in reality, it was just her way of not having to learn anyone's name. I don't respond when people call me 'girl.' It's a pet peeve."

"Fair enough." Bonnie grimaced when Cecily planted her feet and squared her shoulders. She hadn't as much as blinked. "What do you think it means that the footprints led here? Do you think the killer is here?"

"That's what it would seem to indicate," I replied. "I guess I can't be a hundred percent sure. Maybe the footsteps belonged to Hal. He was a member of the church, after all."

"Good point. Still, I think the church bears some looking into."

"Definitely," I agreed, an idea forming when I saw Father Bram ease out from beneath one of the eaves and move in Cecily's direction. The dude was oily. He made me uncomfortable. He was at the church, which meant it was safe to venture elsewhere. "I think I know where we should go next."

"Oh, yeah? Where's that?"

"I don't have an address, but I know where I want to go. I'm hoping you can help me with the rest of it."

BONNIE HAD no idea where Hal lived. Ultimately she had to call Marissa — who was apparently getting her hair done and didn't like being interrupted — to make sure we headed in the right direction.

"This should be it," Bonnie said, checking the coordinates she'd plugged into her phone GPS. "Yeah. This is definitely supposed to be it."

To make sure, I opened the mailbox at the end of the driveway and tugged out an envelope. "It's the right place," I said when I read the name. "Marissa might not be pleasant, but she's helpful when she wants to be."

"Not really," Bonnie countered. "Marissa is all about herself. She's powerful in some aspects. She's also lazy. You don't want to get paired up with her on assignments."

"In Detroit we rarely get paired with anyone," I admitted, starting up the driveway. "We're expected to solve problems ourselves."

"Probably because you have more problems to deal with," Bonnie said pragmatically. "We have specific problems up here, problems that grow huge before we sometimes realize it because everyone is spaced out. Down there, everyone is on top of everyone else and you have more population, which means more creatures that feed on the population."

"Good point." I dug in my pocket until I came back with my lock-picking tools and the wild look that came into Bonnie's eyes when she realized what I was about to do made me laugh out loud.

"You can't be serious," she hissed, glancing around to make sure nobody was watching. I'd already scanned the neighborhood and came up empty when looking for busybodies.

"No, no, no." Bonnie vehemently shook her head, her hair brushing her shoulders. "We could get arrested for this. It's against the law."

I couldn't decide if she was joking. "Only if we get caught. I have no intention of getting caught."

"You might not intend to get caught, but it could happen." She narrowed her eyes. "I'm serious. I ... oh, you're doing it." She threw her hands in the hair, frustration rolling off her. "You're really doing it. I can't believe it. You're breaking and entering. If we end up in jail I'm going to be really angry."

"Duly noted." I chewed my bottom lip until I heard the telltale click I was waiting for and the door fell open. I slipped the lock-pick set back in my pocket before gesturing toward the now-open door. "Shall we?"

She made a face. "This is so wrong."

"Then stay here," I suggested, my agitation getting the better of me. "You can serve as lookout while I break the law."

"I can't be lookout." Bonnie was beside herself. "The lookout is always arrested."

"Then come inside with me."

"I'll definitely be arrested then."

I shook my head. "I don't care what you do," I said finally, slipping through the opening. "Come, don't come, makes no difference to me. We have limited time, and I need to look around."

"What are you expecting to find?" Bonnie timidly poked her head through the door but didn't follow me, uncertainty etching pronounced frown lines across her pretty face. "I'm serious. What do you think you're going to find? Hal wasn't the type to leave a journal and admit that he was into freaky stuff."

"Maybe not a journal," I said, my eyes falling on a distinctive tome that rested on the end table at the far side of the room. "That doesn't mean there's no book that will answer questions." I strode toward the table and scooped up the hefty book, grunting when I realized I needed both hands given its weight. "Good grief."

"What is that?" Her earlier reticence forgotten, Bonnie followed me completely inside. "Is that what I think it is?"

"I don't know. Do you think it's a grimoire?" I flipped open the book and frowned at the handwritten pages. "Geez. I'm pretty sure this isn't English ... although, this page is English." I flipped through five pages before rolling my neck. "It's in several different languages. That can't be normal."

"Definitely not," Bonnie agreed, moving closer. "Can I see that?"

I relinquished the book and watched as she reverently flipped it over. "It's old. This is the sort of thing that's passed down from generation to generation."

"Okay. What is it doing here?"

She shrugged. "I have no idea. I don't even know what's in the book. It's going to take time to dig all the secrets out."

"Well, we can't take that time here." I glanced around to make sure nothing else was sitting out for anybody to see. "We should take it and get out of here. We can always come back if we need to. This place isn't difficult to break into."

Bonnie scowled. "Now you're just trying to annoy me."

I chuckled. "You're a pretty easy mark."

"Maybe." She was somber as she flipped through another few pages. "This grimoire could be a really big find. It's obviously someone's life work."

"That book is so old I'm guessing it's the life work of several someones."

"Good point. I need time to study it."

"I'm taking it to my place to study," I said. "If you want to study it, you can do it there. For now, I want to read it myself."

"I can screenshot what I need and go from there. That's enough for now."

"Great. Let's get it out of here. We don't want to get caught and go to jail."

Her scowl was back. "You're never going to let me live this down, are you?"

"No."

"I guess I deserve that."

"You definitely do," I agreed, the earlier dregs I'd been carrying easing. Finally, we were getting somewhere. "That book has to mean something."

SEVENTEEN

I took the grimoire back to the cabin. It was hard for me to think of it as home – at least so far – but I was starting to get used to my new surroundings.

The kitten met me at the door, but instead of rubbing against my legs as a form of greeting he screeched until I dumped fresh food in his bowl and then promptly forgot me. That allowed me to carry the grimoire to my bed – the only comfortable piece of furniture in the entire place – and start flipping through it.

I'd seen my fair share of magic books. Once, while chasing a group of drudes – nightmare demons who kept trying to feed off the students at the adjoining school – through a church, I was blown through a wall and found an ancient Christian text. It helped me eradicate the drudes, and then an entire cadre of Spells Angels historians descended and spent a full month delving into the book. It turns out that it contained all kinds of spells, most of them beyond our ability to cast. They were from a time long since forgotten.

I hoped this book would be different.

The first page was faded, an illustration that I couldn't quite make out consuming most of the page. There were letters on the bottom, script of some sort, and I was guessing someone had written a name there at some point. It was so long ago that it had worn away, which meant the book had seen frequent use over the years.

The drawing was another matter entirely. It looked like a horned demon stood in front of the fires of Hell, but I couldn't be sure because the right side of the page was much more faded than the left.

When I flipped to the next page, I found something I recognized, but only because I'd seen it a time or two. I didn't understand the words but I verified the language.

"Hebrew," I muttered to myself, rolling my neck. "So there's Latin and Hebrew in this book. That's interesting."

I flipped another page and found a second illustration. This one featured a series of thorns overlapping one another, what looked to be blood dripping from the points. It was a biblical image as far as I could tell. Maybe not a crown of thorns, but definitely a group of them.

I lost myself in the book, turning page after page as I tried to follow a storyline even though there was no prose to read. I was so lost in the book that I almost jumped out of my skin when someone knocked on my door. The sound was loud enough that it shook the thin walls of the cabin and made me slam the book shut in surprise.

It took me a moment to collect my breath and then I slowly climbed off the bed. The cabin was dark thanks to the curtains Gunner and I had installed, and I couldn't see the driveway. Still, no matter how distracted I was by the book, I should've heard a motorcycle pull up. That wasn't something I could simply miss.

The insistent knocking returned and I increased my pace. I figured it was probably Gunner checking up on me – perhaps he wanted to apologize for ducking out on our plans this morning – but I pulled up short when I yanked open the door and found Raisin standing on the front porch.

"What are you doing here?"

If she was offended by the question she didn't show it. Instead, she merely grinned. "I went to school today."

I blinked several times and collected my thoughts. "Do you want a reward or something?"

She snorted. "Of course not. I just don't want you to think you need to order me away. I went to school. It's fine that I'm here."

I turned to look at the clock on the wall to make sure she was telling the truth. It was almost four, so I figured I was safe. "Okay, you went to school. What are you doing here now?"

"I came to see you."

"Why?"

"Because."

"Because why?"

"Can't I just be curious?" Raisin challenged. "I mean ... you are the new witch in town."

Her grin was impish and the twinkle in her eyes was full of charm. I wanted to kick her out, turn her away, dismiss her determination to hang out with me.

I couldn't, though.

"Fine. You're curious." I pushed open the door to allow her entrance. "There's soda in the fridge and cookies on the counter."

"There's also a kitten." Raisin almost knocked me over as she barreled past me and slid to the floor to greet my cuddly roommate. "Oh, I've always wanted a kitten. Where did you get her?"

"Him," I corrected automatically.

"Where did you get him?"

"The lumberyard. You were there."

"I didn't know you found a kitten. Gunner sent me to the front office because I'm a minor and minors aren't allowed to wander around the lumberyard without a designated guardian."

"Oh." I racked my memory. "I guess you didn't see him. Well, you see him now. Gunner said I had to take him or the world would end, so he's here. You can take him if you want."

The second I made the offer I regretted it. I never fancied myself a cat person – a pet person, really – and yet I was already attached to the little monster. Thankfully, Raisin had started shaking her head the moment the words escaped, so I didn't have to rescind the offer.

"Oh, no," she said hurriedly. "I can't have a pet. My father wouldn't like it."

"Oh, is he allergic?"

"No, he just wouldn't like it." For a brief moment the look that crossed Raisin's face was full of emotional distress. I wanted to ask her about it – the panicked glance pierced my heart – but I was afraid that I would be overstepping a boundary that I couldn't uncross. It wasn't that I didn't care about the girl as much as I didn't want to invade her personal business.

"Well, he doesn't know what he's missing." I led her back toward the bedroom. "So far, this little guy has slept on my head and chest and he screams when he's hungry. It's just like having a baby."

Raisin giggled. "That's funny. I love him." She scooped up the kitten and followed me. "What's that?"

I didn't have to turn to know that her eyes were on the grimoire. "It's a book."

"It's a spell book," she corrected, leaving the kitten on the bed as she reached for the book. She looked eager … and somehow knowledgeable, which I found interesting.

"How do you know it's a spell book?" I asked.

"I've seen spell books before. I know what the Spells Angels are."

I wasn't sure that was true. "How do you know? Did Rooster tell you?"

"No." She shook her head, her eyes wide as she opened the book to a random page. "Wow! This is Sanskrit."

I was officially befuddled. "How can you possibly know that?"

"I know things." She puffed out her chest and sat on the bed. "Seriously, where did you get this? It's ancient … and like really impressive."

I wasn't keen on telling her I'd broken into a dead man's house and stole his fancy grimoire. That was not the sort of thing you wanted to own up to, especially to a young and impressionable girl.

"I can't tell you that," I said finally, making up my mind. "What I can tell you is that I'm trying to learn from it. I don't suppose you can read Sanskrit, can you?"

She shot me a "Well, duh" look. "I know what it is, but I can't read it. I can barely keep up with my regular schoolwork. How do you expect me to know Sanskrit?"

That was a good question. "I don't know. I guess I was simply hoping you could. That would certainly make my life easier."

"We can try running it through a program on the internet," she suggested.

"There are programs on the internet to decrypt ancient Sanskrit?"

"There are programs on the internet to decrypt anything," she replied, matter-of-fact. "It won't be exact. All those translation programs come across nutty sometimes, but it might give us a general idea."

I'd heard worse offers. "I have a computer."

She smiled. "Boot it up. Oh, and grab those cookies you mentioned ... and the soda. If you have something salty, bring that, too."

I sighed but kept my smile in place. She was a teenager. She couldn't change the fact that she was annoying. Eventually she would get over it. Er, well, hopefully.

I THINK IT'S TALKING ABOUT dealing with hellmouths," Raisin announced an hour later, her gaze intent as we flipped through the book. She sounded much surer than I felt.

"Really?" I rolled to my back and stared at the ceiling, my mind busy. "Where do you get that?"

"Here." She pointed at a page full of letters that looked almost familiar, but not quite. "This is in Old English."

"I prefer new English," I replied dryly.

She ignored my attitude. "There are a lot of thous and stuff in here, but it clearly says hellmouth." She tapped the page for emphasis. "Do you think that means that Hawthorne Hollow is a hellmouth?"

"No." I had to nip her inclination to assume things in the bud. Her imagination was already huge. If I let her engage in fanciful ideas, it would come back to haunt both of us. "I think we would know if Hawthorne Hollow was a hellmouth."

"How?"

"Well, for one thing, there would be hellhounds everywhere." I meant it as a joke, but Raisin bobbed her head as if what I was saying made perfect sense. "For another, Hawthorne Hollow doesn't have enough people to keep a hellmouth happy."

"A hellmouth isn't a thing with feelings," Raisin argued. "It's a place."

"Have you ever seen a hellmouth?"

She shrugged. "I don't know. Maybe we're sitting on a hellmouth and don't even know it. I can't rule anything out."

I was afraid she would say that. "Listen ... ."

"Have you seen a hellmouth?" She was eager when she locked gazes with me. "You've been all over, right? You must have seen one."

"I've only been to Detroit for the most part," I countered, choosing my words carefully. "I was shuttled around to various parts of the state when I was little, but I don't really remember it. I don't believe I've ever seen a hellmouth."

"But you don't know."

"No, I guess not." I took the book from her and shoved it to the side. Neither of us was getting anywhere with the text, which was dense. The fact that it kept jumping from one dead language to another was beyond frustrating. "The thing is, hellmouths have to be so fantastical that there's no way of missing them. I don't think you could be near one and not realize it."

Raisin pursed her lips and glanced toward the closed window. "Maybe I just want to be part of something," she said finally. "You know, be a part of something that's big and important."

I chuckled. She was serious, but I couldn't understand where the bout of melancholy came from. "You have plenty of time to do something big and important."

"Maybe."

"Of course you do," I insisted. "You're still young. Do you even know what you want to do with your life?"

She nodded without hesitation. "I want to change the world."

"How?"

"I don't know. I want to be important. I want to be like you ... and

Gunner ... and Bonnie. I don't really want to be like Marissa, because I find her annoying, but I definitely want to be like Rooster. You guys change the world all the time; you just don't realize it."

That was a nice way to look at things, if a bit naïve. It did bring up an interesting topic, though. "How do you know about us? About what we do, I mean."

"What do you mean?" Raisin's expression was blank. "I've known for a long time, years ... or maybe months. It feels like years."

"But *how* do you know?" I pressed. "We're not supposed to tell outsiders. I guess it's possible you saw someone slip up."

"I've only seen one person actually use magic," Raisin intoned. "It's the person who lived here before you."

"Rain? I don't know anything about her. In fact, nothing was said when I was recruited. I just know there was a sudden opening and they needed someone to fill it."

"She's not here anymore." Raisin averted her gaze and focused on the cat. "What are you going to name him?" It was an obvious distraction, one that I had no intention of letting her get away with.

"What happened to Rain?"

"I don't ... I don't know." Her eyes were cloudy when she raised them again. "They said she left, but I think something else happened to her. They won't tell me."

"Who won't tell you?"

"None of them. Gunner, Rooster, Whistler ... none of them."

It was possible the mysterious Rain had picked up and left. Something may have come up, forcing her to return to her family or leave for greener pastures. Or perhaps she quit for an entirely different reason. It was also possible she'd died, and I was starting to lean toward that possibility given the secrecy the woman was veiled in.

"I don't get why the cabin was in such disarray when I arrived," I said after a beat. "How long has she been gone?"

"Months."

"Yeah, but ... ."

"She never fixed anything up when she got here," Raisin volunteered. "She wasn't a do-it-yourselfer and she complained about being so far away from everything. Plus, well, she didn't like Tim."

I narrowed my eyes. "You know about Tim?"

"I've heard the others talk. I've never seen him or anything. I'm not magical."

And there, I assumed, was the heart of the problem. What Raisin had been struggling to say earlier was that she wanted to be a member of Spells Angels when she grew up and started making her own way. If she wasn't paranormal, that would severely limit her options. It wouldn't eradicate them, though.

"You can still be part of the group and not have powers," I offered. "It happens all the time."

"But you need powers to be on the frontline."

"Not always."

"Usually."

She wasn't wrong, so I decided to change the subject. "We should start thinking about dinner. Where is there to order from around here that delivers?"

"Dinner?" Her eyes wild, Raisin lifted the curtains and peered outside. "Holy ... why didn't you tell me it was so late?" She scrambled off the bed, the book and potential takeout forgotten. "The curtains made me think it was earlier than it was. Oh, my father is going to kill me!"

I didn't understand her urgency. She seemed panicked, and not in a normal teenager way. "It's okay." I watched her fly through the house, confused. "I'll tell your father you were helping me if you're really worried about getting in trouble. You don't have to freak out. I'm sure he'll understand."

"He won't understand." Raisin threw open the door and stomped out. "He won't ... he'll ... I can't. He's going to be so mad."

She sounded as if she was on the verge of tears, and my heart rate picked up a notch because I recognized that her fear was potent. "Raisin ... ."

"I have to go." She almost stumbled over her own feet as she went down the stairs. "I'll see you around ... probably."

"What do you mean?"

"I have to go." She was firm as she broke into a run toward the road. "I'm sorry about this. I just … my father is strict. I have to go home right now. I just have to."

"Let me go with you," I offered one more time. "I'm sure if I tell him that you were helping me that he'll be fine."

"You can't come with me."

"Why not?"

"Because if you do, he'll kill you, too."

She sounded so certain I came to a full stop and watched her run, her pace impossibly fast. She didn't look back even once, and the fear I felt emanating from her was strong enough to wrap a fist around my heart and squeeze.

EIGHTEEN

I wanted to ask someone about my suspicions regarding Raisin's father — being strict is one thing, but it sounded as if he bordered on something else — but I wasn't sure who to call. In truth, the only one I had a phone number for was Rooster, and I wasn't sure I should bother him over something that wasn't club related.

Because I was antsy, I decided I needed to get out of the cabin. I locked it up, making sure the kitten had plenty of fresh food and water, and headed for town. I wasn't familiar with Hawthorne Hollow. I could go to The Rusty Cauldron and risk running into Gunner, who was pretty much the last person I wanted to see, or I could head out to the dive bar on the highway. Gunner steadfastly warned me against visiting there, but I had a mind of my own ... and a different idea. It was a better idea than either bar – at least that's what I told myself.

I was a block away from All Souls Church before I realized where I was heading. I couldn't shake the idea that something weird was going on within the confines of the facility's walls, so that's where I headed. I parked on a side street and concealed my bike in some bushes not far from the road.

I wore dark jeans and a black leather jacket, which were fine for disappearing into the murk, but my hair was an issue. It stood out in stark contrast to the shadows. I had no way to hide it other than my helmet, so I abandoned my efforts and headed toward the side door I'd seen when watching the property earlier in the afternoon.

I surveyed the parking lot, which was empty, before trying the door handle. I wasn't surprised to find it locked. I wasn't above breaking and entering — not even a little — so I decided to take a look around without risking prying eyes. It was late. There were no services tonight. I had no idea where Father Bram resided, but I was fairly certain it wasn't on the premises. Sure, that could've been wishful thinking, but even if I ran into him I was positive I could take him.

It took longer to pick the lock than normal thanks to the limited light. It was an older mechanism, though, so it slid open with little fuss. It was still relatively early even though darkness had fallen. I took a moment to study the quiet neighborhood before slipping inside. The houses weren't quiet, families flitted across the light from windows, but no eyes appeared to be on the church.

That was exactly how I wanted things.

If I thought it was quiet outside, the lack of noise inside was almost doubly jarring. My boots squeaked on the linoleum floor, making me uncomfortable enough that I made sure to lift them to cut down the noise. I took a moment to get my bearings, and then tilted my head as I debated which way to point myself.

Father Bram had made sure to keep me out of the nave, forcing me to spend most of my visit in the vestibule, where I couldn't see anything. Now that I had my run of the place, I took advantage and walked slowly down the center aisle.

The pews were old school, polished wood that didn't particularly make for a comfortable resting spot. They reminded me of the time I was sent to live with an ultra-religious family that insisted on attending services four times a week. That placement lasted only a month because they didn't like my attitude. They were trying to save souls, but said I was a lost cause. I was fine with that.

I pulled one of the prayer books from the pocket at the back of a pew and opened it, reading the words as I flipped through the pages. I wasn't the religious sort, but they seemed like normal prayers to me. There was nothing in them that stood out, no appeals to demons that ripped off people's faces. They were simple prayers and hymns, at least as far as I could tell.

I returned the book to its place and moved further up the aisle, to where the crossing met the altar. There was a large crucifix on the wall behind the altar, which made me think of Catholicism, but I was fairly certain Father Bram said All Souls was non-denominational. When I moved closer to the sculpture, I noticed an odd feature. The eyes seemed to follow me, which wasn't possible because it was a huge resin sculpture on a wall. Still, it was disconcerting as I watched it, and it in turn watched me head toward the door at the back of the altar. I wasn't sure what lay beyond it. If I had to guess, it was some sort of preparation room for Father Bram. I turned out to be right, but the ornate room was more than I'd envisioned. So much more. It was overloaded with tchotchkes and paintings, all of the bloody and religious variety. Each and every one was disturbing to the point I felt uncomfortable even being in the same room with them. I was about to make my escape when I noticed yet another door at the back of the room. This one was different, smaller and unobtrusive, and the second I saw it I was drawn to it.

I'd already gone his far, I rationalized. There was no reason to turn back now.

The second I pulled open the door I started to doubt my original instincts. The only thing I saw was a staircase that led down, a curvature that was illuminated thanks to a glowing red light from below.

My heart skipped a beat as I tentatively put a foot on the first step, but then, as if by magic, chanting began. I couldn't decide if it was real or in my head, but it was definitely coming from beneath me. I didn't recognize the language — perhaps it was one of the dead ones Raisin had been talking about earlier — but there was an urgency to whatever the words.

I lost myself in the rhythm of the chant, a spell weaving over me as

I began swaying. My eyes drifted from the stairwell to an ornate mirror at my left. It looked old – centuries old, to be precise – and the glass seemed warmed. I almost thought I could see movement in it, which was ridiculous.

Even as I considered the possibility, the chanting continued. I wasn't the sort who would fall under just any spell, but the chants beckoned me to join those assembled in the red glow of destiny. I'm not sure how I knew that I was being invited, but something inside me wanted to acquiesce.

Part of my brain recognized that was an idiotic idea. If congregation members were down there, explaining my sudden appearance would be impossible. They could very well be dangerous. I was cocky enough to believe I could escape, but the other part of me, the one I wasn't completely in control of, thought it was a fine idea to descend into the creepy basement with the evil chanting.

That's when I knew something was terribly wrong. Thankfully, a noise in the nave caught my attention and caused me to force shut the door and focus on what was happening outside the ornate dressing room. I strode to the other door, the one that I'd entered through, and cracked it so I could listen. I recognized Cecily's voice right away.

"You're supposed to be downstairs, not loitering around upstairs."

I listened, certain I would hear Father Bram's voice admonishing Cecily to mind her own business. Instead I heard another woman respond. "I thought I saw someone walking through here a few minutes ago," she protested. I couldn't make out a face, not that I would recognize it even if I could. "I was trying to make sure that no one broke in."

"And who would break in?" Cecily asked, imperious. "Why don't you mind your own business and leave potential thieves to me?" Her tone told me she meant business.

I searched the room again, this time looking for an escape. To my utter relief, there was a window close to the stairwell wall. I pushed the panel open and waved my hand around to make sure a screen wouldn't trip me up when it was time to go through. I wanted to stay and eavesdrop some more, but I'd assumed the building was empty. Now was definitely the time to make my escape.

I went through the window, swearing viciously under my breath when I ended up in a scratchy bush on the other side. I fought my way free, glowering when I landed on my behind and rubbed my scratched arms.

I heard a noise through the open window and instinctively pressed myself closer to the bush to hide. I felt a presence staring out above me, but given my position it was impossible to look without drawing attention. Instead, I held my breath and hoped whoever was poking his or her head out of the window wouldn't look down.

I got my wish, and after a few moments whoever was inside pulled the window shut. After that, I waited even longer before making my escape. I turned to look over my shoulder three times and found the space between the church and me empty, but I still felt eyes on me as I scurried to my motorcycle.

IF I WAS ANTSY BEFORE, my close encounter in the church only exacerbated things. I thought about heading to The Rusty Cauldron to share my adventure with anyone who would listen, but the idea of seeing Gunner irritated me. Even worse, the realization that I was irritated at the thought of seeing him made me want to punch myself in the face.

Instead of heading to the bar, I got out my phone and plugged in the information I had on Raisin. I knew her real name was Ruth Morton, and I figured there couldn't be too many people sharing the same last name in one small town. I lucked out and found two of them: Irene Morton and Steven Morton. Raisin said she lived with her father, so I plugged Steven's address into my GPS. It was only a few minutes from my cabin.

I don't know what I was expecting. Perhaps a nice ranch house with flowers in the front or a colonial with music blaring to signify a teenager was present. Instead, I found a ramshackle cape cod that sagged on one side and was in desperate need of a new roof.

The lights were on inside, but instead of music all I heard was a man raging. I wanted to believe the vile words were being spewed from a television show, but I knew better. I couldn't see him through the windows, but it was clear that whoever lived here was having some sort of a meltdown.

"I set very few rules," he bellowed. "I let you do whatever you want, run all around town with those jerks on the motorcycles, and still you can't be bothered to behave yourself!"

I'd yet to hear Raisin, but I was positive I was in the right spot.

"I said I was sorry," a weak voice sniffled, causing my spine to stiffen. "I just ... I'll do whatever you want. Just tell me what you want."

Raisin. I recognized her voice, even though it was clouded with tears.

"I want you to behave yourself! How many times do I have to tell you that?"

I couldn't be sure, but I was almost positive I heard a piece of furniture being slammed from one side of a room to the other. A kitchen chair maybe, or perhaps a small table of some sort.

"I said I was sorry."

She sounded so pitiful, so terrified, I couldn't hold back. It had been a long day and I'd been searching for a fight from the start. I was still worked up from the adrenalin rush from earlier, so I didn't bother knocking when I reached the front door. Instead, I used my magic and sprung the lock so it flew open.

The house was neat inside, which was mildly amusing considering the exterior, which needed so much work I was convinced they should just start over from scratch. Raisin kept up the inside. That was obviously part of her job. Her father, well, he had other things on his mind ... and he wasn't afraid to express them.

"Who are you?"

Steven Morton wasn't a large man. In fact, he was relatively small. His hands were clenched into fists at his sides, his dark eyes gleamed and his face flushed with rage. He looked nothing like Raisin, for which I was oddly thankful.

"What are you doing here?" Raisin gasped. She was on the floor, tears streaking her cheeks, and she looked terrified as she glanced between her father and me. "You need to go. I told you there was no need to stop by and explain. I ... he ... it's fine."

It was pretty far from fine. "I was out," I explained, never moving my eyes from her father. "I decided to make sure you were okay. I was confused after you took off the way you did."

"It's nothing." She sounded exasperated. "I'm fine. I just ... there are rules that have to be followed."

"Definitely." Steven nodded. "Rules that my daughter always seems to forget. Now, if you'll excuse me, I don't believe I invited you into my home. This is a private matter." He gestured toward the door. "You can show yourself out."

That wasn't going to happen. "No." I shook my head, firm. "I'm not leaving her here with you."

"Excuse me?" His eyebrows flew up his forehead. "Exactly who do you think you are?"

"Scout Randall," I answered without hesitation. "You can act as shocked as you want, put on whatever show you want, but I'm not leaving her here." I looked around to make sure no one else was present. "Are you an only child, Ruthie?" I used her given name because it seemed appropriate, but I was itching to call her to me so I could secure her escape from ... whatever hell she'd been living in.

"Why are you asking that?" Raisin asked, confused.

"I want to make sure no one else is in the house."

"Oh." Realization washed over her face. "Um ... it's just us. You don't have to worry, though. I'm fine. This happens all the time."

The mere thought of that made me sick to my stomach. "Well, it's not happening again." I pinned Steven with a pointed look. "Your daughter is going into her room and packing some things. When she comes out, I'll be taking her to a safe location. What happens after that ... well ... will have to be worked out."

Steven's mouth dropped open in surprise. "What did you just say to me?"

I ignored him and snapped my fingers in Raisin's direction. "Get your things. We're getting out of here."

"But ... where am I supposed to go?" Raisin's eyes brimmed with tears. "I promised my mother I would take care of him."

My heart went out to her, but I recognized a dangerous situation. "Well, I think your mother would understand why you can't keep that particular promise." I refused to back down. "Now, pack your things. Just take the necessities. We'll be back for the rest later."

"But ... ." Fear lit Raisin's eyes as her father viciously swore under his breath and swiveled in her direction. The way she shrank away from him told me all I needed to know.

"You're not going anywhere," he roared at his offspring. "And, you, you're not involved in this. I'm calling the cops and having you locked up. How do you like that?"

I didn't flinch when he turned in my direction. "I think that's a fabulous idea," I replied without hesitation. "I say we call Chief Stratton and get him out here. I'm guessing he would like to hear what's been going on under this roof."

"Get out of my house!" he howled, fury getting the better of him as he took a menacing step in my direction. "I have the legal right to kill you for trespassing on my property."

"You can certainly try."

"Get out!"

He was clearly used to people doing his bidding. I wasn't the sort of person who kowtowed to anyone, especially vicious trolls who mistreated their flesh and blood. "No."

"I can make you," he threatened.

"That, I would like to see."

He was moving almost before I registered it, his hands outstretched. I was expecting him to make some sort of move so I was prepared, and this time the magic I unleashed wasn't from the fire family. No matter how traumatized she was, I knew Raisin wouldn't appreciate me killing her father. That meant I needed to dole out another form of punishment.

"You asked for this," I said, flicking my fingers. "You should've thought long and hard before you put your hands on your daughter. You have this coming."

NINETEEN

*R*ooster wasn't exactly happy when he arrived at Raisin's house to find the girl borderline hysterical and her father in a stupor on the floor.

"What did you do?" he demanded.

I shrugged, refusing to engage in a screaming match. "I saved the day. You should be happy."

"Oh, I'm pretty far from happy." He swore viciously under his breath before pulling out his phone and searching for a contact on his list. When he found it, he hit the button and pressed the phone to his ear as he glared at me. "I knew you were going to be trouble, but I had no idea you were going to be this much trouble."

"First off ... ." I didn't get to finish what I wanted to say because Rooster raised a finger to silence me. I wasn't sure who he was calling until he mentioned keeping the lights and sirens to a minimum. "Graham Stratton?" I asked when he disconnected.

"You didn't think I could just let this go without police involvement, did you?" he challenged.

"Well ... ." I wasn't sure how to respond.

"What's going to happen to me?" Raisin whimpered from the floor. She held her head in her hands and rocked back and forth. "I don't

171

want to go to a state home. I ... he told me what will happen if I go to a state home. I don't want that."

My stomach twisted. I was certain whatever her father told her was an outright lie or a gross exaggeration. That didn't mean a state home would be an exercise in puppies and roses. "I ... ."

"You shut your mouth," Rooster ordered, wagging his finger as he crossed in front of me and went to Raisin. He was gentle when he dropped to one knee and slipped an arm around her shoulders. "It's going to be okay, sweetheart. I don't want you to freak out about this."

"They're going to take me away," the girl sobbed.

"I don't think so, but we'll figure it out." His gaze was cold and accusatory when it fell on me. "What were you thinking?"

Oh, now he wanted to talk to me? What if I didn't want to talk to him? "I was thinking that he was mistreating her and I wasn't going to put up with it," I replied simply.

"How do you know he was mistreating her?"

"I could hear him from the driveway."

"Was he ... hitting her?" Rooster tightened his arm around Raisin when she dissolved into another bout of tears.

"I don't know," I replied honestly. "I heard him yelling ... and I was already worked up. I just saw red. I came in and she was cowering while he raged like a maniac. If you think I'm just going to sit back and watch him do stuff like that, you're crazy."

He didn't immediately say anything, instead rubbing his hand over Raisin's back as her wracking sobs quieted.

"I knew something was wrong this afternoon," I admitted, glaring at Steven as he tried to shift into a sitting position on the floor. He was completely out of it, which was a good thing. "She was terrified when she realized what time it was, yelled about being late and took off. I sensed trouble, but I tried to put it out of my mind. I offered to go with her and she totally freaked out about that, told me he would kill me if I tried. I should've followed my instincts."

Rooster's gaze softened, though only marginally. "I understand the instinct to protect, but did you think we weren't monitoring the situation? Did you think we weren't poised to rush in and save her if it became necessary?"

"You weren't here when it became necessary. I'm not apologizing."

"Fine." He slowly stood. "You'll have to explain yourself to Graham. If he doesn't like what you have to say he'll probably take you in. I hope you're prepared for that."

"Whatever it takes."

"Yeah, well ... ." Rooster moved closer to Steven, who whimpered and turned his face toward the wall. "What did you do to him?"

"Nothing he didn't have coming." I was grim as I glared at the man. "Let's just say I gave him a dose of his own medicine ... magnified to a degree of ten."

"That sounds interesting."

"It didn't suck."

GRAHAM WASN'T nearly as angry as Rooster anticipated. He yelled at me, said they had a plan, and then laughed at the way Steven cringed and cried before locking him in handcuffs and dragging him to his patrol vehicle.

Raisin wasn't in nearly the terrible position I feared. The other Morton in town, Irene, was her grandmother. The woman was expecting her and had no problem taking in the girl. She recognized her son wasn't the best person to raise a child. In fact, she'd been trying to get him to sign over custody for years.

She was standing on her porch when we dropped off Raisin, who had stopped crying when she realized she wasn't going into the system. The girl practically skipped to her grandmother and threw her arms around her in delight when Graham walked her to the porch. Irene was all smiles when she returned her granddaughter's hug.

"We were working toward this solution from the start," Rooster explained, his arms folded across his chest as he regarded the grand-mother-grandchild reunion with a warm smile. "We've been trying to figure out a way to get Raisin out of that house for a long time."

"Why not just take her?"

"We're not in the habit of kidnapping children."

"I didn't kidnap her."

"No, you did something to her father ... and I'm still dying to hear what."

"It was nothing special. I just took all the terror he elicited from her over the years and aimed it at him. Then I magnified it."

Rooster shook his head. "I don't know how you even thought to do that."

"I like making the time fit the crime."

"Yeah, well ... ." He raised his chin when Graham descended the porch stairs and joined us. "Everything is okay?"

"It is," Graham confirmed. "Irene has to sign some papers and we need to get a judge to officially sign off on a permanent custody change, but I'm fairly certain we have everything in order." His eyes slowly tracked to me. "Even though your worker here jumped the gun and put us in a perilous position."

"She did," Rooster agreed. "But she heard Steven yelling from the driveway. You can't expect her to sit back and do nothing when she's worried about Raisin. It's not fair. You and I have had a few go-arounds with Steven, too."

"I guess." Graham rubbed his chin. "I'm not going to congratulate you on a job well done. You saved her, though. You made sure something terrible didn't happen. I don't see where we can ask for more than that."

"I'd do it again." I was feeling fearless. "What's going to happen to him?" I asked, jerking my thumb toward the backseat of Graham's car, where Steven sat and stared at nothing. "You're not going to let him out and give him Raisin again, are you?"

"No. We've been building a case against him for a long time. We should be able to charge him tomorrow. The judge will probably issue a bond, but it will be too high for him to meet."

"Well, then I think my work here is done." I dusted my hands off and grinned. "I don't know about anyone else, but I need a drink. I'm heading off to the Cauldron and getting one."

"Try to stay out of trouble while you're out and about," Graham suggested. "If I get called to another scene because of something you've done tonight, I won't be happy."

"Do I look like I'm in the mood for trouble?" I flashed the sweetest smile in my repertoire.

"You look like you're going to be trouble regardless. Try to remember who's in charge here, okay? If you're wondering who, the answer is me."

I grinned. He was sort of funny ... in a straight-laced way. "I have no intention of getting in trouble. I think I've had my fill for the night."

"See it stays that way."

I WAS FEELING PRETTY GOOD about myself when I strolled into The Rusty Cauldron thirty minutes later. The bar was packed — a lot of faces I didn't recognize bouncing around and having a good time — and I headed to the bar to order a drink.

Whistler was behind the counter by himself, but it didn't take him long to get to me. "What'll you have?"

"I don't know. What's on tap?"

"Corona and some microbrew the locals insist on. I think it tastes like rancid urine, but I'm not paid for my taste."

I snickered. "I'll take a pint of Corona."

"You've got it." He winked as he went to the tap and filled a frosty mug.

While I waited, money in hand, I scanned the faces at the bar. One of the first I saw was Gunner, who sat on a stool in the middle of the huge rectangular monstrosity that took up almost a third of the room. He looked freshly showered, his hair clean and face devoid of dirt that would indicate some manner of battle. He wasn't alone. A beautiful woman sat with him, striking auburn hair and green eyes on full display as she kept up a steady stream of conversation that he seemed to be only half listening to when he caught my gaze.

My heart lodged in my throat, and I felt like a complete and total idiot. His business today had obviously been of the female variety. I'd clearly read more into our interaction than was really there. He was involved ... and I was an idiot.

"Thanks," I mumbled when Whistler delivered the beer. I quickly fumbled with the money, my fingers shaking enough I thought I might drop the ten. I held it together and shoved the bill in his direction. "Keep the change."

I took the mug and turned away from the bar, desperate to put some room between Gunner and me. I never should've come here, I realized. This was his turf ... and I was clearly losing my mind. I couldn't remember the last time I'd had a reaction like this to a man I'd just met. In fact, I was fairly certain it had never happened. There was a reason for that: I didn't fall for men willy-nilly. That was a complication I simply didn't need.

"Scout." I heard someone call after me, but I refused to turn around, instead zeroing in on Bonnie, who sat near one of the pool tables and swilled what looked to be bourbon and soda in a glass. She smiled when she saw me, waved, and I was so relieved to have someone to sit with I almost threw my arms around her for an inappropriate hug.

"Hey." I smiled as I sat. "How are things?"

"Things are good for me," she replied, furrowing her brow as she looked me up and down. "What's up with you? You look ... flustered."

There was no way I could tell her what was really bothering me, so I merely shrugged. "I've had a busy night. I broke into All Souls Church ... and I got in a fight with Raisin's father that resulted in her being removed from the home."

The first part of the statement was heard only by Bonnie because of the blaring music. The second part, unfortunately, floated over the entire bar because I uttered the words at the exact second the music died.

"You did what?" Bonnie was dumbfounded. "I can't ... you ... are you kidding me?"

I forced a tight-lipped grin as I sipped my beer. It was good, and I needed it to keep myself from looking over my shoulder and staring at Gunner and his date. Honestly, I couldn't believe I so badly misjudged the signs. I felt like a total moron.

"I think I'm going to need you to tell me the story from the beginning," Bonnie prodded, downing half her drink as she stared at my face. "Don't leave anything out."

I told her everything, not because she ordered me to, but because I needed someone to bounce ideas off. Gunner was clearly out of the picture, so Bonnie was my sounding board. "I couldn't not go in there," I said finally, scowling when I remembered the way Steven went off on his daughter. "She needed help ... so I helped."

"No one blames you for going in there." Bonnie adjusted her tone so she sounded conciliatory. "We've been trying to get her out for some time. We've never been able to actually catch him in the act and we were afraid that if we jumped the gun he would retaliate and isolate her. That's not what we wanted."

I thought back over Raisin's interaction with the club since I'd been introduced to her. "That's why you guys were so keen to make sure she was going to school, not riding on motorcycles and all that other stuff," I mused. "You didn't want to give her father a reason to cut off contact."

"She latched onto us because she was a sad girl in dire straits," Bonnie countered. "We're all attached to her in our own ways. But we were terrified we would screw things up. Do you think Gunner, Rooster and Whistler didn't want to go in there and bash his head in? We had to talk them out of it. If Steven met a violent end there was every chance Raisin would've been shipped away from Hawthorne Hollow.

"You said she's with her grandmother now." she continued. "That's good. Irene is strict, but she's not abusive. She'll give Raisin the attention she needs. I just hope the custody sticks."

"Oh, it will stick." I turned dark as I thought of the things I'd seen in Steven's mind before I slammed home the nightmare I created for him. "He's not getting her back. If I have to convince him that she belongs with her grandmother, I'll do it."

Bonnie pursed her lips. "I ... you ... what do you mean?" she asked finally. "Are you saying you can control his mind and make him sign over custody of Raisin?"

The question threw me for a loop. "Well, basically, yeah. I told you I was a hereditary witch. I've been able to convince people to do things since I was nine or ten. It's been very beneficial, especially when I was locked up in a variety of bad foster homes."

"Oh, geez!" Bonnie slapped her hand to her forehead. "I can't believe you can do that. I'm dying to know what your mother could do. If you're this strong and you weren't raised in a coven ... I just ... we should really test your magic one day. I bet you don't even know all the things you can do."

"I have a pretty good idea," I countered. "I'm not sorry for helping Raisin. If it comes to it, I can offer more help. There's no limit to what we can do for her. I'm not afraid to do what needs to be done."

"Clearly not." Bonnie heaved out a sigh and leaned back in her chair. "You're well and truly a badass. I think I'm going to like hanging out with you."

"That's good. You're stuck with me for the foreseeable future." I drained the rest of my beer. "I'm running to the bathroom and grabbing another drink. Do you want one?"

"Absolutely." Bonnie nodded. "I'll order them. Once you get back, I insist on hearing about you breaking into that crazy church. What were you thinking?"

That was a very good question. "I don't know, but the entire thing was weird. Like ... really weird."

"Well, I can't wait to hear about it."

"You say that now, but I'm not sure you'll feel the same way in twenty minutes. Either way, I'm running to the bathroom. Get me another Corona draft."

TWENTY

Gunner was standing by the jukebox when I exited the restroom. He made a big show of looking at the song selections, his elbows resting on the glass as he leaned over and stared, making for a tall and fit package that was ridiculously attractive.

I'm not kidding. He was causing quite the stir with a group of women who had taken over one of the larger tables in the corner. They kept pointing and giggling, whispering behind their hands as they stared. For his part, he remained focused on the music.

Of course, I knew why he was really there. He wanted to talk to me. If he thought I was going to be the first to speak, he had another think coming. Instead of going the obvious route and skirting around him, which would've forced me to brush against him, I opted for the scenic route and headed down a dark hallway. It was a longer walk to get back to the main part of the bar, but it was worth it.

I thought that right up until I realized there was no opening in the hallway that led to the bar. Instead, it led to what was obviously Whistler's office and a storage room. There was no escape.

"Are you trying to hide from someone down here?"

I jumped at the sound of Gunner's voice, turning quickly to find him standing behind me in the hallway. He looked amused.

"I thought this led back to the bar," I replied, forcing myself to remain calm. "I didn't realize there was no exit."

"There is one by the bathroom."

That proved he'd been waiting for me by the jukebox. "Yes, well, I thought it would be easier if I came this way."

He crossed his arms and tilted his head, considering. "Why?"

"What do you mean? I thought it would be easier. I was wrong. Are you going to sue me for being wrong or something?"

"Not last time I checked," he replied simply. "Why are you acting weird?"

That had to be a loaded question. "I'm not acting weird. I'm acting like a normal person. You're the one acting weird."

"No, you're definitely acting weird." He shifted from one foot to the other. "What did you do today?"

Oh, well, that was just the limit. "What does it matter?" It took everything I had not to explode. As it was, my voice was a bit shriller than necessary. "You wanted off the team and you're off. I have everything under control."

"Off the team?" He furrowed his brow. "That's not what I said. I ... something came up."

"Oh, really?" I rolled my eyes. "You were here drinking. I doubt that was as important as you're making it out to be." I caught myself before I could descend into melodrama. "It doesn't matter. We were forced together from the start and you didn't like the pairing. I won't make you keep coming around when you obviously don't want to. It's fine. You can wash your hands of me."

His next statement was enough to drive me bonkers. "Are you drunk or something?"

I wanted to pull my hair and scream. I managed to refrain, but it was a struggle. "I'm not drunk. I'm being honest. You don't need to hang around with me. You obviously have other things — other people — on your mind. I'm no longer your concern."

"Other people?" He looked confused, something that frustrated me to no end. "I ... you ... are you talking about the woman at the bar?"

She was the last person I wanted to talk about. I actually felt sorry for her because her boyfriend couldn't keep his hormones in check and repeatedly sent the wrong signals. Hey, it was easier blaming him than me.

"I have to go." I pushed past him with enough force that he had no choice but to step aside unless he wanted to get physical. "Bonnie is waiting for me. I have to get out of here."

"Wait." He moved to grab my arm but thought better of it and pulled back. "I want to talk to you."

"There's nothing to talk about." I forced a smile for his benefit before continuing down the hallway. "Have fun on your date. You don't have to worry about me. I've been doing this a very long time. I have everything completely under control."

I STOPPED AT TWO BEERS EVEN though my mood would've allowed for ten. I hated hangovers as much as the next person, so I said goodbye to Bonnie after explaining my breaking-and-entering excursion at the church and headed home.

As much as I didn't want to admit it, I remained annoyed that Gunner blew me off to hang with his girlfriend. Part of it was that he refused to admit he had a girlfriend. The other part was that I noted serious sparks between us the night before ... and it was very obvious that had all been in my head. I hated looking like a fool, but there was no other way to see myself now.

I removed my bike helmet as I strode toward the cabin, uneven earth to my left catching my attention as I made the trek. On a whim, I detoured to look more closely at the ground. I was confused when I got closer, pulling out my key ring so I could use the flashlight attachment on it to get a better look.

"That's ... weird," I muttered, frowning when I realized what I was looking at. I dipped a finger in the upturned dirt and touched it to my tongue, ignoring how gross other people would find the action and instead focusing on the task at hand. I wasn't surprised at the tart taste and spit out the grit as I scanned the nearby tree line for hints of movement.

"It's salt," a voice announced, causing me to jerk my head in the opposite direction. Instead of finding a creature about to attack I found a ghost about to ... well, peep, I guess.

"Peeping Tim," I noted, turning back to the mess in the yard. "Did you see who did this?"

He shook his head. "I wish you wouldn't call me that, by the way. I'm not a peeper."

"Really? What do you call staring at women as they undress without them knowing it?"

"A victimless crime."

If he were corporeal, this is where I would punch him. "I think we're going to have to agree to disagree there. That's not my biggest concern, though. The ground wasn't like this when I left. That means someone came here and disturbed it. What I want to know is, why."

"I can't answer that. I only just got here myself." Tim moved closer to study the ground. "Did you know the ground was salted?"

"Yes. I assumed Rooster did it to keep away unwanted pests. It doesn't work for everyone — especially with unwanted peeping ghosts coming and going as they please — but it holds back some basic enemies."

"Rooster didn't do this." Tim was matter-of-fact. "He would prefer taking on an enemy rather than hiding behind a line. Rain did this."

And back to the mysterious Rain. "What happened to her?" I'd meant to ask Rooster when I saw him earlier — the question was becoming more and more necessary to ask — but it didn't seem appropriate given the other things we were dealing with.

"She left."

It was a simple response, but I could read between the lines. "No, it's not that easy." I shook my head. "Something happened to her, didn't it?"

"I didn't do anything." He sounded offended that I would dare insinuate anything of the sort. The problem was, I didn't insinuate anything even remotely close to that.

"I'm guessing she could put up with you, which makes you miss her," I said. "I'm more interested in the things she couldn't put up with. What happened to her?"

"I don't know. Honestly, I don't." He turned earnest. "She was here one day and gone the next."

"Did she leave of her own volition?"

"I don't know."

I hated that I didn't have the answers I wanted. Tim seemed the type to fold under questioning and he appeared more confused than reticent. He was probably a dead end, at least on this particular track. "Well, I guess I should go inside." I turned my attention back to the cabin. "Would you know if anyone was in there?"

"I could check if there weren't curtains over every window," Tim scowled. "Curtains are the worst."

"Yeah, yeah, yeah." I made sympathetic noises. "What if I give you permission, just this once, to go inside? Could you see if anyone is in there if I allowed it?"

He shook his head, taking me by surprise. "The salt is too strong the closer you get. I can't get very close."

"Oh." I straightened. "If you can't I guess other creatures have the same problem."

"Maybe." He didn't look as if he cared. "But from now on I think it would behoove all of us if you simply left your curtains open — especially in your bedroom — so I can check these things from afar when you're not here."

"And I think you're dreaming." Resigned, I moved toward the door. "If someone attacks and manages to kill me, make sure you wake Rooster so he can take care of the kitten. I don't want him to go hungry."

"You really should name that thing," he chided. "A kitten without a name is like a pickle without a toothpick."

I wasn't sure what that was supposed to mean and I didn't care enough to ask the obvious question. "I'm sure it will be fine. Just in case, though, I'm putting you on kitten duty."

He offered up a salute. "I won't let you down, Ma'am."

"Awesome. But ... don't call me ma'am. I'm not old enough to be a ma'am."

"Of course, madame."

I wasn't sure that was better, but I let it go. I was too tired to argue. I needed to put this day behind me.

THERE WAS NO ONE inside. As far as I could tell, no one had even tried the door. Still, I made sure to lock it before stumbling to the bedroom. There, I found the kitten stretched out on the bed. He didn't look to be ceding the center spot, so I crowded in at the edge, even though it wasn't exactly comfortable, and curled around him.

That's how I fell asleep. I didn't wake until someone started pounding on the front door.

"Geez." I turned on my back and found the kitten staring at me with a look that could only be described as disdain. "Don't look at me, buddy," I groused, rolling out of the bed. "I know exactly three people in this town. It's not my fault they keep showing up."

I'd slept in the same shirt I'd worn to the bar and a pair of flannel boxer shorts. I didn't think about the fact that I wasn't wearing a bra or socks until I'd already thrown open the door ... and found Gunner waiting on the other side. He had a box of doughnuts in one hand and a tray holding two coffee cups in the other.

"How did you even manage to drive out here on a motorcycle with that thing?" I asked, genuinely baffled. "That's impossible."

"Anything is possible if you put your mind to it." He grinned as he took in my outfit. "I take it you're sleeping in."

"I didn't mean to." I turned and padded into the kitchen, leaving him to follow. I'd mostly forgotten I was trying to cut him out of my life, which is why I allowed him into the cabin. Truth be told, the caffeine and doughnuts didn't hurt. I would remind myself that he was no good once I was sugared up and ready to face the day. "I guess I slept later than I thought."

"Maybe you needed the sleep," he suggested, resting the coffee tray and doughnut box on the counter and grinning when the kitten came racing into the room. "Hello, little guy." He reached over and scooped up the wriggling mass of purrs. "I take it you're hungry. Is your mother not feeding you enough?"

"Don't call me his mother," I shot back, automatically reaching for the Iams bag on the counter. "As for feeding him, he can eat whatever he wants. He slept the entire night away, too. It wasn't just me."

"You look rather well rested," he noted as he lowered the cat to the ground and watched as I filled his bowl. "I was a little worried after the way you left last night."

The way he phrased it grated. "Why? I wasn't drunk and I'm fully capable of taking care of myself."

"I didn't say you weren't." He held up his hands. "There's no reason to go crazy."

"I'm not going crazy. Why do men always say that? Just because a woman is agitated doesn't mean she's going crazy."

"Uh-huh." He ran his tongue over his teeth and regarded me. "That's something my sister would say. That's who I was with at the bar last night, by the way. My sister ... Ashley."

I pressed my lips together, mortified. "I ... ."

"She wanted to meet you," he continued, a hint of his charming smirk back in place. "I told her I would make it happen, but apparently I didn't keep my word. She's angry with me, too, in case you're wondering."

I collected myself as fast as humanly possible. "I didn't know you had a sister. I was under the impression you were an only child. That's how you made it sound ... I mean, with the stories you told about your mother."

"I guess I should explain," he said. "Ashley is my half-sister. My father had an affair with a woman while married to my mother — something that didn't help her mental instability — and she completely went over the edge when she realized his mistress was pregnant."

I worked my jaw but kept quiet.

He smiled as he watched my reaction. "It's okay," he assured me. "I've come to terms with my father's part in my mother's breakdown, and I'm over it. She would've always ended up where she is. Whether it was sooner is the ultimate question."

I found my voice. "I'm sorry. That's awful."

"It's not Ashley's fault," he noted, opening the doughnut box. "She's all right. We get along ... okay. I'm older than her. Her mother doesn't want her spending time with me because Ashley doesn't shift. She found out my father was a shifter and, thankfully for them, Ashley's genes appear to be dormant."

It was a lot to take in. "I'm sorry," I repeated because I didn't know what else to say. "It's nice you spend time with her even if you don't like her."

"She insists on spending time with me," he corrected. "We're casual half-siblings. She comes around once a month and catches up on life. She doesn't generally announce herself when she does and simply inserts herself into what's going on.

"She has a natural curiosity when it comes to Spells Angels," he continued. "She wants to be part of it but can't because of her mother. When she showed up out of the blue yesterday, I felt it was necessary to take the day off so she didn't get too involved with what we have going on. The last thing I want is for her face to go missing."

I felt like a dolt ... and then some. Still, he could've admitted that's why he was taking the day off from the start instead of playing it cryptic. Ah, well. It was in the past. "What kind of doughnuts did you get?" I peered into the box and immediately reached for a cake doughnut with chocolate icing and sprinkles. "How did you know this is my favorite?"

He reached for an identical doughnut. "I didn't. It's my favorite, and that's all that matters. Between these and the powdered dough-nuts, I always know how to get my sugar fix."

I laughed, some of the weight from the previous day floating away.

I felt better, which would only serve to infuriate me later when I had time to think about it. For now, I pushed it out of my head.

"So, I should probably catch you up on everything I did yesterday," I noted, remembering how far behind he was. "You're probably not going to be happy."

"If you're talking about Raisin, I already know. I wish you would've waited for me, but I'm not sorry she's out of that house. Things will be better for her now."

"Yeah. I figured you would hear about that from your father. That's not what I was referring to, though. There are other … things."

"Oh, yeah?" He lifted an eyebrow and stared at me. "What things are we talking about?"

"You're not going to like it."

"You already said that."

"Okay, well … I cast a spell to follow footprints from the site where we found Hal's body. They led to All Souls Church. Then, because everyone was at the church, I took Bonnie with me to Hal's house and we broke in. Everything seemed normal except for this really old grimoire he had, so we stole it."

Gunner's mouth dropped open. "What? You cannot be serious."

"I'm not done." I figured it was best to get it all out there. "I came home and looked at the grimoire. It's, like, eight different languages, most of them dead, and a lot of freaky images. Later, when I was feeling antsy, I broke into the church because I thought it was empty. It turns out it wasn't.

"There were people inside, including Cecily, and when I went into that little room behind the altar I found a stairwell that leads to the basement … and I heard chanting down there, and not fun 'Let's dance in a circle' chanting, either," I continued. "Cecily came into the room right after I escaped. I don't think she saw me, but I can't be certain. Also, when I got back last night, someone had been digging in the yard. I have no idea why, but I'm guessing it's to dislodge the salt that Rain placed around the cabin."

Gunner's eyes flashed with something I couldn't identify. "Is that it?"

"Pretty much."

"Well, great." He braced his hands on the counter. "Now I have all the facts and we can talk about what an idiot you are and how I'm going to kill you."

Instead of rising to the bait, I grinned. "It's nice to be back to normal, huh?"

He didn't answer, his eyes flashing murder instead of merriment.

"If you're going to yell it'll have to wait until after I take a shower," I insisted, grabbing my coffee and doughnut and heading toward the bathroom. "The grimoire is in my bedroom if you want a look. I figure a twenty-minute shower should be long enough for you to calm yourself."

"Better make it twenty-five," he growled.

"Consider it done."

TWENTY-ONE

$\mathcal{G}$unner was reclining on the bed, the kitten stretched out across his chest and the book resting on his stomach, when I exited the bathroom. I'd changed into jeans and a T-shirt, my hair wet, and I felt exposed when I joined him.

"Anything?" I asked, rubbing my hands together.

"I guess that depends on how much you trust my ancient Sumerian."

I was surprised "It has to be better than mine."

"Don't get too excited," he admonished. "I was joking. I have no idea if this is Sumerian." He tapped a page for emphasis, causing me to lean closer.

"That's Sanskrit."

"Oh, well, my Sanskrit is even worse."

I grinned. "Yeah, well ... ." I slid onto the bed and positioned myself so I was close but not touching him. He gave me a heavy-lidded look and for a moment I wondered what he was thinking. There was no way I could ask, because I simply wasn't mature enough to put myself out there that way. Honestly, it was fairly obvious he felt the same way.

So, in lieu of either of us growing a backbone, we would simply suffer.

"It's definitely dark magic," Gunner said after a beat, his eyes back on the book. "I don't understand where it came from. More than what it can do — which is an issue, granted, but not one we can solve yet — I'm worried about where it came from. Hal doesn't strike me as the sort of guy who went to antique shows to buy old spell books."

"Probably not," I agreed, absently rubbing my finger over the kitten's nose as it purred maniacally. "Do you have occult stores in this area?"

He shrugged. "Not in town. There are some magic shops around, most scattered across other small towns, but none of them are havens of dark magic. Almost all of them are places for tarot readings and incense. That's about it."

I smirked at the image he conjured. "I know the places you're talking about."

"There's a store in Hemlock Cove that offers real magical items, but I very much doubt they'd be putting grimoires on the racks. They're not reckless, despite the stories I've heard about the eldest witch. Apparently she's all kinds of nuts."

I snickered. "You've mentioned Hemlock Cove twice now. I'll have to take a trip over there."

"I'll go with you. I haven't been in years and wouldn't mind a refresher. But that's for another day. We need to focus on this." He flipped a page, bringing up a bright red illustration. It looked like flames leaping from a cave and threatening to take over the wooded expanse surrounding the stony edifice.

Something occurred to me. "Do you believe in hellmouths?"

Whatever he was expecting, that wasn't it. Gunner straightened on the bed and stared at me. "That's a weird question."

"I know. It came up when Raisin was here yesterday. She says she believes Hawthorne Hollow is located on a hellmouth."

"And what do you think?"

I shrugged, holding out my hands, unsure. "I don't know." That was the truth. "I would like to think I would recognize a hellmouth if I were standing over it. I know Raisin's imagination tends to get away from her, but this book is full of fiery illustrations."

"It is," he agreed, thoughtful. "I'm not a witch, so I'm not as sensitive as you, but wolf shifters sense things, too ... especially about the environment. I have trouble believing we're sitting on a hellmouth and don't realize it. I think we would know."

"Right." I agreed with him, at least for the most part. "Why all the illustrations revolving around fiery death, though?"

"I don't know. You have to think back to when this book was written. Given all the dead languages, I think someone was trying to hide the spells collected here. Maybe the person who found all of them simply didn't know how to translate them, or maybe it's something more nefarious.

"Either way, the book is old," he continued. "Depictions of Hell have accompanied dark magic from the beginning of time. It might not be a reflection of what's really happening as much as the author's fear — or maybe even fervent wish — of what he or she wants to come."

I regarded him a moment, amused. "That was almost poetic."

He offered up a self-assured wink. It was as close to flirting as either of us had managed so far, and he backed off immediately.

"Tell me about what happened at the church again," he prodded, clearing his throat as he sobered.

"There's not much to tell." I was glad he redirected the conversation, because I was starting to feel increasingly uncomfortable. "I thought it was empty so I broke in. The prayer books seem normal — I mean, as far as I can tell — and the back room is weird.

"I figured it was a place for Father Bram to change, collect himself before sermons," I continued. "I was right about that. It's a very ornate little room, a lot of weird statues and art. There's also a really weird mirror that I'm pretty sure is evil."

He arched an eyebrow, surprised. "You think the mirror is evil?"

"Yeah."

"How so?"

I shrugged, unsure how to answer. "I don't know how to explain it.

I saw myself in the mirror and, for a second, it was almost as if I wasn't by myself, as if someone was in the mirror with me. The entire thing was weird, because the chants from the basement were kind of lulling me. It was almost as if I was getting very close to drifting into a trance."

He closed the grimoire and leaned forward, forgetting about the cat in the process and ignoring the way it protested as it moved from his chest to me. "You think you were in a trance?"

"I was getting close to a trance," I corrected. "I was fully aware of everything going on around me. Weird movement was happening in an old mirror that was really close to the stairwell. I think it's possible I could've fallen into a trance if Cecily hadn't picked that moment to arrive."

"And who was she talking to?"

"I don't know. For some reason, I assumed it was Father Bram, but it wasn't. I don't recognize faces because I haven't been here long enough, and I'd never heard the voice before. I don't know who she was talking to."

Gunner lapsed into silence, stroking his chin as he considered everything I'd related. Finally, he raised his eyebrows and snagged my gaze. "I have an idea."

"Coming from you, I'm not sure that I'm comfortable with whatever you're about to suggest."

His grin widened. "I think you're going to like it."

"And why is that?"

"All Souls Church is due for a lumber delivery. It's scheduled for tomorrow, but I'll bet I can get Brandon to move it up a day."

I leaned forward, intrigued. "And then what? Are we going to enchant the lumber to show us the congregation's secrets?"

He snorted. "No. I'm going to distract Father Bram and Cecily with an unexpected delivery while you get into that basement and have a look around."

I balked. "You want me to break into the basement? How is that a good idea?"

"We need to see what's down there." He was calm. "You said there was chanting. We have a ritual death on our plate and a dead guy who died weeks ago yet somehow got up the strength to climb out of his casket and visit you in the middle of the night."

I squirmed, uncomfortable. "But ... you said you don't like it when I break into places."

"I don't like it when you do it and I'm not there," he clarified. "I'll be there today. If you run into trouble, then I will call the cavalry and we'll swoop in to get you."

"Big, fat load of good that will do me if whatever is in the basement eats me," I groused, making a face.

He flicked my ear and smirked. "Do you have a better suggestion? I don't want to make you do something you don't want to, but I don't see where we have any other option. Our one lead is the church. If they're doing funky stuff, we need to know what that funky stuff is."

"So, basically you're saying I'm on funky patrol?"

"Pretty much."

I let loose a resigned sigh. "Okay, well ... I guess I'm up to the challenge. How exactly are we going to make this happen?"

"Leave that to me."

TRUE TO HIS WORD, GUNNER arranged for the church's delivery to be moved up a day. Brandon didn't argue when Gunner insisted it was necessary, instead putting an entire team on the order. In less than two hours, the lumber was ready for delivery, which meant our plan was ready to put into action.

"Okay, I'm going in the front," Gunner noted as he dropped me off on the street behind the church. I was hidden from prying eyes at this location, which meant it was the perfect place to serve as a rendezvous point. "You need to get as close as you can to the church without anyone seeing you. As soon as Father Bram and Cecily are with me in the parking lot, I'll text you the all clear.

"Now, I'm going to do my best to keep them busy but you need to be prepared to run if it comes to it," he continued. "I can't account for everyone in the church. Cecily might be Bram's right-hand woman, but that doesn't mean there aren't other equally zealous acolytes.

"Don't use your magic unless you absolutely have to," he ordered. "We don't want to explain how you managed to set Willa Frederickson on fire without any matches if she stops you and starts asking invasive questions."

I rolled my eyes. "I'm not new. I know exactly what I'm doing. Don't worry about me."

"I don't think I'll be able to stop worrying about you, but we'll take it one step at a time. I'll text when it's clear to go inside. If you run into trouble ... ."

"You'll be the first one I call," I promised, forcing a smile for his benefit. I wasn't exactly keen to return to the church, but I didn't see many options. "Don't turn yourself inside out. I've handled much more dangerous assignments than this one."

"Not on my watch."

"Well, you'll have to get used to it. We're working together, right? That means we need to trust one another."

"I'll keep that in mind," he said dryly. "Now, get moving. Hopefully, if everything goes as planned, you'll be inside within five minutes."

"Here's hoping."

AS FAR AS PLANS GO, OURS WAS solid. True to his word, Gunner caused a ruckus when he pulled into the parking lot with the huge load of wood. The church members weren't expecting him, so they kicked up enough of a fuss that Cecily and Father Bram exited the building. They looked to be questioning Gunner when I slipped in through the same side door I'd used the night before. I couldn't hear them, but trusted that Gunner would keep them distracted as long as possible.

That left me to search the basement. I was a bit nervous. I kept picturing monsters living there, demons that required chanting as part of a tribute. The church was empty, so it was easy for me to slip through it without detection. I was back in Father Bram's private room in less than sixty seconds, and once there, I took a moment to stand in front of the mirror again to see if I could sense the second presence. When it didn't immediately occur, I pushed the notion to the back of my brain and headed for the stairwell. The basement was my highest priority for the day. The mirror would have to wait.

I cocked my head and listened at the top of the stairs. Unlike the previous evening, there was no eerie light to lead the way. And there was no chanting, which allowed me to tamp down the fear that threatened to grab me by the throat and push past it.

I was careful as I descended the spiral staircase that led to what felt like a dank underground cavern. The room I ended up in was poorly lit, and almost entirely empty except for three boxes stacked against the nearest wall. I peered into the top box, furrowing my brow as I tried to make out the contents. I couldn't be sure, but it looked like the same prayer books I'd spied upstairs. I shoved one in the waistband of my pants, pressing it flush against my back, and continued through the claustrophobic space. I figured I could look more closely later. The odds of Father Bram putting his nefarious plans in prayer books and then putting them on display for anybody to see were slim, but I was curious enough that I wanted to be sure.

The next room I visited looked to be a dressing room of some sort. I had no idea if the church used to belong to another denomination, but the more I stared at the setup of the room, the more it looked like a way to segregate the sexes ... or perhaps serve as a crying room for small children to get them away from the sermon when they were in foul moods. But I was almost positive I'd seen a crying room on the main floor. Perhaps that room was newer and replaced this one.

The next room I found contained more boxes. I didn't have a lot of time, but I peeked in a few of the open ones. The first seemed to include dirt, which frankly baffled me. I touched the substance to be sure, lifted it to my nose, and then shook my head as I brushed off my hand. It was definitely dirt. What I didn't understand is why anybody would keep dirt in a box in a church basement. Perhaps it was special dirt ... or perhaps the congregants were even nuttier than I first thought.

My inner map told me I should be getting close to the end of the basement, so I wasn't surprised when I walked into the final room and realized the only way out was another stairwell, this one exiting near the front door. I'd seen it the first day I visited.

This final room contained a symbol painted on the floor, one I didn't recognize but which gave me shivers all the same. I dug for my phone so I could take a photo of it, frowning as something niggled the back of my brain. I didn't recognize the symbol. It wasn't from a pagan textbook or anything that I'd read while preparing to join the club. It was somehow familiar, though. I simply couldn't remember where I'd seen it before.

To make sure I got the symbol from every angle, I slowly circled and snapped at least five photos. I was almost back to where I'd started and ready to head back the way I came when I walked past a small alcove that I hadn't immediately seen because it was set behind a recessed wall.

"That's weird," I muttered, poking my head in. The space was small, probably only three feet across and eight feet deep. I had no idea the purpose of the room. I honestly didn't care, though, because it was now being used to store a dead body.

"Holy ... !" My mouth dropped open when I caught sight of the dead man resting in the far corner. His features were pale, waxy. His clothes were torn and ragged. There was a definite stench.

Oh, and his hand was moving. Wait ... so was his head! He was dead, very clearly dead, and yet he was moving.

I let loose a strangled gasp as the man slowly rose to unsteady feet. I wasn't sure how he managed it, because he didn't bend his appendages as much as he suddenly appeared on his feet ... and focused on me.

His eyes glowed an unearthly color, something of a muddy cross between red and green, and he moaned as he took a lurching step toward me.

My heart was pounding, my head clouded, and yet one thought managed to make it to the forefront of my brain. I had to run ... and I had to do it now.

Instinctively I raised the phone in my hand long enough to take a photo of the man before I bolted. I had enough sense not to race up the stairs that led to the vestibule. That wouldn't go over well if Father Bram and Cecily saw me escaping during the distraction Gunner just happened to serve up.

I didn't stop to investigate anything as I blew through the rooms, and I forced myself not to look over my shoulder when I hit the staircase. I heard the man — zombie, ghoul, whatever he was — moaning behind me, but he hadn't managed to catch up. I didn't trip climbing the stairs, but that felt like a miracle because my limbs were ungainly thanks to the panic coursing through me.

Once back in Father Bram's room, I strode straight for the door to escape, casting one look at the mirror as I passed. Even though I was moving quickly, I swore I saw what looked to be a pair of eyes staring back. I blinked hard and looked again. This time it appeared to be a normal mirror, but I couldn't shake the feeling that I'd definitely glimpsed something inside, something beyond the glass that wasn't supposed to be there.

I didn't bother checking to make sure the nave was empty before exiting. I was so eager to escape from the building that I ran to the side door. I burst out, exhaling in relief when the sun hit my face, and then headed straight for the street where Gunner had dropped me. He was supposed to pick me up there the second he finished delivering the lumber.

I could only hope he would be quick about it, because I was terrified to stay in a remote area alone. If I did, I would be forced to ask the obvious questions: Who was that? Where did he come from? How was he moving when he was very clearly dead? Oh, and who reanimated him and why?

Because I couldn't answer any of those questions, I assumed a panic attack was incoming. I simply had to get clear of the church before it hit.

TWENTY-TWO

*I*t took Gunner twenty minutes to make it back to our meeting place. I was so antsy, prone to scouring every bush and ditch for signs of movement, that I considered leaving without saying a word. I figured he would eventually find me, and if he didn't ... well ... it was nice knowing him.

Gunner was all smiles when he pulled up, offering me a saucy salute. It wasn't until he got closer that he saw the look on my face, and he was out of the truck and by my side before I could form words.

"What happened to you?" He tipped back my head so he could stare at my features under the limited light filtering through the tree-tops. "You look as if you're going to pass out."

I wasn't far from it. "They have a ... something ... in the basement."

"A something? Can you be more specific?"

"A ... man."

"They have a man in the basement? Is he shackled or locked in a room? I mean ... it's not like *The Goonies*, is it?"

The absurd question snapped me out of my haze. "That isn't funny."

He snickered. "It was kind of funny. I love that movie."

198

I loved that movie, too. Now wasn't the time to reminisce about pirate ships and Baby Ruth candy bars, though. "The basement is odd," I announced, pulling myself together. "It's like a chain of rooms. The first one was empty except for some boxes. Then there's a weird changing room. There's another room that has boxes of dirt. I mean ... dirt. It's as if someone went out, dug a big hole, collected the dirt and put it in boxes for some reason."

"Dirt?" Gunner's eyebrow flew up. "Why would they need boxes of dirt?"

The look I shot him was withering. "I have no idea. Perhaps you should ask them. I know I want to. I thought the dirt was going to be the weirdest thing I saw down there ... and then I went into the last room."

To my surprise, Gunner gently raised a hand and slid a strand of hair behind my ear instead of asking the obvious question. He was calm as he waited for me to spit it out. I couldn't decide if that made me feel better or worse.

"There was a symbol on the floor." My hand was steady as I retrieved my phone and flipped to the photos I'd taken. Gunner wordlessly took the phone from me and stared at the symbol, furrowing his brow as he tilted his head left and right to look at it from various angles. "That's ... weird."

"You think?"

We could both laugh at my reaction now, and it felt good to give in to the mirth for a full twenty seconds. I was starting to feel better until the sound of a snapping twig in the woods behind us caused me to jerk my head in that direction. Instead of an undead man with glazed eyes, I found a squirrel playing around the base of a tree.

"That's not all?" Gunner turned serious.

"That's not even close to all," I confirmed, sucking in a breath. "I circled the room to get photos of the symbol at every angle. I didn't want to miss anything because there's a lot of fine detail in there and I can't possibly remember all of it."

He nodded to propel me to continue.

"I was almost back to where I started when I realized there was this recessed area that I hadn't noticed from the other side," I explained. "It hid a small alcove."

"I take it you went into the alcove."

"I really wish I hadn't," I admitted, pressing the heel of my hand to my forehead. "There was a man inside. I didn't recognize him, before you ask. He was clearly dead. I mean ... absolutely dead.

"His skin was hanging and waxy," I continued. "You know how bodies get when they've been dead for a while?"

He nodded and brushed his hand over my shoulder to sweep my hair from my face.

"I've seen dead bodies before. They never freak me out. I'm not some big baby who can't handle her job. I don't want you to think that."

"I don't think that," he said. "Just tell me what happened. I can't help unless you tell me."

I sucked in a breath. "He started moving when I made a noise. I was surprised. I scuffed my feet. I'm positive that's what woke him, although I didn't realize it at the time."

"He woke and went after you?" Gunner challenged, surprised. "Did he say anything?"

"I already told you he was dead. The only dead things doing any talking are ghosts, and he was most definitely not a ghost. Besides, he opened his mouth a few times and I could see inside. I ... could see that his mouth had been sutured shut at some point. They only do that before embalming."

"Oh, geez." Gunner made a face. "You think the body was embalmed."

"I do. Bodies don't last forever despite embalming. It depends on the strength of the solution used and the specific process. He was clearly dead – and rotting."

"Thank you for that lovely picture," Gunner complained, dragging a hand through his hair. "What happened then?"

"I snapped a photo and took off. I heard him following, but ... I couldn't make myself look back."

"That's okay." He shocked me when he pulled me forward for a hug. "Stop beating yourself up over this. Anyone would've freaked seeing that." He rocked back and forth and I felt his free arm moving behind me.

"What are you doing?" I asked, twisting so I could watch him. Then I realized he still had my phone and he was looking for the photo I mentioned. "I have no idea if it's any good," I offered. "I just took it and ran. I felt as if I was caught in a nightmare."

"You're fine." He absently stroked his hand over the back of my hair, causing me to stop swaying and tilt my head so I could look up at him. He was intent on the phone as he searched for the photo. "Here it is. I ... oh, holy water ... no way!"

I swallowed hard at his reaction. "I take it that means you know him."

"Fred Melcher."

"Should I know that name?"

"No. He ... well, he's my former wrestling coach. He died about six months ago. I don't understand why he would be in the church basement."

"It's not as if he's living there," I volunteered. "Er, well, he is sort of living there. He's not living, though, so it's more like he's un-living there. What? That's a thing."

Despite the serious nature of the situation, Gunner cracked a smile. "It's totally a thing," he agreed, giving me an additional squeeze before releasing me. "I can't believe he's down there. He was a good man. He understood I had issues with my father and he stood between us a few times. He always tried to protect me, do what's best for me. There was no stopping my father, but Coach Fred always tried."

He looked melancholy as he thought back on his beloved wrestling coach. I felt bad for him. I also had questions. "I can't believe you wrestled. Did you wear tights? Did you wear one of those tiny little rubber uniforms? Did you like it when you were rolling around on the mats with other guys?"

Gunner's lips curved down. "Oh, you're so funny. I'll have you know wrestling is a manly sport. There's a reason it has survived for centuries."

"Yes, I'm sure there is." I poked his side to let him know I was teasing ... mostly. "Your coach is in the basement. Was he a member of the church?"

"Not that I know of. His wife, who died a good five years ago, she might've been a member of the church. Mable will know. We should head over there for lunch."

I wasn't sure I could eat anything, but I was eager to put distance between the church and me. "Yeah, sure, whatever. Let's get out of here."

Gunner chuckled as we moved toward the truck, which was still running and had a door gaping open. "The zombie really frightened you, huh? I would've thought you'd seen plenty of zombies during your time as a Spells Angel."

I slowed my pace. "He's not a zombie."

"Then ... what is he?"

"I don't know, but he's not a zombie. Zombies aren't embalmed. They turn quickly after a bite. They never make it to embalming. Your coach was very clearly embalmed."

Gunner worked his jaw. "So, what comes back from the dead beside ghosts and zombies?"

"I don't know, but I'm guessing the symbol will lead us to an answer. We need to figure out what it is."

"Okay. Lunch first. Research after."

"You're so bossy."

"I want to talk to Mable." He was grim. "I can't remember much about coach's wife, but Mable will know."

"Why?"

"Because the coach's wife was Mable's mother's best friend."

"Oh, well ... ."

"Yeah." He smiled. "It's a small town. You're going to find we're all related in one way or other. So far, no one has been born with webbed fingers and toes because of close family lines. That should make you happy."

I scowled. "You really know how to put a smiley face on a crap afternoon."

"Don't I, though?"

MABLE'S COUNTRY TABLE WAS packed. I didn't think we would find a place to sit until an eager woman started waving from the corner booth. It took me a few seconds to realize she was trying to get Gunner's attention, and when I did, amusement washed over me fast and hard.

"Um ... I believe you have a fan."

"What?" He knit his eyebrows as he met my gaze. "What are you talking about?"

"In the corner." I inclined my chin toward the auburn-haired siren who was practically giving herself a stroke to get Gunner's attention. "That's your sister, right?"

His smile was grim as his hands landed on his hips. "Yup. That's my sister."

He didn't look happy. "I thought you said she came to town all the time. This shouldn't be a surprise."

"I was under the impression she was leaving this morning," Gunner replied, waving to Ashley to let her know he saw her and then nodding to indicate we would sit with her. "I don't see where I can get out of eating with her."

"It's fine." His reaction amused me. "I'm looking forward to meeting her."

"Yeah, well, you might not say that after she grills you about our relationship."

"What do you mean?"

"She's determined to get me married before the year is out. She says it's pathetic for men in their thirties to be single."

"I'm almost thirty," I noted. "Is it pathetic for women, too?"

"You'll have to ask her." He put his hand to the small of my back and prodded me forward. "I'm warning you she'll try to set us up. She won't be able to help herself. Don't take it personally."

"I'll try to refrain from jumping you in excitement," I said dryly.

"Oh, well, jumping me is another story." His lips twitched. He was getting more comfortable with the flirting. "Let's just get through this meal and we'll talk about jumping games later."

"No problem." I was thrilled that Ashley was here, because that meant I could forget about my problems for a bit. The more I could put distance between myself and the memory of Gunner's dead wrestling coach, the better. "This should be fun."

"Just remember you said that."

ASHLEY STRATTON was a bundle of energy that simply could not be contained. She was bubbly, friendly and a bit overwhelming. While I found her manic nature entertaining, I could see why Gunner seemed drained by her visits.

"So, how do you know Graham?" she wheedled once the waitress had taken our orders.

"I've only met him briefly," I replied. "I met him the day I arrived, when your brother and I stumbled over a dead body, and then yesterday when I got in trouble for hurting an abusive father."

Ashley stared at me for a long beat, her eyes wide. "What?" she finally squeaked out.

"She thinks you're asking about Dad, Ashley," Gunner volunteered. "You should realize, Scout, that Ashley calls me Graham because she knows it irritates me."

"Oh." Whoops. That question made so much more sense now. "Ignore everything I just said."

"Even the part about you and my brother stumbling over a dead body together?" Ashley was indignant as she glared at her brother, who was sharing a booth bench with me. I was starting to think that was by design because he didn't want to be within swiping distance of her long fingernails.

"That part is true," Gunner said, choosing his words carefully. "We found a body together."

"And why didn't you mention that?"

"Because I didn't think it was a big deal. I turned the case over to Dad. He's investigating it."

"Uh-huh." Ashley didn't look convinced when she shifted her eyes to me. "You're my brother's co-worker. That's how he kept referring to you yesterday when I asked why he was staring at you at the Cauldron."

Gunner moved his jaw but didn't say anything.

"We work together," I agreed. "I haven't been in town very long, so it's a relatively new relationship."

"What can you tell me about your work?"

Gunner cleared his throat and shot me a warning look. He was clearly used to his sister's curiosity regarding Spells Angels. Even if we weren't sworn to secrecy, I knew better than to share information with Ashley. She had "blabber" written all over her.

"We can't talk to you about work and you know it, Ashley," Gunner warned, clearly frustrated. When he said his sister irritated him I thought he was exaggerating. Obviously he was telling the truth. "Let's talk about something else, huh? Scout has a new kitten she refuses to name. Let's talk about that."

"Kittens are cute," Ashley said automatically. "Why is your name Scout? Is that your biker handle? I know certain people have biker names — like Gunner." She rolled her eyes in dramatic fashion, forcing me to bite the inside of my cheek to keep from laughing. "Why did you pick Scout?"

"Oh, geez." Gunner leaned back in his seat. "I'm sorry." The apology was aimed at me, but it was unnecessary.

"It's fine." I waved off his concern. "I'm used to it."

Ashley wrinkled her pert little nose. "Used to what?"

Thankfully, Mable picked that moment to stop at the table and ask how we were doing. Gunner seized on the distraction and focused solely on the restaurant proprietress.

"Hey, do you remember Dolly Melcher?"

"Who could forget a woman named Dolly?" Mable asked, making a face. "I remember her. She had blond hair from a bottle and boobs from a surgeon's office."

I choked on the water I was sipping, causing Gunner to smack my back to clear my airway.

"That's the woman I'm talking about," he confirmed with a smile. "She's been dead a few years, but I was wondering if you remembered when she was alive. Was she a member of All Souls Church?"

"Dolly? I don't think so." Mable squinted as she searched her memory. "Or, you know what? I think she was kind of a member. She got talked into joining by Cecily Duncan — they were friends for a hot minute, although I don't know how anyone could stand either one of them — but she didn't last at the church for more than a few months.

"I remember she was really into everything they had going on there because it made me want to punch her even more than normal," she continued. "Then she walked away from the church just as fast as she joined. That was about six weeks before her heart attack claimed her."

"I forgot she died of a heart attack." Gunner rubbed his chin as he slid me a sidelong look. "You haven't heard about anyone at the church doing anything ... weird ... have you?"

One look at Mable told me she was instantly suspicious.

"Define weird," she instructed.

"Oh, I don't know ... holding services late at night, threatening people in the town, buying weird things at estate sales. That sort of weird."

"Not that I've heard of," Mable replied.

"What about worshipping demons?" I asked, avoiding Gunner's well-aimed elbow as it careened toward my ribs. "You haven't heard about them doing that, have you?"

"Oh, *that?*" Mable snorted. "Half the town is talking about that. I don't ever listen to gossip like that."

Gunner froze. "Wait ... you have heard about them worshipping demons?"

Mable nodded without hesitation. "Marie Adler says that they're sacrificing chickens and raising the dead. She swears up and down she saw Herbert Jones outside the gas station four nights ago. You can't listen to town gossip. It's always a bunch of nonsense."

Perhaps not always. I rubbed my hands over my arms to ward off the sudden chill that permeated the air. When I remembered we weren't alone, I lifted my chin and found Ashley watching me with suspicious eyes. Whatever she was thinking couldn't possibly be good.

TWENTY-THREE

*a*fter lunch, Gunner insisted we track down Rooster — which led us to The Rusty Cauldron — leaving Ashley to pout because she hadn't gotten anywhere with her interrogation. Gunner didn't appear to feel guilty about leaving her behind, so I pushed similar thoughts out of my mind and focused on the problem at hand.

"So ... what is it?" Marissa asked as she swiveled on a bar stool, her long legs on full display in tight pants and knee-high boots. Honestly, I didn't know how she managed to get into those boots in the first place, let alone walk in them. The heels were six inches high and razor thin.

"It's a zombie," Bonnie automatically volunteered. "We've dealt with zombies before."

"It's not a zombie," Gunner countered, walking behind the bar and reaching for a bottle of Jack Daniels. Whistler, who was rubbing down the counter, apparently didn't mind; he didn't admonish him to stop.

"If it's not a zombie, what is it?"

He shrugged. "I don't know. Why do you think we're here? Whatever it is, the church obviously has something to do with it. I don't know if it's Cecily or Father Bram — or both of them working together — but they're up to no good."

"Okay, they're up to no good," Rooster conceded. "I think we've known that since Bram showed up."

That was an interesting statement. "Wait ... he's not local?"

Gunner shook his head as he poured whiskey over ice. "No. He didn't show up in Hawthorne Hollow until about ten years ago."

"He had to come from somewhere," I noted. "Call your father and have him track Bram's history."

"Call my father?" Gunner arched a dubious eyebrow. "I don't know what sort of cops you've been working with, but my father doesn't share information unless he absolutely has to. That's not how 'real' cops work." He made the appropriate air quotes before downing the whiskey in one gulp. Lunch with his sister really had put him on edge.

"So ... you guys don't have any cops working with you?" I asked, confused. "How do you manage?"

"Are you saying you do have cops working with you in Detroit?" Rooster challenged. "How does that work with the whole, 'We swear to keep the secret until our dying day' thing?"

"Most of the cops we deal with have stumbled across us in the middle of a job," I admitted. "When that happens ... ."

"You have to make a judgment call," he finished, shaking his head. "Well, we've never had to make that call here. Graham knows what we are, what we do, but he doesn't get involved. He doesn't want us to get involved with his business."

"Well ... ." I made a hissing sound with my tongue as I surveyed the room. Then, something occurred to me. "I can make a call. I know someone who might be able to help. I'll need Father Bram's information, everything you have on him."

"That is all we have on him," Bonnie noted. "He's Father Bram and he works at All Souls Church."

She had to be kidding. "That's all you know?"

"Yeah. Do you think it will be enough?"

"WHAT TOOK YOU SO LONG TO ANSWER?"

Mike Foley, a desk jockey from Detroit's seventh precinct, picked up the Skype call on the third ring. He didn't look surprised to see me.

"Do you miss me yet?" He was young, in his twenties, and suffered from a debilitating case of post-traumatic stress disorder that arrived on the heels of a school shooting that caused him to lose his nerve after he shot a student sniper in the midst of the massacre. The shooting was justified, and he was cleared, but he was no longer comfortable on the streets.

During a bout of melancholy at the bar one evening, he confessed that he dreamed of the dead students' faces every night. He didn't want to add new faces to the lineup because he didn't want to forget ... and he also didn't want to be forced to remember more. He was a computer whiz, so ultimately his superiors put him on desk duty and he was happy with his new assignment.

"Every moment without you is a torment," I replied, grinning.

"Hello," Marissa purred, grabbing a chair and sliding closer to me so the computer camera could pick her up. "Who are you? Are you Scout's boyfriend?"

Mike looked her up and down with an amused expression before shaking his head. "We came close, but I'm too good-looking for her."

I glared at him, annoyance bubbling up. "Keep it up."

"When did you come close?" Gunner asked out of nowhere, catching me by surprise.

I glanced over my shoulder and frowned at him. "He's making that up. We never came close."

"We did," Mike protested, grinning so widely a dimple creased his cheek. "Do you remember that night we all went to the haunted maze at the orchard? You were freaked out and held my hand. We almost did it you were so afraid."

That was the most ludicrous thing I'd ever heard. "We held hands because you were afraid of the guy with the chainsaw," I countered, my temper getting the better of me. "You whined like a little girl."

"Hey!" Mike jabbed a finger at the screen. "I maintain that it should be illegal for haunted houses to use real chainsaws. That cannot be safe. I mean ... those are people who can't get anything but seasonal positions and they're using dangerous equipment."

Bonnie snickered behind me as Gunner folded his arms over his chest and glared at the computer screen.

"Also, you tried to rub yourself all over me," Mike challenged. "I remember. It's all up here in the vault." He tapped the side of his head for emphasis.

"Actually, I'm contacting you because of the vault," I said, turning to the business at hand. "You know I've been transferred to Hawthorne Hollow?"

"I do." Mike's smile slipped. "I complained to Buzz as soon as I heard."

Buzz was my former superior, a crabby individual with a rough voice and a pocked face, so I had a feeling I knew how that conversation went. "Did he acquiesce to your demands?"

"He told me to suck it up," Mike replied. "He said he didn't know if you'd be coming back. You're not staying up there, are you?"

I slid a gaze to my left and found Gunner watching me with expressive eyes. "That's up in the air," I replied. "We're in the middle of a case and I need your help." I explained what we were up against, hitting the salient points and leaving some of the more fantastical tidbits out. "I need to know more about this Father Bram. Can you run him for me?"

"I can try," Mike replied, turning to business. I heard his fingers on the keyboard. "What do you have on him?"

"Not much." I felt stupid for providing him with so little information. "All Souls Church and Father Bram. That's all I have ... but he must have an address in Hawthorne Hollow." I turned to Rooster for confirmation. "Where does he live?"

"I ... ." Rooster's expression was blank as he worked his jaw. "You know what? I don't know."

"Me either," Gunner admitted, sliding into the chair next to me and peering into the camera. He and Mike spent a moment sharing eye contact, perhaps sizing each other up, and then he focused on me. "I've never really asked myself where he lives. I'm sorry about that."

"Who are you?" Mike asked, his fingers ceasing their tapping.

"This is Gunner," I replied. "He works with me."

Mike tilted his head back and gave Gunner a long look. "Have you run him to make sure he's kosher? I mean ... he could be a plant or something. Perhaps the bad guys recruited him and he infiltrated that chapter with nefarious designs or something."

Oh, geez. This was the last thing I needed. "I'm pretty sure he's okay," I countered. "He's been here for a long time ... and his father is the chief of police."

"Really?" Mike made a face as his shoulders relaxed. "If you have a law enforcement in, why are you calling me?" He went back to typing without waiting for an answer.

"Gunner's father is a 'by-the-rules' guy. We can't use him on this," I explained.

"Okay, well, let me see what I can find." He was quiet for a few minutes, his eyes busy as they scanned multiple files. Mike was quick on his feet, so I wasn't surprised when he started relaying information. It was a relief, because I didn't know how long I could sit here pretending that I wasn't aware of Gunner's steady glare.

"Well, this is interesting," Mike started. "The church isn't listed as a non-profit."

I stilled, surprised. "How does that work?"

"Your guess is as good as mine, but there are a few notes in here that might explain things." Mike was getting into the spirit of the search now as he happily clicked away on his keyboard. "Okay, twenty years ago the church was a Mennonite church. It looked to have a small congregation, but retained non-profit status."

"He's right," Rooster interjected. "That was a Mennonite church. We had, like, fifteen Mennonites in town. The church had been abandoned years before, so it was sold to them at a song because they promised to fix it up ... and they did a pretty good job of it. Last time I was inside, it looked nice."

"I bet you didn't look in the basement," I grumbled, earning a smirk from Gunner.

"What's in the basement?" Mike asked, understandably curious.

"Nothing. We need to know more about the church. Why did the Mennonites leave?"

"It doesn't say," Mike answered. "That would take more digging than I'm capable of."

"It was because of September 11th," Whistler offered, taking everyone by surprise.

"September 11th?" That made zero sense to me. "How do you figure?"

"Mennonites are pacifists," he replied. "They don't believe in war ... or fighting. When September 11th happened, military recruiters were all over the place. The Mennonites refused to pray at some of the assemblies and that didn't go over well, even though they weren't making a judgment on what happened.

"Anyway, things got ugly and a few of our more benevolent souls decided to go over and pick a fight," he continued. "The head of the church was severely beaten, and the next day the group picked up and left town."

A sickening sense of dread filled my stomach. "You're sure they really left of their own volition? They're not dead in that basement, are they?"

Whistler chuckled. "I know they moved to Ohio to join with a group there. My niece married one of the men in the group, and she's safe in Ohio, with her husband and children and everyone else who was part of that group. They're safe."

"Well, that's a relief." I exhaled heavily. "If the Mennonites left in 2001 and Father Bram didn't get here until ten years ago, that means the church sat empty for a good eight years or so."

"It did," Rooster confirmed. "As you've seen, we have an abundance of churches in town. Once a month, the bank sent somebody inside to clean. They also kept up the lawn. Nothing else was done with the building during that time."

"And you're sure nobody killed the maids sent in there to clean and tried to resurrect them?"

"I'm fairly certain we would've heard about that," he replied with a straight face.

"So Bram showed up in 2009 and bought the building?" I asked. "With what money?"

"He probably got it on a land contract," Rooster supplied. "As long as he kept up on his monthly payments he didn't have to provide a down payment. The bank was so eager to unload that building I can see it doing that. I can try to feel out a source tomorrow and see if my hunch is true."

"Why aren't they a non-profit though?" Gunner asked, focusing on Mike. "There has to be a reason."

"There is," Mike confirmed. "They're not listed as an accredited religion thanks to a problem with the filing documents."

"What does that mean?" Bonnie asked.

Mike shrugged. "No idea. I'm not up on the inner-workings of churches and how they get their non-profit status. I suppose I could make a few calls if you want, Scout, but I honestly don't know how important it is to what you're doing."

"I don't know that the non-profit status is the thing we should be focusing on," I argued. "I mean ... what about Bram himself? I'm mostly interested in his background. He's all sorts of crazy."

"Crazy how?"

"Like ... he has crazy eyes. Remember old Gordon Buttons, the guy who lived under the bridge near the Cass Corridor even though he had a three-story house in Grosse Pointe that was paid off and modernized?"

Mike chuckled. "Yeah. He was a nut."

"He was," I agreed. "He also had crazy eyes. You could tell the first time you sat down with him that he wasn't normal, that it wasn't some temporary condition he was suffering from. Bram is that crazy, but he's manipulative, too. He's got a diabolical streak. Something else is going on at that church beside the non-profit snafu."

"I can dig on him, but you haven't given me much to go on," Mike offered. "There are a few threads here. I can tug on them in my free time and see what unravels."

"Would you?" I beamed at him. "I would really appreciate it."

"I'll see what I can find out," Mike said. "I'll be in contact tomorrow if I dig anything up. As an aside, you're going to owe me big time if I find the smoking gun you're looking for."

He sounded serious, but I knew better. "Oh, yeah? Exactly how do you expect me to pay up?"

"You know exactly what I'm talking about." He winked. "You know exactly what I'm talking about."

"Well, great," Gunner announced, hopping to his feet. "We appreciate you helping us. We'll be in contact tomorrow." He killed the connection on the call before I could utter a goodbye.

"That was a little abrupt," Bonnie noted.

"I thought everyone was done," Gunner said as he moved away from the group and strolled behind me. "In fact ... ." He fell silent, which I thought was weird. I imagined him running out of the building when he thought no one was looking because he wanted to end the conversation, so I turned quickly to make sure he wasn't fleeing.

Instead of something to laugh at, I found something to weep about. Sometime in the middle of the conversation, Raisin had entered the building ... and she was a bloody mess. Her red hair was tousled, blood caking it on the left side. Her face was puffy, one eye almost swollen shut.

She had bruises all over her arms and walked on unsteady legs. Gunner made a beeline for her, our earlier conversation forgotten. He caught her as she began to sway and threatened to topple over.

"Sweetheart, what happened to you?" he gasped as the rest of us hopped to our feet to help her.

"He came for me," she slurred, struggling to remain conscious. "He came for me ... and took her."

"Who?" Rooster asked, alarmed.

"Grandma. He took Grandma. He's going to ... !" She swallowed whatever else she was going to say as she cringed. "You have to save my Grandma!"

I looked to Rooster for help as Gunner soothed the battered child. "Her father must've got out of jail. I thought they were keeping him?"

"I thought so, too," Rooster muttered. "I guess that didn't go as planned. We need to get Graham on the phone and figure out what's going on. We also need to get an ambulance here for Raisin. I'm guessing she has internal injuries."

"I'm floating," the girl muttered. "Do you think anyone will notice if I float away?"

"I'll notice," Gunner barked, tension radiating off him. "I'll notice. You stay right here with me. Don't you float anywhere!"

My heart skipped a beat at his plea. "We need to get help for Raisin and then track down her father before he can hurt the grandmother. If that means killing him ... I'm fine with that. I should've done it the first time."

"No, *I* should've done it the first time," Rooster countered. "This is my fault. I shouldn't have waited for the right moment to act. I should've just done it. I ... if that guy has killed Irene, I swear, I will end him."

"I think you'll have to get in line," I countered. "I ... ." I didn't get a chance to finish what I was about to say because someone started laying on a horn in the parking lot. The blare drowned out the outgoing words for a long time, and then died. Someone screamed obscenities into the silence that followed before the horn blared again. Then more screams.

I looked to Rooster for confirmation. "That's him, right?"

Rooster nodded. "He either followed Raisin here to finish what he started or planned to use her as bait to get back at us." He was grim. "Either way, it doesn't matter now. We have to end this here and now."

I couldn't agree more.

TWENTY-FOUR

Fury bubbled in my throat as I strode toward the door. I could taste the revenge I wanted to unleash.

"Just where do you think you're going?" Rooster caught me by the arm and spun me around, our eyes meeting as he let out a hiss and I vented some of the building magic by shooting sparks through the door and into the night. "Geez, girl. How much power do you have building in there?" He looked worried.

"He's outside," I prodded. "All we have to do is go out there and get him. That's what we agreed on twenty seconds ago."

"And we're keeping to that," he shot back. "We need to ascertain where Irene is first. She's key to this. We're not doing anything that will put her at risk, which means you can't run out there half-cocked."

"Is that what you assume I'm going to do?"

He didn't back down, instead shrugging as he held his hands out. "I don't know. I've never seen you in action. All I know is that so far you set a spriggan on fire even though it could've raced through the woods and ignited the entire town and you smacked a fire spell against an ice spell and are lucky you didn't detonate something in the process."

If his words were meant to temper my determination, he'd failed ...

miserably. "I'm going out there." I wasn't in the mood to be trifled with. "That man ... he ... I'm not letting him carry on like this."

"So, you're going to kill him, are you?" Rooster pinned me with a serious gaze. "Do you think that's the best way to go about things?"

"Look what he did to her." I gestured toward Raisin, who had rolled into a ball on the floor and started sobbing as Marissa and Bonnie flanked her. "I'm not going to let that stand. If you think I am, well ... ."

"Don't walk away from me, girl." Rooster grabbed at me again when I moved to storm through the door.

"Don't call me 'girl,'" I snapped as frustration, hot and acidic, spewed forth. "I hate that. You have no idea how much I hate it when people call me that. It's rude ... and demeaning. I have a name."

"Fine. *Scout.*" Annoyance flashed in the depths of Rooster's eyes as he shook his head. "I'm not done talking to you." He was firm. "I don't know how they do things in Detroit, but you can't simply roll through that door and blow up Steven Morton. That will make things worse for Raisin."

"How do you figure? He won't be able to touch her again. Isn't that the most important thing? Other than saving her grandmother, I mean."

"Keeping Raisin safe is most definitely important," he agreed. "But if you kill Steven you'll change the course of her life."

"How is that the wrong move?" I wanted to slam him into a wall of itchy magic to get him out of my face, but I managed to rein in my temper. "If he's gone he can never touch her again. That's a better course for her life."

"Maybe. But killing him won't fix what's been done to her." Rooster kept his voice low so Raisin couldn't hear. "She'll always wonder if she's responsible for his death if you do this. She'll blame herself even though she's the victim here, and you know it."

I swallowed hard. He had a point, loath as I was to admit it. Still, I wasn't ready to back down. "A man like him shouldn't be allowed to live. He's been terrorizing her her whole life."

"And yet she still loves him." Rooster looked sad. "Children have an instinctive need to please their parents. You probably don't under-stand that because ... well ... you have your own trauma that revolves around absent parental figures. She still loves him, and killing him will make her a victim twice.

"Besides that, if you kill him, the state could be called in as part of the investigation," he continued. "They could overrule Graham and remove Raisin from Irene's home. Depending on what sort of shape she's in, we can take care of her and Raisin. If she's not on her feet, the state won't let Raisin stay ... and then her entire world will be erased. Is that what you want?"

I hated being put on the spot. "No. I ... no. But he has to be punished."

"Of course he does. That's where Graham comes in."

"Graham already let him out once."

"And that will eat away at him something fierce. I know him better than you do. He won't let it happen a second time."

I didn't have the same faith he did, but I knew he spoke from the heart and had Raisin's best interests in mind. "Fine. What are you thinking?"

He offered me a cocky grin. "Well, you've got a lot of magic ready to burst out and pull a horror movie maneuver. Let's give Steven a show. We need to get Irene first. More than anything, she's our prior-ity. Once that happens, if you give Steven a nightmare or two — or ten — I wouldn't be opposed to it. The more he rants and raves, the better it is for Raisin."

I understood what he was saying and nodded, squaring my shoul-ders. "Let's do this."

"Wait," Gunner called out from several feet away as he straight-ened. The look on his face was murderous. "I'm coming with you."

"I think we have all the firepower we need," Rooster countered.

"I'm coming with you." Gunner's tone told me he meant business. "We're doing this together. We can't screw it up."

Rooster sighed, resigned. "Fine. But don't you go losing your head either. I just had to talk this one down off a mountain. I don't have another inspirational speech in me right now."

"I'm sure I can handle myself." Gunner slid between us and walked through the door.

THE PARKING LOT WAS DARK and it took my eyes a moment to adjust. Gunner took the center position, so Rooster and I flanked him. The noise was coming from a sports-utility vehicle parked sideways in the middle of the lot. I heard movement inside, but it was too dark to see what was happening.

"I'm going to get on Whistler about adding more lights out here," Rooster growled.

On impulse, I waved my hand and sent a fistful of magic sparkles into the sky directly above the car. They illuminated the vehicle without shining a beacon, and the scene through the glass caused my heart to skip a beat.

Irene was alive, which was the good news. She looked terrified, tears streaming down her cheeks, but she was alive. If I had to guess, she was sporting some new bruises. That was nothing compared to the violence he'd doled out to Raisin.

"Oh, well, look who it is," Steven drawled as he lit a cigarette and focused on me. "It's the woman of the hour, the stupid lady who broke up my happy home."

Rooster didn't immediately acknowledge Steven. Instead, he focused on the other side of the vehicle. "Are you okay, Irene?"

The older woman nodded stiffly. "I'll live. I'm embarrassed this piece of crap is my son, but I'll live. Is Ruthie okay?"

"She's inside," Rooster replied. "We're going to get her some help."

"She'll be fine," I offered. I didn't want the woman worrying about anything other than her own survival. "We're more worried about you right now."

"Don't worry about me." Irene was grim. "Whatever you do, don't let Ruthie come back out here. He's done enough to her."

"Don't worry about that," Gunner growled, glaring at Steven, who looked a bit too smug given the circumstances. His eyes were glassy, a smile playing at the corners of his mouth, and he was covered in a thin sheen of sweat.

Realization dawned hot and fast. "He's lit," I announced, narrowing my eyes. "He's completely and totally hammered."

"Drunk?" Gunner asked, sliding me a look.

I shook my head. "I don't think so. I'd say meth. His pupils are dilated and he keeps picking at the skin around his hairline. I think he's tweaking."

Gunner worked his jaw. "How do you know that?"

All I could do was shrug. "We saw it enough in Detroit. I'm used to the signs."

"That would explain a few things," Rooster noted, thoughtful. "He's been pulling in extra money. We couldn't figure out from where. He might be cooking it somewhere."

"We should be able to find the location easy enough." I moved closer to the SUV. "I don't think we should drag this out. He has a gun." I could see that easily enough through the window. It was pointed at Irene. "The longer this goes on, the more trigger happy he's going to be."

"Do you have a suggestion for getting the gun?" Rooster asked.

Steven cackled like a maniac. "I'm never giving up this gun. Never! I'm going to use it on all of you." He stopped aiming it at Irene and turned it in my direction. "I want to start with you because you're the busybody who ruined everything."

A low growl, one that reminded me of a territorial animal about to strike, ripped from Gunner's throat. "Do not point that at her," he hissed.

"It's okay." I held up a hand to still him. The last thing we needed was for Gunner to terrify Steven to the point he started squeezing the trigger. "Let's not get worked up here."

Gunner stretched his fingers as he clenched and unclenched his fists. "We need to move."

"We do," I agreed. "I'm going to start. In fact ... ." I jerked my chin to the left, gathering my magic quickly and funneling it toward one goal.

The look on Steven's face would've been comical under different circumstances. His eyes went wide as the gun was ripped from his hand and flew in my direction. I reached up and snagged it as it flew through the air. I was familiar with weapons and checked the chamber and clip quickly before handing the firearm to Rooster. "Only two bullets."

Rooster accepted it with half a smile as Steven howled about evil demons. "That was ... interesting."

"It was nothing." I meant it. I'd disarmed so many men — and a few women — I'd lost count over the years. "Now we need to get Irene out of that vehicle. I think she's hurt, so we have to be gentle."

"We're going to talk about your magic once this is over and we can sit down," Rooster supplied. "I mean ... seriously. You've got magic at your disposal I've only ever heard about. It's ... impressive."

"I guess I'm just used to it." I narrowed my eyes when I realized Steven was reaching for Irene. "Hey!" My voice was loud and booming, deep enough that Irene looked at me with terrified eyes. Steven didn't turn away from his mother; he was clearly determined to kill her.

I had no intention of letting that happen.

"Stop," I ordered, my voice deepening as the fingers on my right hand lit with red fire magic. The fingers on my left hand turned a more muted shade of green as I froze Steven in his place. His eyes went wide as he struggled to fight what I was doing to him. He wasn't exactly strong, but I couldn't risk leaving him in the vehicle.

"I said stop," I repeated, my voice low and dark, a chill emanating from inside me as I issued what I hoped would be a final warning. I yanked with my left hand, and the door of his vehicle flew off as he was dragged bodily from inside. I wasn't gentle. I let him hit the pavement and then proceeded to rake him over it as I dragged him in my direction. "Just stop," I hissed, when he skidded to a halt at my feet.

"What was that?" Steven screamed. "Demons! Demons! They're demons!" He was most definitely lit, which meant anything he said would be discarded. That was a bonus for us.

"Good grief," Rooster muttered, shaking his head as he crossed the front of the vehicle and headed toward Irene. "We're definitely going to talk."

Gunner, his face drowned in wonder, made a strangled sound as he moved closer to me. "What did you just do?"

"Created a mess," Rooster answered, yanking open the passenger door. "She created a mess."

"You're welcome," I called out, posturing a bit because I enjoyed making Steven cringe. "I believe I managed to save all of us a lot of trouble."

"Oh, yeah?" Rooster was gentle as he helped Irene from the vehicle. "How are we going to explain the door being ripped off? That should go over well."

"Is that what you're worried about?" I made a face as I moved away from Steven, leaving Gunner to watch over him, and strode toward the door. "Geez. Don't be such a baby. It's easy enough to fix."

"We're not mechanics," Rooster shot back. "Er, at least the types of mechanics who can weld a car door in place in less than five minutes. I think that's out of our wheelhouse."

I ignored him and gathered the power pooling in my belly. It had been edgily calling out for me to use it again. It was like a drug at times, and when I started using it I often struggled to stop. Upon release, the magic barreled into the door with enough force that it was lifted from the ground and slammed back to its original resting place. The magic wasn't done; it inched over the door with a glimmering sheen that twinkled and crackled, repairing the damage I'd wrought, and within seconds the vehicle was back to the way it was ... perhaps even a little nicer as some of the dents were now smoothed out.

"Happy?" I brushed my hands off and smiled serenely at Rooster as he shook his head.

"We're definitely going to talk," he warned as he led Irene toward the Cauldron, their steps slow and shuffling. "We're going to talk and talk and talk until we no longer have voices."

I looked to Gunner for approval. "I handled things and nobody got hurt. What does he want?"

"He's not angry with you," Gunner said finally, his voice low and gravelly. "He's just ... we've never seen anyone use that much power in one go. You must understand, you're more than a simple witch."

His awe made me uncomfortable. "I don't think so. It's nice that you think so, but I'm positive I'm just a normal witch."

"No, you're not." He blew out a sigh. "I ... ." He didn't finish what he was going to say, the sound of approaching sirens tearing his attention to the highway. "Go inside. I'll handle my father."

"I'm sure he'll want to question me, too."

"He will. I want to talk to him first. Alone."

I nodded, understanding. "I'll go fix Raisin and then we should be pretty well set to call it a night."

"That sounds like a great idea. I ... wait, how are you going to fix Raisin?"

I didn't answer, instead strolling back toward the door. There was one thing left to do, and I was looking forward to it.

RAISIN WAS HAPPY TO SEE her grandmother, but the pain rolling through the girl in potent waves was so intense it hit me like a tsunami when I entered the bar.

"Is everything okay out there?" Rooster asked as he helped Irene sit.

"Gunner has Steven. Graham is pulling into the parking lot. He wants a moment alone with his father." I didn't mention who *he* was, but I figured it was a given.

"I'm sure he does," Rooster muttered. "That should be a lovely conversation."

"They'll figure it out." I crouched next to Raisin. Her eyes were filled with pain and she was sweating profusely.

"The ambulance should be here soon," Whistler noted, pressing a cold compress to her face. "I think she has internal injuries."

"Yeah." I lifted my hands, which were now glowing blue, and let them hover over Raisin's body. "Two broken ribs," I muttered. "Her spleen is bleeding. She has multiple contusions and a concussion."

Whistler's mouth dropped open. "You can't be serious. Are you a doctor, too?"

"No, but I know how to gauge an injury ... and fix it." I flashed a tight smile for Raisin's benefit. "Just relax. This will be over before you know it and you'll feel like a new person."

"What will be over?" Raisin asked, confused.

"I can heal you."

"What?" Rooster must have been listening from across the room because he jerked up his head. "What do you mean? How can you heal her?"

I shrugged. "I just can. It's something I've always been able to do. Chill out." I started moving my hands, applying the soothing blue magic that accompanied healing without giving it much thought. "It's much better than casts, surgery and aching bones. Trust me."

"But ... ."

If Rooster kept talking, I didn't hear him. I lost myself in my work, floating with the magic as it worked to mend bones and eradicate pain. I moved into a trance, as I always did when utilizing this branch of my magic, and frowned when I heard screaming in the back of my head.

I didn't mean to do it. I should've been prepared for the possibility, but it was already too late when I slipped into Raisin's memories and saw the terror her father had brought to her doorstep tonight. The beating she took at that man's hands as she cried and begged would stay with me for a very long time.

Her screams chilled me to the bone.

And then I realized she wasn't the only one screaming. Someone else was screaming in my head. It was another memory, one from someplace I didn't immediately recognize, and I was being dragged into it. I was already captive in a shard of the past when the reality set in that this wasn't Raisin's memory.

It was my own.

TWENTY-FIVE

*T*he screaming came from a small girl with blond hair and blue eyes. She was tiny — perhaps four years old at the most — and the pain roving her face was enough to turn my bowels into water.

"What am I doing here?" I asked the two women buzzing around the room. They both ignored me, one in favor of taking care of the girl and the other focused on the window.

"I only see one of them," the woman by the window announced. "There's only one. We can still run."

"Not until we heal her," the second woman countered, kneeling by the girl and placing a cold compress to her forehead. "There you go, little one. You'll feel better soon."

The girl had stopped screaming and taken to sniffling as tears dried on her cheeks. There was an open wound on her shoulder, a jagged cut that looked to be deep.

"We need to heal her and get out of here," the woman closest to the window announced. "We can't stay. There's only one of them out there, but soon there will be more." She turned toward the scene on the floor. "We have to pool our resources and heal her magically ... and then flee. There's no time to waste."

"She would do better with time to recover," the second woman protested.

"In an ideal situation, yes." She put her hand to the girl's shoulder and watched as she flinched ... and whimpered. "I'm sorry. You shouldn't have been outside, though. You know better."

"It's probably better for us that she was outside," the other woman noted. "Now we know that they've found us ... again."

"She's hurt."

"It's not the first time. It won't be the last." She sighed and forced a smile for the girl's benefit. "We'll heal you and then get moving. Just ... hold still. This is going to hurt."

The screams started again, forcing me to close my eyes. When I finally opened them again, the wound was gone. All that was left was an oddly-shaped scar, one I recognized.

Instinctively, I reached toward my own shoulder and frowned when I traced the exact same shape that marred my skin. That's when reality hit me, although part of me already recognized what I was seeing.

This wasn't some random child, or a scene from a long-ago horror. This was me ... and it was from the time before I was abandoned at the fire station. It was the only memory I had of my life before everything changed.

The realization sent me spinning, and when I pulled out of the memory I was falling backward to the floor. Raisin, completely healed, chased after me with wide eyes as she tried to catch me.

She was already too late.

"What's wrong?" Bonnie asked, confused. "I don't understand. What just happened?"

That made two of us who didn't understand. I closed my eyes in an attempt to shut out the world. I didn't want to deal with this ... especially now.

"What's going on?" I recognized Gunner's voice as he entered the bar. "What happened?"

"I'm healed," Raisin announced, and I could practically see her grinning even though my eyes remained closed. "I think Scout did something to herself while healing me. She fell over."

"So you guys just left her there?" Gunner's fury was palpable. I felt him growing closer and it sent a shiver down my spine. "Hey." He gentled his voice as he slid an arm under my shoulders and tugged me to a sitting position as he dropped to his knees. "Hey there, superstar." He forced a smile as I slitted my eyes. "I know you're awake. You need to do a better job if you want me to believe you're asleep."

I didn't initially speak. I couldn't. I had no idea what to say.

"Scout, tell me where it hurts." His fingers were gentle as they brushed against my face. "Please, I need to know what's going on here so I can help you."

"What happened to her?" Graham asked, striding into the room. "Is she dying?"

He didn't sound broken up at the prospect, which was enough to get my juices going. I opened my eyes the rest of the way.

"I'm fine," I rasped, frowning at how ragged my voice sounded. "I'm fine," I repeated, trying to clear the phlegm from my voice. It didn't work.

"You don't sound fine," Gunner noted, forcing a smile for my benefit as he brushed my hair from my face. "You sound sick."

"I'm fine." I was determined to prove it, so I fought to remain upright. "I don't get sick."

Gunner didn't look convinced. "Everyone gets sick."

"I don't. Well, other than hangovers. I can get a hangover like everyone else. Other than that, I've never been sick a day in my life."

He looked dubious. "That's not possible."

"Yeah, well ... ."

"You're warm," he pointed out, pressing his hand to my forehead. "I think you might have a fever."

"She probably overloaded," Raisin said sagely. Now healed, she'd gone back to her exuberant self in a matter of seconds. "Maybe she absorbed all the pain I was feeling. That's a thing, right? I've read about empathic witches who take on emotional and physical pain. She took what I was feeling and absorbed it into herself."

"Is that what you did?" Frustration lined Gunner's handsome face. "You really shouldn't have done that. The ambulance is in the parking lot. They could've fixed her."

"That's not what happened," I gritted out, making a face when Graham joined his son on the floor and stared at me. "Stop looking at me as if I'm a circus freak," I barked. "I didn't absorb her pain. That's not how it works."

"How what works?" Graham asked his son.

"I'm not sure," Gunner replied. "She's put on quite the display this evening. Her magic is ... I've never seen anything like it. I don't know anyone who has as much power. She was fine when she walked into the building.

"I was only outside with you a few minutes," he continued. "In that time she healed Raisin and somehow did this to herself."

"I'm fine," I repeated, the dregs from before slowly receding. "Don't worry about me." I was determined to put on a brave face, so I slapped Gunner's hands away. "I don't need to be coddled."

"You're weak," he shot back. "It's not coddling when you're taking care of someone who is genuinely sick."

"I'm not sick!" I thought I would explode. Instead, I rolled to my feet. Sadly, my legs were shaky, as if I was walking on pudding. "See. I'm fine."

"Your hands are shaking," Graham noted. "I don't think you're fine."

"Well, I am." I needed to get out of this place, put some distance between me and the others so I could reflect on what I'd seen in the vision. It was the first time I'd seen myself before the fire station. There had to be a reason I was dragged back to that time and place now. I couldn't think about it in front of an audience, though. "I'm going to head home. If you need me to make a statement, I can come into the station tomorrow."

"You're not driving like this," Graham argued. "It's not going to happen ... especially since you have a motorcycle. You'll crack open your head on the highway."

"I'm fine."

"You're not."

"I am."

Graham refused to back down. "I will arrest you if you try to drive."

Oh, well, he was going to be like that, was he? "Fine. I'll walk."

OKAY, I'M OBSTINATE.

That's the one thing everyone who has ever met me can agree upon. I'm stubborn to a fault and refuse to back down, even on occasions when I would be better off admitting I'm wrong. In this particular case, I couldn't do that. My obstinacy was the only thing holding me upright when I stormed out of the Cauldron.

The parking lot was full of cops and an ambulance. I skirted the side of the building and headed toward the path in the woods. I knew where it led — and it was nowhere near my cabin — but I had to get away.

I didn't think about spriggans lurking in the dark. If they attacked I would fight them off. A quick bout of violence might be good, wash away what I was feeling. I was convinced I wouldn't get that lucky, but when I heard noises behind me my heart skipped a beat and I readied myself.

Instead of an unknown enemy, I found Gunner trailing me in the darkness ... and he didn't look happy.

"I'm fine," I repeated, my voice cracking. "Don't worry about me. I ... I'm fine."

"You're pretty far from fine." His tone wasn't accusatory, just matter-of-fact. "I'm not letting you wander around in the dark on your own."

The sickness from earlier rolled through me. "I'm fine."

"Stop saying that!" His eyes flared with annoyance. "You're the exact opposite of fine. Just ... tell me what happened."

"Nothing happened."

"Something bloody well did happen. I don't know what, but I felt you shaking. Your whole body was quaking to your bones. That's not normal."

"I was just weak from expending so much power." I said the words, but they weren't exactly true. I'd expended double the amount of power on a variety of different occasions and never once felt weak. The reason I was reacting this way was mental ... and that shamed me for some reason.

"It's something else. Tell me."

"I ... ."

"Tell me." He refused to back down and instead invaded my personal space as he gently wrapped his hands around my arms. "If you tell me, I'll do everything in my power to help. Please ... I need to know."

He sounded so sincere I couldn't ignore his pleading. "I saw something."

"What?"

"I don't know." That was the truth, although it felt like a lame answer. "We need to keep walking." I gestured toward the dark pathway. "I can't sit still. It's too much."

"Okay." He didn't object. He also didn't allow me the chance to escape, grabbing my hand and linking our fingers before I could drift too far in front of him. "Let's walk."

I stared at our joined hands for what felt like forever and then, because there was nothing else to do, I started walking.

"This is weird," I said after a few minutes.

"Walking in the dark after the night we've had? I agree, totally weird. You need to decompress. I find walking is the best way to decompress."

"Not *that*." I gestured toward our hands. "That!"

"People hold hands all the time." He didn't back down. "I happen to like it. You'll get used to it."

He sounded sure of himself, which set my teeth on edge.

"Tell me what happened." This time when he spoke his tone was gentle. "I want to hear it."

I heaved out a sigh. There would be no getting out of this. He wouldn't allow it. "I don't know what happened. One second I was healing Raisin. I know better than to slip into memories when I'm using that particular magic, but I think I was a little tired because my defenses were down and I accidentally slipped through realities before I realized what was happening.

"I saw what happened to her earlier," I continued. "The fear was close to the surface for her, the memory was right there, so I saw it. It's happened before. It's not ideal, but I've never had trouble turning it off before."

"Something changed tonight," he prodded.

"I ... ."

"I won't judge you," he repeated. "I want to help. Don't put up a wall now. That will only tick me off."

He sounded so frustrated all I could do was laugh. It was a weak chuckle, but it loosened one of the knots in my chest. "We wouldn't want that."

"No," he agreed.

"I started in one memory and then hopped to another," I volunteered. "I don't know how to explain it. I just ... hopped to a different time and place."

"I don't understand how you do any of it, but I believe you're extremely powerful. I've seen you in action. You can do anything," he said. "What was the second memory?"

"Me." My voice was barely a whisper.

"You? Are you saying you saw yourself going through Raisin's ordeal in her place?" He looked stricken at the thought.

"I'm saying that I slipped from her memory to one of mine. The thing is, it was from before."

"Before when?"

"Before I was dropped off at the fire station."

"Oh." His face drained of color. "Oh." He gripped my hand tighter. "Seeing Raisin abused by her father made you remember something. God, I don't want to know what that something is, but ... if you need to tell me ... ." He left it hanging.

"That's not what I saw," I corrected quickly. "I saw myself as a child. I was hurt, my shoulder was bleeding. There were two women with me. One was staring out a window, talking about some enemy we had to run from. The other was trying to treat my wound."

"Well, that doesn't sound terrible," he said. "They weren't yelling at you or anything, right?"

"No. But I was crying. I was in pain. They insisted on healing me."

"They had healing magic, too? You know that's not a normal gift, right? In fact, I've never heard of a witch having the power to heal. I've heard of kitchen witches who could brew powerful remedies, but what you pulled off today is entirely different."

"I researched my gifts when I first joined Spells Angels," I countered. "There were witches in the past who could heal people. It's one of those gifts that have sort of disappeared over the years, probably because medical science has advanced."

"I don't know that I believe that, but it's hardly the most important thing to focus on this evening," he said. "They healed you and then what?"

"Nothing. It hurt. It hurt more than what I did to Raisin. I screamed again – or little me did, to be more exact – and it was shocking to hear that coming from ... me. It was weird, like I was an interloper in my own life. I don't know how to explain it."

"I don't blame you for feeling weird. I don't know what I would do in similar circumstances."

"It shook me, but the worst part was when I saw the scar. I still have that scar on my shoulder."

By now we'd made it to the neighborhood on the other side of the pathway and were standing under a streetlight. Gunner motioned for me to slow down and then inclined his chin toward my shoulder. "Show me," he prodded.

"It's just a scar."

"Show me. I want to see."

Because I needed to share my ordeal with someone, I pulled my hand from his and tugged on the neckline of my shirt, dragging it to the side so he could see the scar. His fingers lightly traced the puffy residue of an old injury I didn't remember getting until this very night, his expression grave.

"That's a distinctive scar," he said finally. "It looks as if you were stabbed with a jagged knife."

"I don't remember how I got it. I don't even remember healing from it. What I saw was from a position outside the memory. It didn't really belong to me ... and yet it did."

"Well ... ." He broke off, clearly unsure what to say. Instead of finishing, he rubbed his hands up and down my shoulders and leaned forward to rest his forehead against mine. "You've had quite the night."

"Yup."

"I don't know how to help you, but I'm going to figure something out. Clearly there is part of you that is trying to remember what happened."

"I never really thought about it before," I admitted. "It was too painful. I got this buzzing in my ear when I tried. But tonight seeing myself was sort of a revelation. It made things more real."

"We'll figure it out." He pulled me in tight against him and brushed his lips over the corner of my mouth, causing me to freeze in his arms as a tingling sensation rushed through my body, like a magic beacon of warmth taking me over. "Don't do that," he admonished. "I'm not going to pressure you to do anything. I just ... felt the urge to kiss you. That wasn't a real kiss anyway. It was only half a kiss."

"Why?"

"Because it wasn't a full on-the-mouth kiss."

I rolled my eyes. "Not that. Why did you feel the urge to kiss me?"

"I have no idea." He chuckled as he pulled back and stared into my eyes. "I'm feeling a lot of feelings I can't explain."

"It's probably the adrenalin," I said hurriedly. "Those feelings will fade."

"I don't think so, but we're definitely not talking about that tonight. In fact ... ." He trailed off, and when I tilted my head I realized he was staring at someone else entirely.

Even though I'd barely registered it, we were in front of All Souls

Church ... and Cecily was standing in the parking lot watching us. She didn't look thrilled with our sudden appearance.

"Hey." Gunner offered her a lame wave. "Nice, night, huh?" He took a step in her direction. I had no idea what he had planned. Instead of crossing the border of the church's property, he smacked into an invisible barrier that bounced him back. "What the ... ?"

I was as confused as he was. "What is that?" I extended my fingers, frowning when they ran into something hard, something that was somehow transparent and solid at the same time. "It's a force field of some sort," I murmured.

"I noticed." Gunner drilled a smug-looking Cecily with a pointed look. "What's going on?"

"He is the resurrection and the light," Cecily replied. "Only true believers may pray with us. You're not true believers."

"Yeah, but ... do you really think no one is going to notice ... this?"

"He doesn't care who notices. He only cares that we do his bidding. We have, so ... nighty-night." She gave us a finger wave before climbing into her car. All the while, she laughed like a loon.

"Okay, that was creepy," I muttered, watching as she pulled out of the parking lot and drove in the opposite direction. Whatever the barrier was, it clearly didn't stop her from leaving ... just us from crossing over and invading their territory. "What do you make of that?"

"Nothing good."

TWENTY-SIX

*G*unner and I spent thirty minutes trying to breach the barrier surrounding the church to no avail. I had a few ideas, but I wanted to rest and recharge before unleashing them. Besides, it was getting late and Gunner wanted to check on those we'd left behind at The Rusty Cauldron.

By the time we returned, the place was mostly empty. Only Graham, Rooster and Whistler remained, all drinking whiskey at a table.

"I wondered if you were coming back," Graham said before he downed a shot. "I guess I lost that bet."

Whistler snickered and held out his hand. "I told you they'd be back. Where's my twenty bucks?"

"Yeah, yeah, yeah." Graham's expression was hard to read as he dug in his wallet and came back with a crisp twenty-dollar bill. "I thought maybe you two decided to work out your frustrations together."

I was mortified by what he insinuated. "Excuse me?"

"Ignore him," Gunner instructed, his expression dark. "He's not digging at you. He's digging at me."

"Hey, I'm just glad you're finally showing interest in a woman," Graham drawled. "I thought for sure there were no grandchildren in my future. My worry, however, is that this particular woman apparently has the ability to blow Hawthorne Hollow off the map."

I stiffened, frustrated. "I do not."

"She's fine," Gunner countered, rubbing his hand against my back. "But if you truly believe she's that powerful you might not want to mess with her right now. I mean ... she is dangerous."

Graham's expression darkened as Gunner led me closer to the table. "Point taken. Why are you guys back?"

"We went for a walk so Scout could calm down," Gunner responded. "She's fine now, feeling frisky and fun." He sent me a flirty wink. "We discovered another problem while we were out, though, and we think it bears discussing."

"Oh, geez." Rooster dropped his head into his hand. "Do I even want to know?"

"Probably not," Gunner replied. "But you're part of the team. We all have to deal with this issue."

Rooster was resigned. "Lay it on me."

"There's a barrier around All Souls Church."

The three men sat in silence for a beat. Graham was the first to speak.

"They put up a fence?"

"No, they didn't put up a fence," Gunner sneered at his father. "They put up a magical barrier ... and we can't cross it. We spent thirty minutes trying."

"I actually have some ideas on that," I offered, "but I need to sleep on it first."

"So ... they erected a magical barrier?" Rooster rubbed his chin, thoughtful. "How?"

"I don't know," Gunner replied.

"Why would they erect it?" Whistler asked.

"I don't know for sure, but I think it has something to do with our visit earlier." Gunner cast me a sidelong look. "They must know Scout was in the basement."

"Hold up." Graham waved a hand to get everybody's attention. "Why were you in the church basement, young lady?"

"Because I was trying to find the source of the chanting," I replied automatically. "And don't call me 'young lady.'"

"What chanting?"

"The chanting I heard the night I broke in."

Graham looked exasperated. "Oh, good grief! I can't even believe ... I just ... way to go, son." He flashed Gunner a sarcastic thumbs-up. "You finally found someone you like, and she's crazy."

Gunner didn't appear bothered by his father's response. "We're not here to talk about that. I'm taking Scout home. She's had a long day and needs some sleep. We just wanted you to know about the barrier so you can start dealing with it tomorrow."

"I can't tell you how much I look forward to that," Graham snarked.

"Speaking of tonight," I interrupted, "are Raisin and Irene okay?"

"They are," Rooster confirmed. "Bonnie took them home, got them settled, performed a little magic to get the house back in order. She's sleeping on the couch tonight so they feel safe, although it doesn't really matter. Steven is locked up and there's no chance he'll be getting out anytime soon."

"I believe our esteemed chief said the same thing yesterday," I pointed out.

Graham scowled. "Hey, it's not my fault he called an attorney who actually managed to bend the ear of a judge and get bail. Heck, I didn't think he had the money to cover bail."

"Yeah, well, I'm pretty sure he got that money selling meth," I noted.

"I've heard your hunch. I'll need you to point me in the right direction for his cook house. If you can find it for me, he won't ever get out of jail. That will be the best thing for Ruthie."

"I'll find it," I promised, rubbing my forehead. "I need some sleep right now. Come tomorrow, we'll have to figure a way around that barrier."

Rooster nodded at Gunner, something unsaid passing between them. "You guys get some sleep. We'll talk about the rest of it tomorrow."

"I'll also need a written statement from you," Graham added, his eyes on me. "I need it on the record to make sure there are no questions about what happened tonight."

"No problem. I'll get right on that for you."

"Yeah. I'll be reminding you in case you forget."

"I really will type it up."

"I look forward to reading that particular piece of fiction."

GUNNER LOADED MY BIKE in the back of the furniture truck — which he seemed to have endless access to — and drove me home. I helped him unload it and park it in the driveway.

He insisted on walking me to the door, which had the butterflies in my stomach dancing a particularly festive jig, but he didn't make a move when I stepped over the threshold.

"Well, um, thanks for bringing me home. Sorry about the whole meltdown thing."

He chuckled. "It's okay. I think you held it together much better than most people would have."

"I'm not sure I believe that, but thanks anyway." I stepped completely inside and moved to shut the door. "I guess I'll see you tomorrow. I ... ." I couldn't shut the door because he was blocking my effort and following me inside. "What are you doing?"

"Spending the night," he replied without hesitation. "You're too upset to stay by yourself."

"I am not upset." My voice was shriller than I intended. "I am completely put together. Like ... totally awesome and great."

"You *are* awesome and great," he agreed, refusing to move no matter how much I jiggled the door. "But you're not staying alone. It's not just what happened with Steven ... and the memory. It's also what happened at the church. The only reason they would erect that barrier is because they're suspicious.

"I don't know if they're suspicious of you, but I'm not risking it," he continued. "I'm sticking close ... and that means sleeping here."

I was flustered, a rarity. "The couch is uncomfortable. It's meant for a short person. You won't be able to sleep there."

"I know. That's why I'm sharing your bed."

"Excuse me?"

His grin widened. "I promise I won't take advantage of you. I won't kiss you ... or touch you ... or cuddle under the covers. I just want to sleep. I might cuddle with the cat."

"You can't just share a bed with me," I complained, making a face. "That's not normal."

"Perhaps not, but we'll make it work." He pushed open the door to step inside before shutting and locking it. "We're grownups. We both need sleep. Neither one of us are going to get it if you're here alone. This is the best compromise."

I wasn't convinced. "What if you can't keep your hands off me?" I challenged. "That will create a situation in which I'll be forced to kill you."

Rather than be offended, he leaned closer. "I can control myself."

While a welcome sentiment, it didn't do much for my ego. "What if you can't?"

"I think you'll be surprised." He pointed toward the bedroom. "Now, march. I'm asleep on my feet and we've got a busy day tomorrow."

I thought back on the invisible barrier, the magic I felt rippling beneath it, and sighed. "We are," I agreed. "You'd better keep your hands to yourself."

"I was just about to give you the same warning."

I WOKE TO DARKNESS.

I didn't remember falling asleep. So certain was I that I would never be able to rest thanks to Gunner's presence in my bed — in nothing more than boxer shorts, no less — I resigned myself to counting sheep. I didn't make it past five before I passed out, and I didn't wake once throughout the night.

I had no idea what time it was, and when I looked to the nightstand for my phone I realized I'd left it in the kitchen the previous evening. A quick glance at the empty spot next to me said Gunner was already up, but I didn't know if he was still in the cabin or had returned to his house to get ready for the day.

I ran my hand over the empty spot, found it still warm, and decided to check the kitchen. If he'd left, he'd done so recently. It was a better guess that he was in the kitchen, perhaps hanging out with the traitorous cat who had snuggled between us, a paw on his chest, the entire night.

Sure enough, I found Gunner in the kitchen. He was still in his boxer shorts, his hair messy from sleep. He was staring at the instructions on the coffee can. He smiled when he heard me approaching. Even though I was annoyed by his insistence on spending the night, I couldn't deny he looked appealing ... which made me hate every hormone coursing through my body.

"Good morning," I murmured.

"Good morning, Sunshine," he teased. "How did you sleep?"

"Hard."

"I noticed the snoring."

"Ha, ha." I padded closer to him. "Why is there no coffee?"

"I have a Keurig. I was trying to figure out how much coffee I'm supposed to put in the filter. It's been a while since I've seen one of these."

"Oh, let me." I used my hip to nudge him out of the way. "I like my coffee strong. You'll have to suffer through it if you don't like it. I ... ." I trailed off when I realized we weren't alone. Honestly, I should've picked up on the fact that another person was sitting at the kitchen table, but I was still waking up and it hadn't occurred to me that someone could possibly visit without me being aware.

"Mama Moon?" I made a face as I immediately moved my hands to my clothes to make sure I was covered.

Gunner chuckled at my reaction. "I like that you would've been fine if you were naked in front of me. That's progress."

I shot him a withering look. "Why didn't you tell me she was here?"

"I thought you saw her. You're clearly a bit slow in the morning."

"Not usually." I scowled at Mama Moon, who was relaxing in her chair ... and looking completely at ease with the situation. "Hello, young lady."

"My name is Scout," I said automatically. "You can either call me that or Ms. Randall. I don't care which. Don't call me 'young lady.' I don't like it."

She snickered. "I see you're getting fired up. That's good. I like seeing that."

"Yeah, yeah, yeah." I shook my head, frustrated. "Why are you here? I don't remember inviting you to my house."

"I wouldn't exactly call this a house, but it has potential if you're willing to put in the effort." She pursed her lips as she regarded me. Gunner had supplied her with a bottle of water, but she'd yet to crack it open. "I'm here because news is spreading fast in magical circles. The folks at All Souls Church are up to something."

Oh, well, she was here to rat on others. I should've seen that coming. "And how many magical circles are buzzing about this area?" I asked, genuinely curious.

She shrugged. "Enough that we can take care of ourselves when trouble hits. The problem is, this trouble has been building for a long time."

"If you believe that, why didn't you say something sooner?" Gunner challenged, taking the filter away from me so he could keep measuring coffee. "Why not warn everyone that they posed a threat?"

"I did warn people. I warned your father."

Gunner stilled. "He failed to mention that."

"Your father and I don't have the easiest of relationships," Mama Moon conceded. "It goes back a long time, and I doubt things will get better between us. That doesn't change the fact that I've always been suspicious of that group."

"What do you think they're doing?" I asked, easing a hip against the counter as Gunner snapped the filter drawer in place and pressed the button to percolate the coffee. "You must have a few suspicions."

"I do. I'm not sure you'll believe me."

"Try us," Gunner suggested, taking me by surprise when he moved behind me and slipped an arm around my waist.

I slid him a sidelong look. "What are you doing?"

"Trying this on for size," he replied, unruffled. "It's kind of nice. We're sharing a quiet morning together, coffee and conversation. Sure, we're dealing with the woman who got blown across a room a few days ago because she tried to see inside your head and we haven't really defined anything yet. Still, it's nice."

I had no idea how to respond. "I think you're getting nuttier with every passing moment."

"Yeah? I think I'm awesome." He gave me a wink. "We'll talk about that later." He didn't move his arm from my waist, and curse the blue moon, it felt nice. I wanted to smack him around, exert dominance, but I couldn't make myself push him away. It was utterly disgusting.

"Tell us what you think is going on with the group," he instructed Mama Moon, whose eyes sparkled as she chuckled.

"I think they're playing with forces they don't understand and trying to raise the dead."

I ran my tongue over my teeth as I exchanged a quick look with Gunner. "You mean like zombies?" I asked finally in an attempt to test her.

"Not zombies, no," she countered. "Something else. Something ... different. The magic we're dealing with is older and it's being wielded by people who don't understand it."

I was understandably confused. "How old?"

"Try ancient Egypt."

I stilled, something clicking in the back of my head. "Mummies," I blurted out suddenly, my heart skipping a beat. "They're mummies. That's why they didn't check off all the boxes for zombies. They're kind of like zombies, but not really."

"You're smarter than you look." Mama Moon winked at me as she tapped the side of her head. "Mummies is correct."

"Mummies are draped in rags," Gunner argued. "Also, they're not real."

"They're not common," Mama Moon corrected. "They haven't

been popular in a very long time. Zombies get all the attention now because they're easier to raise. Mummies are stronger, though. There was a time they were even capable of passing as human, which I think is what our esteemed group is trying to do."

I didn't understand. "They're trying to raise a dead man who can pass for human? But ... why?"

"Not necessarily a dead *man*."

I stared at her for a beat. "A creature from another plane. That's what they're trying to call to."

"He is the resurrection and the light," Mama Moon intoned, grinning.

"Oh, geez." I felt sick to my stomach. "They're trying to create their own prophet, essentially prove their own religion. It's a game."

"Not a game." She tsked as she shook her head. "This is pretty far from a game. It's real, and the stakes are real."

"They've erected a barrier," Gunner noted. "We can't get in. We think it's because they know we've been spying on them."

Mama Moon nodded. "Some sort of alarm was sounded yesterday afternoon. I'd say it's because of something you did."

"We broke in and found a zombie — er, mummy — in the basement," I said. "That must mean they intend to accelerate their timetable." I dragged a hand through my snarled hair. "We've got to figure out a way to get through that barrier if we want to take them down. They're protecting themselves in the hope that they can hold out until they finish ... well, whatever it is they're doing."

"That barrier is strong, but you're stronger," Mama Moon said. "You can break it if you put your mind to it. It will take some time, but you're smart enough to do it. More importantly, you're strong enough to do it."

The words were nice, but I felt helpless. "I don't know what to do."

"You'll figure it out." Mama Moon winked. "You're more than a normal witch, after all. I figured that out the moment I saw you. Now you simply need to have faith in yourself and let the magic flow. You were born to do this."

"Do you know what I am?" I asked, suspicious.

"No, but you're powerful. I think you have all the answers you need locked up here." She tapped her forehead. "Unlocking them won't be easy, but you're strong enough to make it happen."

"We have to make this happen first," Gunner said. "We have to take down that church. How do we do that?"

"I can't help you there." Mama Moon slowly got to her feet. "That's Rooster's domain. He should be able to figure it out. He always does."

TWENTY-SEVEN

$\mathcal{W}$e started by fortifying ourselves, eating the leftover doughnuts from the previous day. The sugar was good, and got me going. I thought we would leave after that, get cleaned up and head back to the church. Instead, Gunner climbed back into bed and started flipping through the grimoire.

"What are you doing?" I asked, nervously following him and hovering in the open doorway. "I ... are you taking a nap?"

He smirked, obviously amused. "I'm trying to figure out this book. I want to know why Hal had it. More importantly, I want to know why Cecily — or Father Bram, for that matter — didn't reclaim it once he was dead."

"Maybe they didn't realize he had it," I suggested, grunting when I stubbed my toe against something on the floor and swearing under my breath as I bent over to pick it up. It was buried under my jeans from the previous day, which were in desperate need of being washed after all the excitement and magical upheaval.

"I guess that's possible. Listen, we need to talk."

The abrupt shift in his demeanor had me standing straight. "What? I didn't do anything."

He chuckled. "I didn't say you did. Come over here." He patted the side of the bed, making me instantly suspicious.

"We don't have time for that," I complained. "We have research to conduct."

"I know we don't have time. Please, sit with me."

I remained alert as I crossed to the other side of the bed and climbed on. I told myself this was only happening because I didn't have any decent furniture in the living room — something that would be corrected quickly — and the amount of time we were spending together meant absolutely nothing.

Yeah, I didn't really believe it either.

"There's something here," he started, wagging his finger between the two of us. "I know you feel it."

"I ... ."

"Shh." He pressed the finger to my lips and grinned at my outrage. "We can't deal with it right now. We can't even talk about it right now, because it's a lot of stuff. After this is over we'll have time to discuss things.

"Until then, I want you to stop worrying about me making a move on you," he continued. "It won't happen. I want time to get to know you, perhaps a night out that doesn't involve breaking and entering or ripping the door off a vehicle to get at a horrible man.

"I'm attracted to you," he admitted. "It makes me feel weird because I'm not keen on the idea of dating a co-worker. Still, I can't stop thinking about you, so I'm going to try dating you. Do you think you can handle that?"

I narrowed my eyes. "You keep bringing it up. I want to pretend it's not happening."

"Yes, well, I don't think that's wise either. For now, we have to focus on work. I know it's going to be difficult for you because of all that drooling you do whenever I'm around, but try to hold it together."

The impish light in his eyes was charming. His ego was not. "You might get a surprise if you're not careful," I warned. "There's a very good chance I won't want to date you once everything is done."

"Oh, I don't believe that." He winked. "I plan to knock your socks off ... maybe even literally. This is more important, though ... for the time being."

At least we agreed on that. "Let's focus on the book. There has to be a key we're missing."

"Right. That's exactly what I was saying." Gunner shifted so he could get comfortable, his eyes momentarily tracking to the item I picked up from the floor before getting distracted. "What's that?"

"What?" I glanced at the prayer book I'd lifted from the box in the basement before I'd been distracted by the mummy. "I stole it from the church yesterday and forgot about it."

He took the book from me and flipped it open, making a face when he read the first page. "He is the resurrection and the light. He will cross boundaries from one plane to the next, rendering this world his playground and the previous one a wasteland." He frowned. "That's cheery."

"Yeah, well ... ." I pursed my lips when I caught sight of the illustration below the words. "Is that a mirror?"

"It is," he confirmed. "It looks to be an antique mirror."

"Yeah." I took the book and stared at the hand-drawn illustration. "I've seen this mirror."

"I have, too, now that you mention it." Gunner started flipping through the grimoire. "I've seen it in here."

I flicked my eyes to the page he indicated, bolting upright at the two illustrations side by side. "Holy ... !"

"Do you think the mirror is important?" he asked.

"This grimoire is a hodgepodge of texts and illustrations that spans a great number of years," I noted. "There's Sanskrit, Aramaic, Biblical Hebrew and Middle English. We talked about it before, but I'm starting to think this book was written long after those languages were considered dead."

"Because people wanted to hide what they were writing in here?"

"That would be my guess. The book is in too good of shape to have been written when those languages were in use. There's every possibility the information was traced over every few years and included in a different book, but at some point they were all joined together like this ... and there has to be a reason."

"You think the mirror is the reason," Gunner mused, his eyes drifting back to the illustration. "Do you think it's a talisman?"

"I think it's a portal." I thought back to what I saw in Father Bram's dressing room. "I think it's an active portal at that."

"What sort of portal?"

"One that allows you to travel between two planes, one living and dead. It might explain what happened to Hal's body to boot."

"Oh, well, now you have my full attention." Gunner was rapt as he pushed my hair from my face. "You think this mirror is in Hawthorne Hollow, don't you?"

"I know it is. I saw it." I related my two interactions with the mirror, leaving nothing out. When I was done, he was irate.

"You failed to mention the mirror to me," he complained, his tone accusatory.

"I forgot." That was mostly true. The red eyes I saw in the mirror as I was fleeing jolted me, but the mummy giving chase had eradicated almost everything else from my mind. "I was worried about other things ... like the mummy."

"And then Raisin," he surmised, exhaling heavily. "Okay. I don't want to argue, so I'll accept your apology."

"I didn't apologize."

"Close enough."

He was annoying when he wanted to be. "That doesn't change the fact that the mirror is in the church ... and we're now closed off from the mirror."

"You said that you think the mirror explains what happened to Hal's body," he prodded. "How?"

"A mirror is a flat surface," I replied, my mind working overtime. "Hal's face wasn't cut off, it was simply missing, flat."

"You think he somehow tried to travel between two worlds and something went wrong."

"Definitely." I tapped my chin as I stared at the prayer book. "What if Hal wasn't working with the church, but instead wanted to master the secrets of the mirror for a different reason?"

"What reason would that be?"

I shrugged. "He's older. Maybe he wanted to cheat death."

"Okay, he wanted to live forever. He found the grimoire and he was doing research and somehow managed to track the mirror. That's taking a few leaps, but I can believe it."

"It also explains why the church members didn't break into his house after his death and steal the grimoire," I noted. "They didn't know it existed. He ended up dead ... and not in that field. They found him at the church. Either his trip was cut short or someone cut it short, and he died. That left them with a body they had to dispose of."

"And the trail isn't far from the church," Gunner mused. "They waited until night, carried him out and dumped him on the other side of the woods."

"Close to the Cauldron," I added. "Perhaps they thought we would make good suspects because we ride motorcycles and hang out at a bar all day."

"Weirder things have happened." He held up both books so he could compare the mirrors. "These are illustrations of the same mirror. There's no doubt about that."

"It's a portal." I was certain of it. "I saw what lived on the other side. I have no idea if they're trying to resurrect someone specific or if a demon somehow bamboozled them and he's the one they're trying to help, but whatever that thing I saw is, it wants to come to this side."

"Which would be disastrous."

"Definitely." I bobbed my head. "They've been experimenting with bringing people back. They started with Herbert. It worked relatively well, and they could order him around because he was mindless. He was a toy. They weren't thrilled about losing him, but it was an experiment and they learned from it.

"Then came your wrestling coach," I continued. "His body was old, but it didn't look as if it had been underground long. Heck, he might've been raised not long after his death for all we know. He could've been in that basement the entire time."

"We need to release him." Gunner was grim. "I can't stand the idea of him being dragged back to this side like that ... and before you say his soul might've remained behind, I don't think so. You said Herbert had a pulse. I think his soul was attached to his body."

I wanted to comfort him, but he wasn't wrong. The odds of the souls being separated from the bodies were slim. That was the main difference between mummies and zombies. "We'll make sure we release him." I patted his hand before turning to the nightstand and grabbing my computer. "I need to call Mike."

Gunner's eyebrows flew up his forehead. "Why? Is now really the time for that?"

"Um, yeah. Father Bram is hiding something important and we need to figure out what it is before we move on them. That barrier will take work to come down. I have an idea about that."

"If it involves fire, I strongly suggest you come up with a different plan."

I shot him a look. "Listen, smarty pants ... ."

He caught my finger as I wagged it in his face. "Oh, it's cute how we already have nicknames for each other," he drawled. "I'm going to call you droopy drawers."

I scowled. "I'll kill you if you try."

He chuckled. "What's your idea?"

"We need to talk to Mike first." I was firm on that. My idea didn't necessarily hinge on the information he could provide, but I wasn't quite finished sorting through my magical options. "I'll tell you as soon as I'm done talking to him."

"Yes, let's talk to Mike." Gunner shifted so he could stare at the screen with me. "Have you ever seen this guy naked?"

I slid him a sidelong look as I hit the "connect" button to place the call. "Why do you care?"

"Because he bugs me."

"Maybe you bug him."

"I hope so." He offered me a saucy wink. "I'm good at bugging people."

"I noticed."

Mike, bleary-eyed and still in his pajamas, answered the call. "This had better be good."

"And don't you look fresh as a daisy this morning," I supplied, enjoying the way he glared at me. "I forgot you're not a morning person."

"You're usually not a morning person either," he pointed out, throwing himself into the chair with an exaggerated sigh. "Why are you up at this ungodly hour?"

"It's almost ten," Gunner pointed out.

Mike shifted his gaze to him. "Are you two in bed together?" He knit his eyebrows, frustration evident. "Ugh. I'm so grossed out."

"Join the club," Gunner said. "You wouldn't believe the way she drools. Really, it's disgusting. It's a good thing she looks good naked, because otherwise ... yuck."

It took everything I had not to roll over and smother him with a pillow. "You are a disgusting individual."

"I am," he agreed, grinning.

"I don't even want to know what's going on between the two of you," Mike complained. "It will seriously turn my stomach. I can't stand either one of you right now."

"Oh, poor baby." I offered a teasing smile and then sobered. "Please tell me you have more information on Father Bram. We have something of a situation here, and it's going to come to a head today. The more information we have, the better off everyone will be."

"I have something," he confirmed. "It's weird, but I have information."

"Lay it on me."

"Okay." Mike rubbed his eyes and then focused on his screen. "Brian McNamara grew up in Minnesota. His father was a grifter who was arrested a good twenty times on a variety of charges. Most of those instances involved romancing older women who happened to be lonely and then draining their bank accounts."

"He sounds lovely," I muttered, shaking my head.

"Yeah, well, he romanced the wrong woman and her son got involved," Mike explained. "He was irate because he felt that money should've gone to him — he was a real jackass, quite frankly, and only took care of his mother for the inheritance — and he lost his mind and shot and killed him!"

"Oh, wow." I rubbed my forehead. "That is ... wow!"

"Pretty much," Mike confirmed. "Brian was sixteen at the time. He'd been learning from his father for years. I'm not sure what happened to his mother. She's listed on the birth certificate, but she disappeared when he was eight."

"Is it possible that his father killed his mother?" Gunner asked.

"Anything is possible, but there's no record of that. She simply fell off the face of the earth. It's possible she took off because she didn't like the life she was living."

"I guess."

"Brian lived with an aunt until he was eighteen and could strike out on his own," Mike said. "He picked up right where his father left off. He was too young to play gigolo — at least at first — so he ran property scams and the like. It was one of those old property scams that caused the church to lose its non-profit status."

I perked up, intrigued. "Do tell."

"There's not much to tell. Twenty years ago he convinced a bunch of people to invest in waterfront condos that never came to fruition. He ran with the money, left Chicago, where he was living at the time under the name Brian Markham.

"I don't know where he went after that," he continued. "I'm sure he was grifting, perhaps living off the stolen money for a long time, but he didn't reappear on the radar screen until he adopted the Father Bram persona twelve years ago.

"He started out learning in Unitarian and Methodist churches, but I don't know why he chose them. It could be because they're more open or something, but you'll have to ask him that question. His upward mobility was stymied in both outfits after a short time."

"That must be why he decided to start his own religion," Gunner said. "He couldn't be the boss if he followed someone else's rules, so he had to make his own."

"I'm guessing you're right," Mike said. "He registered the religion, jumped through all the necessary hoops relatively quickly, and secured non-profit status. He probably thought he'd found a goldmine or something.

"The problem is, to get the non-profit status he had to register under his real Social Security number," he continued. "He was wanted for fraud in Minnesota under that number, so eventually the government caught up to him. It took a full two years."

"So, they stripped his nonprofit status, which essentially takes money out of his pockets," I said. "How does that lead him to discovering the magic mirror and raising mummies? I just don't understand the jump."

Mike's mouth dropped open. "Mummies?"

"Er ... ."

"Way to go, big mouth," Gunner chided, grinning.

"Don't worry about the mummies," I said. "They're not important. Thanks for the information, though. I think it will prove helpful."

"No problem." Mike waved off the gratitude. "Talk to you soon. I want to hear more about the mummies ... and that dude." He glared at Gunner. "I definitely want to know what you're doing with that dude."

"It's a really long story."

"And it has a happy ending," Gunner added, reaching for the disconnect button. "Thank you so much, Mike. We'll take it from here."

I glared at him when the screen went dark. "That was rude."

"I don't like the way he looks at you."

"You realize we've known each other less than a week, right?" I challenged. "I had a long and fulfilling life before we collided."

"Yes, but things are going to be better now. Just you wait." He grinned as I rolled my eyes. "Now, tell me your plan for the barrier. You have your information. Does it involve fire?"

"You really don't want to know the answer to that."

His smile slipped. "Oh, I just knew you were going to burn something before this was all over. This is going to suck."

"You don't know that. It could be fun."

"No, it's going to suck."

"Well, at least your head is in a good place for this mission. I would hate to think you were looking at the dark side of things."

"Yup. It's definitely going to suck."

I couldn't decide if he was right. Things really were up in the air.

TWENTY-EIGHT

*R*ooster, Bonnie, Marissa and Whistler were waiting for us when we arrived at All Souls Church. They looked ready for battle, but the barrier was obviously in place and they were stuck on the opposite side of the road.

"We're starting to draw looky-loos," Rooster complained as he greeted us. "There's no way we can move on the church with so many people watching."

I glanced over his shoulder to where a group of residents had grouped together. There had to be at least six of them, and they had their heads bent together as they whispered. Clearly they sensed something was about to go down. "Don't worry about them."

Rooster arched a dubious eyebrow. "Don't worry? Secrecy is important, young lady. You haven't forgotten that, have you?"

"No. I have the crowd under control. And don't call me 'young lady.'"

"Would you like to explain to the class how you're going to ensure that?"

"Sure." I flashed a tight smile. "Will you hold this for me?" I handed him the prayer book and raised my hands. "Just give me one second."

"What is she doing?" Bonnie asked, ambling over.

"Probably showing off some more," Marissa muttered. "Does anyone else think all she's done since arriving is show off?"

"No." Gunner shot her a look. "It's not as if she's trying to get people to call her Foxy or anything."

"I am foxy," Marissa shot back.

"Whatever." He turned back to me as I gathered my magic. "What are you going to do?"

"Don't worry. The fire portion of today's festivities isn't up yet. This is more of a ... wet thing."

"Wet? I ... ." He broke off at the rumble of thunder, his eyes flying to the sky as storm clouds appeared out of nowhere and obliterated the sun. They rolled in so fast it was almost as if someone had pressed "fast forward" on a remote control.

The people across the road started murmuring, as if they were surprised to be caught in a storm. Within seconds, they started hurrying toward their homes. None of them made it before the rain came. With a terrific crack of lightning, followed closely by a deafening roar of thunder, a deluge started ... and forced prying eyes indoors, where they belonged.

"Well, that's great," Rooster commented, wiping his hand over his forehead as rain drenched us. "That is just ... awesome."

"I hate it when my hair gets wet," Marissa groused. "It curls when it's wet. Do you have any idea how difficult poodle hair is to deal with?"

Whistler snorted. "Poodle hair. Now that's funny."

"The storm won't last forever," I warned, drawing everyone's attention. "We have to be quick."

"The rain is great for getting them off the street," Rooster said, "but that won't stop them from looking out their windows."

"No," I agreed. "But they won't be able to see anything. The storm is a glamour. It obliterates what we're doing. I designed the spell so it was two-fold, a way to give us cover and also a way to protect them, keep them away from the action, so to speak."

Bonnie's mouth dropped open. "Are you kidding? That's some freaking deep magic."

"We're definitely going to talk," Rooster stressed. "I mean ... it could take days at this rate."

"I can't wait. For now, though, we need to get through the barrier and to that mirror. I'm guessing they didn't move it. They thought the barrier would be enough to keep us out until they finished whatever ritual they're enacting.

"Look at the windows," I instructed. "A few people are watching from inside. Notice they didn't come out to greet us. They'll be the ones standing between us and the mirror."

"We have to be careful," Gunner intoned. "The people inside ... some of them aren't our enemies. They're simply misguided souls who were bamboozled. The problem is going to be deciding who the enemy is. Does anyone have any suggestions on that?"

I automatically raised my hand.

"Oh, I was afraid you were going to be the one with the suggestion," he lamented, briefly pressing his eyes shut. "I just ... you're so much work."

I grinned at him. "We'll drop a sleeping spell on them. It's basically a modified version of a fairytale sleeping curse, only they don't have to eat or drink anything. I can tailor it to put the innocents to sleep so we'll know the people left standing are truly evil."

"And how do you know how to do that?" Marissa asked, incredulous.

I shrugged. "I read about sleeping curses when I was a kid and tried one in the group home where I lived. It worked like a charm ... except for the fact that the two people who were left awake were murderers and I had to take care of them before anyone else woke up."

Rooster shook his head. "Geez. I just ... geez."

I flashed a smile. "It's okay. There's no reason to get worked up. I know what I'm doing."

"You're terrifying," he muttered.

"She's also our best shot at ending this," Gunner noted. "We have to follow her lead. She'll get us past the barrier ... and knock out the innocent people. Once we get to the mirror, do you have any suggestions for destroying it?"

I'd been thinking about that, too. "I don't know. I'm hoping we can just break it and call it a day."

"Like ... with a hammer?" Bonnie asked.

"Why?" I was intrigued. "Do you have a hammer with you?" I flicked my gaze to Gunner. "We totally should've brought a hammer."

"I have one in my truck," Whistler offered. "Should I get it?"

"That would be great." I beamed at him. "See, we're completely prepared. Is everyone ready for me to take down the barrier?"

"I know I am," Marissa said. "I want to get home and hide my poodle hair as soon as possible."

"Will you shut up about your hair?" Rooster barked.

"I wish you all would shut up," Gunner muttered under his breath. I was the only one close enough to hear him and I slid him a sidelong look.

"What?" he complained. "This day already feels endless and it's barely started."

"You need to chill." Instinctively, I reached over and squeezed his hand. "Everything will be okay. Trust me."

He returned the squeeze. "I do trust you. I'm freaked out by what you can do, but I totally trust you. Now, let's get this show on the road."

I released his hand and strode closer to the barrier, extending my fingers until I found the wall. "Back up," I instructed everyone, glancing over my shoulder to make sure they weren't crowding me. I shouldn't have been surprised that they were increasing the distance to laughable lengths. "Yeah, you guys have faith in me," I muttered, turning back to the barrier. "Here we go."

I pressed my eyes shut and murmured under my breath, calling the ice magic I'd used several nights prior to freeze Tim. It was my interaction with him — the explosion of sorts that happened after the fact — that had convinced me of what I needed to do.

The barrier hardened quickly, turning into an icy igloo that covered the church. The rain bounced off it, causing the ice to steam. This was going to work, I realized, as I took a step back and waved my hands, fire burning at my fingertips.

"What is she doing?" Marissa asked from behind me.

"I think I know," Gunner replied. "She's going to blow a hole in the barrier now that it's solid."

"How?"

"With fire."

"Oh, well ... ." Her statement died on her lips.

The fire magic whooshed out and slammed into the ice. I thought it would take time for the magic to wriggle through the solid structure I'd managed to create, but instead it was like a bomb detonated. The barrier shattered, like a snow globe dropped on the floor, and I had to shield my face to keep the smaller ice fragments from cutting me.

"Good grief," Gunner grunted as he grabbed my arm. I hadn't seen him break from the rest of the group to join me. "Did you know it was going to do that?" He had a shallow cut on his cheek, and I swiped at it when I straightened.

"Of course," I lied. "I have everything under control."

"Uh-huh." He didn't look convinced. "Well, it's down. Are you ready for the next part? It's time."

THE FACES AT THE WINDOWS had drawn together into a protective circle when we barreled into the church. I heard the whispers, felt the dread, and there was no doubt the congregants believed they were about to die at the hands of evil.

"I'm sorry about all this," I offered. "You don't realize it, but you're being used. The people in the back, the ones who left you out here to fight, they're hoping you'll serve as battle fodder and hold us off for a few minutes so they can reap the rewards."

"We know what you are, demons." A woman, brown hair pulled back in a severe bun, held up a crucifix and pointed it at us. "We will not bow to your evil whims."

"Oh, that was a little over the top." I smiled at her. "For those worried, by the way, you can calm down right now. Nothing is going to happen. I just need you to remain calm and things will be over before you know it."

"Demon!" the woman shrieked and pitched the crucifix at me.

Gunner, his reflexes top notch, reached out and plucked it from the air before it could strike me. The woman's eyes went wide, but I was already humming to put her to sleep before she could respond.

Most of the people in the circles began swaying as the humming increased in intensity. Then, just as a wave coming to shore, the spell rolled out and knocked them over. The only one left standing was a man in the middle of the circle, and he looked absolutely terrified.

"Why am I not surprised that you're the one left standing, George?" Rooster shook his head. "I should've seen that coming."

"George is the former mayor," Gunner volunteered for my benefit. "He was fired from his position for appropriating township funds."

"I was framed!" George shrieked.

"He couldn't be prosecuted because the prosecutor took a payout right before the arrest came and refused to bring charges."

"That's a lie." George's eyes darkened. "Why is everyone else dead? Why did I survive?"

"They're asleep," I corrected. "As for why, it's pretty simple. We wanted to make sure those who were innocent didn't get caught in the crossfire."

"Are you saying I'm guilty of something?" he challenged.

I shrugged. "If the black hat fits."

"Well, I'm not guilty," he barked. "I'm innocent ... totally innocent."

"The spell says otherwise."

He straightened, his eyes turning murderous. "Why do I even care what you think? Can you answer me that? You can think whatever you want about me. It doesn't matter. I know you're the real demons."

"Yes, well, you should feel right at home then with them trying to raise a demon in the back room," Rooster noted. "You need to step aside, George."

"And if I don't?"

"Then we'll make you." Rooster was matter-of-fact. "Do you want us to make you?"

George worriedly glanced between faces. He was a coward, outnumbered, but he was hedging his bets. The people in the other room frightened him more than we did. "I'm not afraid of you." He said the words, but there was little strength behind them. "I won't let you pass."

"Oh, yeah?" Rooster was menacing as he stepped closer and faced off with George. I left him to fight however he wanted and strode into the nave. It was empty, which didn't surprise me. I heard chanting from the back of the church, and knew exactly where to go.

"You should stay here," I instructed Gunner, putting my best "I'm being reasonable so you should listen to what I say" face in place. "I'll go in. You can catch any stragglers as they escape."

He narrowed his eyes. "Right. You want me to let you go in there alone and deal with the stragglers out here, where it's safe."

"We don't want anyone getting away." I thought I was being pragmatic. He obviously thought otherwise.

"I'm not leaving you." He was firm. "We're doing this together."

"It's not about leaving me to fight on my own," I argued.

"I know. You don't want me to see you get down and dirty. I don't care about that. We're doing this together."

I stared at him for a long beat, wondering if I could change his mind. He was as stubborn as me in most ways, which meant he wouldn't back down. "Fine. Don't be afraid if I go all 'woo-woo' and scare the crap out of them. It would be best if you didn't react."

He pursed his lips, a hint of amusement flitting over his handsome features. "I'll try to keep it together."

"Good." I sucked in a breath and glanced over my shoulder to where Rooster was still fighting with George, and Bonnie and Marissa were watching me with trepidation. "This is going to be fun," I promised. "Just let me do all the talking."

"I think that's definitely best," Bonnie agreed.

I turned back to the door and grabbed the handle. It was locked, but the hold was weak and I easily blew past it with my magic. Now was not the time for finesse. We were well past that.

"Hello, kids." I greeted the four people in the room with what I hoped was a trustworthy smile. "How's it going?"

Father Bram and Cecily held hands in front of the mirror. The glass was swirling, telling me they'd completed whatever ritual they were conducting and simply waiting for the outcome. I didn't recognize the woman standing to the left. She had an interesting dark countenance, but she didn't speak. The other person in the room was Gunner's beloved wrestling coach, who took a lumbering step in our direction as he moaned.

"Kill them," Father Bram ordered Fred, his demeanor calm. "Kill them and we will fully bring you back to life."

I slid my eyes to Gunner to see how he would react. As I expected, he was shaken ... but resigned.

"They're lying to you, Coach Fred," he called out, watching the mummy with hopeful eyes. "They can't bring you back. What they're doing ... well ... it's not for you. They're trying to raise a demon."

"Yeah, what's up with that?" I asked Father Bram, keeping one eye on the mummy as Gunner tried to reason with a man who wasn't entirely there. "Why would you want to bring forth a demon?"

"You have no idea what you're talking about." Bram was haughty as he squared his shoulders. "You're the demons in this scenario."

"I'm a witch," I countered, blasé. "What you're dealing with in that mirror is different. In fact ... ." I trailed off, something occurring to me. "Mammon. You're trying raise Mammon."

"Who is Mammon?" Gunner asked, making sure to keep himself between me and his coach as the mummy paced back and forth, clearly confused. Whatever part of the coach that remained appeared to remember Gunner ... and it was torn.

"Mammon is a fallen angel in mythology," I explained. "That's mythology, not theology. He was supposedly one of the brightest and best ... until he became enamored with wealth and lost his soul in the process.

"The story goes that he got so greedy the other angels joined together to banish him," I continued. "He was sent to another plane of existence, where nothing of wealth could be achieved, and where he would spend the rest of his days thinking about what he'd done."

"How do you know all this?" Bonnie asked from behind me.

I shrugged. "I read a lot."

"We're going to turn your attention to a nice romance," Gunner said. "For now, I don't like the way that glass is swirling."

He wasn't the only one. I had a feeling I understood what was to come. "You finally cast the spell to bring him forth even though you're not sure it will work. Hal tried the spell, too, right? He realized what the mirror was and tried to bring forth Mammon for his own needs."

"Hal was not a true believer," Bram replied. "He was a pretender to the throne."

That was rich. "Really, *Brian?*" I smirked when he jolted. "You're a user who was taught by a grifter. You're not exactly a true believer either."

"Who is Brian?" Cecily asked, confused. I couldn't get a true read on her. Potentially, she was dangerous. Of course, her brother said she was "nutty." She could be innocent in a lot of respects. There was a possibility she didn't understand what she was doing or saying.

"This is Brian." I jerked my thumb at Bram. "He's a grifter from Minnesota. He's been bopping around for years. His father was a confidence man who romanced women for money ... until he tried to get in with the wrong woman and her son killed him."

"How do you even know that?" Bram asked, frustrated. "I put that life behind me."

"Wait ... it's true?" Cecily furrowed her brow. "How can that possibly be true? You're a prophet. I mean ... you are a prophet, aren't you?"

Bram growled as he shook his head. "I'm a prophet. I already told you that."

"He's not a prophet," I argued. "He's a man trying to find an easy button for life. Where did you find the mirror? How did you discover its purpose?"

Bram snorted. "Believe it or not, I found it at an estate sale. I was there with a ... date ... and I couldn't turn away from it. I thought I saw someone who wasn't me staring back."

In an odd sort of way, that made sense. "You did. I saw him, too."

"He showed himself to you?" Bram looked surprised. "Why would he do that? I'm his vessel. I'm the one who will play host to him."

That's when the final piece of the puzzle fell into place. "Oh, geez. That's how it works. You have to meld with him. That's why Hal was missing his face. He tried to meld with him and something went wrong. He got in but couldn't get completely out, and the solidifying mirror sheared off his face."

"That is absolutely gross," Marissa whined.

"That's what happened," Bram confirmed. "I'm thankful for Hal's attempt to betray us. We learned from it."

"Yeah?" I felt sick to my stomach. "Well, he got his. Something tells me you're going to get yours."

"The ritual has begun," Bram shot back. "There's nothing you can do to stop it. In a few minutes, Mammon and I will join and then I'll be rich beyond my wildest dreams."

"Good for you." I slid my eyes to Cecily, who looked legitimately confused. "You didn't know that, did you? You thought he was a real man of God."

"I ... ." Cecily managed only the one word before falling silent.

I exchanged a quick look with Rooster, who had blood on his shirt. "I don't think she realizes what's happening," I offered.

He nodded. "Yeah. I'm right there with her. We'll get her to her brother. He'll know what to do."

"That's smart." I turned back to Bram. "As for you ... ."

"There's nothing you can do," he repeated, raising his voice to an uncomfortable level. "I am the resurrection and the light."

"Right." The conversation was going in circles and I was officially sick of it. "Well, I guess I should leave you to your business."

Hope momentarily flared to life on Bram's face. "Really?"

"No. Not really." I took the crucifix Gunner still clutched in his hand, the one thrown at me in the nave, and wrapped my fingers around it. Metal and heavy, it made an impressive weapon. I gathered my magic, wrapping it around the crucifix and turning it into a spinning ball that flew into the air and careened toward the mirror.

Bram realized what was happening too late. He tried to throw himself in the path of the projectile, but he couldn't move fast enough.

The crucifix hit the mirror with such force it almost sounded as if a grenade exploded. Glass shattered in a million different directions, a low growl emanating from the world behind the mirror before the connection died and the swirling ceased.

"No!" Bram grabbed his hair and stared at the wreckage. "What did you do?"

"Honestly, not much." I was blasé. "It was a lot easier than I thought it would be." I turned to Gunner, who was on the floor next to his coach's lifeless body. His hands shook as he held the shell of a man who once meant a great deal to him. Apparently destroying the mirror had severed whatever spell tethered Fred between this world and the next. "Oh, I didn't know." I moved toward Gunner, my heart heaving. "I'm sorry."

"It's okay." He gripped the hand I rested on his shoulder. "I saw him the moment it happened. He looked relieved. This is what he wanted."

I didn't know if Gunner really witnessed what he thought he did or he simply convinced himself he had. In the end, it didn't matter. It was over.

"Well, that's that." I squeezed his shoulder. "Anyone up for lunch? I'm starving."

Rooster groaned as he rubbed his forehead and looked around at the mess, which was going to take days to clean up thanks to the force I put behind the spell. "We definitely need to talk."

TWENTY-NINE

I had the next day off, which meant more work around the cabin. Because it was the afternoon (and I was already dressed) I opened all the windows to let the sunlight in. I figured I could air out the space for the afternoon and then make some decisions on the furniture. Almost everything would have to go if I wanted to be comfortable. The problem was, I had no idea how long I would be staying ... or how comfortable I truly wanted to be here.

"Hey."

I jumped at the voice, turning swiftly to find Gunner standing in the driveway. I'd been standing on the front porch, lost in thought, and hadn't heard him drive up. Had he been on his motorcycle that would've been impossible. He was leaning out the driver's window of one of the lumberyard trucks, and the smile he shot me was smug.

"I'm going to get a bell for you," I complained, descending from the porch. "You need to learn to make a noise or something."

"I wasn't being purposely quiet," he countered. "I think you were lost in your own little world."

That was entirely possible. "So ... what's up?"

He grinned. "I brought some more supplies to work on the cabin."

"So I see." I made sure to keep a least a foot between us as we circled to the rear of the truck. It was indeed full of supplies ... and a picnic basket, which made me furrow my brow. "What's this?" I plucked out the basket and lifted it.

"That is lunch."

"For who?"

"Us."

I pinned him with a pointed look. "We're having lunch together?"

His grin widened. "We are," he confirmed, smirking. "I brought a blanket and everything."

"That sounds ... cozy."

"Don't worry, your virtue is safe with me."

"I'm pretty sure I lost that in high school."

He chuckled as he grabbed the blanket from the back and pointed toward a spot in the shade. "Come on. We have some things to talk about."

I wasn't particularly worried that he was going to jump in feet first and ask me on a date. We were still dealing with the fallout from the takedown at the church. Until that was completely resolved, we weren't free to look forward ... which was a very small comfort.

"What did you bring?" I peered into the basket as he spread the blanket, much to the kitten's delight as it raced after the fluttering edges and tried to wrestle them to the ground.

"I see you have your buddy with you." Gunner chuckled as he captured the kitten and sat on the blanket with him, watching as I placed the basket on the center of the rectangle and opened it. "I hope you like potato salad."

"I happen to be a big fan of potato salad," I admitted, grinning as I sat cross-legged across from him. "What else is in here?"

"Macaroni salad."

"I like that, too."

"And sandwiches."

"What kind of sandwiches?"

"Ham and cheese."

"Oh, you went all out." I winked at him, genuinely amused. "May I ask why you brought the picnic? Don't get me wrong, I appreciate it, but you could've just stopped by and said whatever it is you want to say."

"And what do you think I want to say?"

I shrugged, unsure how to proceed. "I'm guessing Rooster is angry."

"Why would he be angry?"

"Because ... ." I trailed off, uncertain.

"He's not angry," Gunner said, catching my eye to be certain I was listening. "He is surprised, like the rest of us. You do understand that you're more powerful than the average witch, right?"

"I've never really thought about it."

"No?" He waited a beat. "I'm not sure I believe that. I think you wonder about it all the time, but you push it out of your head because you want to appear strong. If you look back, you can't look forward."

"You sound like a fortune cookie."

He flicked the end of my nose. "That won't work on me. I know the secret you're hiding."

"Oh, yeah?"

"You're really a soft touch." He leaned forward, his finger scratching behind the kitten's ears, and didn't stop until his lips were inches from mine. I was torn between wanting to lean closer or run in the other direction. "I think you have a puffy pillow for a heart." His smirk was ridiculously attractive.

"And I think you're full of it." I found the strength to pull back, and grabbed the container of potato salad. Changing the subject was in order, so that's what I did. "How are things with Father Bram?"

"Oh, you mean Brian?" Gunner leaned back on his elbows, allowing the kitten to sprawl on his stomach and fall asleep. "He claims that we can't prove he was doing anything because mummies aren't real and nothing came through the mirror."

I stilled, running the scenario through my head. "Huh. He has a point."

"Don't worry about it. My father isn't an idiot. We told him what happened, what Bram was planning, and we're working on something that will make sure he's locked away for life."

"Do I want to know?"

He shrugged. "Probably not, but it's up to you."

"I think I'll pass. As long as he stays locked up, that's all I care about."

"I figured that." He accepted the plate I handed him, potato salad and a sandwich prominently displayed. "I talked to Bart. Cecily has been put on an involuntary hold at the same hospital my mother is in. They're going to figure out a treatment plan that hopefully has her living on her own again down the line."

"Not right now, though?"

"No."

"That's probably a good thing. I mean ... ultimately I felt sorry for her. She's still a danger to society right now."

"She is. And she won't be wandering around getting into mischief for the foreseeable future."

"That's good."

He forked up a mouthful of potato salad. "She admitted to painting the symbol in the basement, by the way. It was the same symbol on her tree. It's part of the ritual for calling Mammon, which she thought would be a good thing. Apparently she didn't realize Mammon was a demon, not an angel."

"I don't think she's all there." I twirled my finger near my head for emphasis.

"I agree."

We ate in amiable silence, which Gunner was the first to break.

"How are you after that display you put on yesterday? I wanted to talk to you after the fact, but you disappeared."

"I needed time to think."

"About?"

That was a hard question to answer. "I'm not sure. There's a lot going on in my head these days."

"It might help to talk about it."

He sounded sure of himself, but I wasn't convinced it was the right move. Still, I didn't have many outlets. He was the person I knew best here, the one individual I knew I could talk to openly.

"I've been thinking about what I saw in the vision."

"You mean the two women?"

I nodded.

"Do you think one of them was your mother?" he asked, his tone gentle.

"I don't know. Neither one of them looked like me, if that's what you're asking. They both had darker hair. I've spent some time thinking about their noses, and those were different, too."

His eyes lit with amusement, he shifted and pinned me with an amused look. "Their noses?"

"You know what I mean."

"I do. I'm not making fun of you."

"That's not how it sounds."

"Yeah, well ... fair enough." He pivoted quickly. "The mirror has been destroyed. The fragments were taken to a local industrial lot and melted down. Marissa was in charge of that. She complained about the smell, but because she didn't have to lift a finger in the fight Rooster thought it was only fair she contribute."

"I guess I'm sorry I missed that." I played with my potato salad. "There was another woman in the room." I'd almost forgotten about her, but I'd woken in the middle of the night, bolting upright from a bad dream, and hers was the face I remembered. "Who was she?"

"You mean Caroline Boston." He wiped the corners of his mouth with a napkin. "She's an odd duck. I don't know how to explain her. She's been in tight with that crowd since they came to town. She denied being in on it — and Bram and Cecily are keeping quiet, at least about her — but I'm not sure I believe her."

"She has a bad aura."

"You can see auras, too?"

"Sometimes," I hedged. "Hers was dark. She's got a dark soul."

"Well, she's not under arrest. She didn't make a move on any of us, and my father says he can't hold her."

"I guess that means we'll have to watch her."

"Pretty much." Gunner abandoned his food and snagged my

fingers, taking me by surprise. "Do you want to go on a date with me?"

The invitation was out of left field. "I ... right now?"

"I figure we're on a different sort of date right now," he replied with a chuckle. "It's a fun date, relaxing. I was hoping we could do something more formal."

"What did you have in mind?"

"Dinner. A walk on the beach."

"No dancing?"

"I'm not much of a dancer. If you want to go dancing, I might be able to figure something out."

I should say no. That's what I told myself. I wasn't even sure I was staying. I couldn't, though. My heart would've revolted. The attraction I felt for him was almost chemical, and there really was no turning back. "I guess we can go on a date."

His grin widened. "Good. I'm definitely looking forward to it."

"I'm sure you are." I went back to poking my potato salad. "When do you want this date to occur?"

"I haven't decided yet. I want to plan a nice evening. I have a feeling Rooster will want to talk to you first. Just remember ... he's a big softie, just like you."

"Ha, ha, ha." I rolled my eyes as he broke off a piece of ham and fed it to the suddenly-awake kitten. "Oh, by the way, I named him."

"Really?" Gunner cocked his head and met my gaze. "I'm dying to hear what you came up with after all this time. Is it three names, like Theodore Wayne Booth? You know, like a serial killer?" He chuckled at his own joke.

"No. It came to me last night ... in my dreams."

"Okay. I'm listening. What's his name?"

"Merlin."

He was quiet for a bit and then he burst out laughing. "All this build-up for the name Merlin? That seems a bit on-the-nose. Still, he's your cat. It's your decision."

"I think he told me his name." The words were out of my mouth before I thought better about uttering them.

"Excuse me?" He arched an eyebrow. "The cat told you his name? When did he start talking?"

"I don't know." I averted my gaze because I felt a bit daft. "I just heard someone whispering it in my dreams last night. It's not a big deal."

He opened his mouth — perhaps to say something annoying that would send me right over the edge — but then he snapped it shut. "Merlin is a fine name. We should get him a collar and tag ... and take him to the vet."

"I already have an appointment for next week."

"That's convenient."

"I might be a new pet owner, but I'm not an idiot."

"No one could ever call you that." He moved his fork to my plate and stole some of my potato salad. "So, where do you want to go on our date? I mean ... what's your favorite sort of food?"

"The kind you can eat."

"Such a funny girl." He shook his head. "Do you like seafood?"

"Yes."

"Steak?"

"Yes."

"Is there anything you don't like?"

"Endless questions."

"Ugh. You're going to be a lot of work." He poked my side before breaking out in another grin. "Do you want me to surprise you?"

I'd had worse offers. "Sure. That sounds nice."

"Great. Liver it is."

"Don't make me hurt you."

He scrubbed his cheek, considering. "What would a geek eat? I mean, on *Star Trek*, what did they eat? We could go that route. You know, make it a themed evening."

"You should probably start running now," I threatened.

"Oh, it's too late to run. We're stuck with each other ... at least for now."

He spoke the truth. I couldn't have walked away even if I'd wanted to. There was definitely something there.

"Let's go with steak," I suggested. "I love a good steak. You're buying, though."

"But of course. I'm nothing if not a gentleman."

"I'll be the judge of that."

"Don't worry. My reputation precedes me. Ask anyone. I'm going to totally sweep you off your feet."

That's exactly what I was afraid of.

Made in the USA
Las Vegas, NV
26 October 2023

79743980R10162